Mournin
Evan's Story

Written by Jeremy A. Harper
Edited by Sky West

First Printing, 2019

ISBN: 9781076475190

This is a work of fiction. Names, characters, business, events and incidents are the products of the author's imagination. Any resemblance to actual persons, living or dead, or actual events is purely coincidental.

Table of Contents

Prologue

Alexa

Hanging up in the vast black sea, the full moon rested neatly above a small suburban neighborhood. The pale light flooded the area, illuminating the surrounding streets. In one particular one-story home, a teenage girl lies on her back, with her boyfriend arched over her.

"Qu…quieter," the girl breathed out hastily.

"I'm trying," the boy groaned.

She sat up, her auburn hair sliding back off of her pale shoulders. She ran her fingers through his dark hair, wrapping her arms around his neck. She kissed him, her body shuddering, her back arched, moaning as she climaxed. As he followed suit, she leaned up, her lips pressed against his, closing her eyes as she crashed down onto her bed.

"I love you," she whispered softly.

A few moments passed.

"…yeah," he replied flatly.

She opened her eyes to see his black bangs swaying as he pulled his pants up, his shirt already back on.

"Can't you stay a bit?" She pleaded insistently.

"Better if I go, babe," he said. "See you at school, Alex."

"Okay…" She exhaled, pouting.

He climbed back out the window from which he came, dropping into the yard. Once again alone, she stared up at her ceiling, closing her eyes as a single tear began to slide down her cheek.

The next morning, she entered the kitchen to a familiar sight. At the table sat a man captivated by his laptop. The sound of the latest headline filled the kitchen.

"International tension mounts as a veritable arms race ensues between budding nations…" A man's voice droned on, adding to the perpetual misery of everyday adulthood.

"Where's Mom?" Alexa asked.

The man ignored her, completely engrossed in today's top story. With no food to be seen, it looked like she was once again going without breakfast.

She sighed, "See you later, Dad."

And with that, she left the house, taking her usual route to school.

"Hey Mike, have you heard?" Alexa whispered to the ebony skinned boy sitting next to her. "There's supposedly a new game out!"

"Oh yeah? Rumors like that pop up all the time," he said, dismissing her. "Gaming production has all but come to a halt due to the war, remember?"

"This is supposed to be more than a rumor!" she exclaimed.

"Uh huh," he replied sarcastically. "What's it all about then?"

"It's a world based entirely --"

"How about you go ahead and explain to the class how one would go about finding the volume of a cylinder?" the teacher suddenly interjected.

"Oh... um," Alexa stuttered.

"That's what I thought." The teacher scoffed. "If I hear another word from you, it'll be detention! Now let's continue."

Half an hour later, the lunch bell rang. The students began packing their bags, making their way out of the classroom, and funneling into the hallway.

"So, Alexa," Mike called out, catching up to his friend. "What's this game about?"

"Right!" Alexa beamed, picking up where she left off. "It's a world immersed completely in magic!"

"...So?" he replied, unenthused.

"It's supposed to be really lifelike, though!" she exclaimed. "Real! Virtual reality! Isn't that exciting?!"

Mike shook his head. "I thought they gave up on virtual reality ten years ago. You know, because of the sudden war?"

She paused. "Maybe someone kept researching it in secret?"

"Didn't you say it was just a rumor?" he asked. "Why are you getting so excited?"

"I just want it to be true!" she sighed, exasperated. "Wouldn't it be exciting?! To be immersed in a world of magic, where we have actual power and influence! Let's be late to lunch — I'll show you the website in the library!"

With that, they made their way to the library where they saw a familiar dark-haired boy sitting at one of the computers, typing away.

"There's Gerard," Alexa told Mike.

"What's up, Gerard?" Mike asked as they approached him.

"Oh, hey, what are you guys doing here? "Gerard continued typing. "Isn't it your lunch period?"

"We're going to be late so your girlfriend can show me some website," Mike said.

"Oh..." Gerard rolled his eyes.

"What?!" Alexa's cheeks turned bright red. "Things have developed since before!"

Gerard nodded listlessly, accommodating her newest obsession once again and allowing Alexa to take his seat. Without missing a beat, she typed in the URL, bringing up the website within seconds. The site's front page was a single picture split into five horizontal sections. The first was a lush forest brimming with life juxtaposed against the second — mountains so high they kissed the sky. At the base of the mountains, the third section started: a vast ocean which bled into the fourth, a desolate plain. The plain eventually built into the fifth, a modern city. Two words stretched across all five sections; JOIN TODAY.

"See?" Alexa exclaimed. "Each section is a separate link that takes you to more information. Races, spells, equipment, locations, everything you need to know! If it's a prank, it's quite elaborate!"

"Any screen shots?" Mike asked.

"Well...." Alexa began.

"No," Gerard smirked.

"There is a ton of concept art though!" Alexa pouted.

"Still, it doesn't have any download link, or release information," Mike added.

"Well, that's the thing." Alexa paused. "Just the other day, the 'join now' became a hyperlink."

"Have you clicked on it yet?" Gerard asked.

Glancing to the side, Alexa clicked the link. "…Yes." Obviously, she hadn't.

Mike chuckled.

The page changed, loading a map of their city, with a red circle on a street corner.

Mike's eyes widened. "I know that street."

Alexa turned to face him. "What's on it?"

"Nothing, really; mostly just specialty shops," Mike stated. "Is there a specific address?"

"Yeah. Want to stop and get food on the way there?" Alexa glanced from Mike to Gerard.

Mike nodded. "Sounds good."

"How am I getting dragged into this?" Gerard sighed. "I didn't agree to ditching school today."

"Come on, man!" Mike exclaimed. "There's a good chance this city will be leveled by the end of the year. It won't matter if we miss a day or two of school. We should focus on enjoying the time we have not living in a war zone!"

Gerard rolled his eyes, "Fine."

After taking the liberty of printing out a copy of the map, the group left the library, making their way out of the school and wandering deep into the city.

"Well, this is the place," Alexa said as they turned a corner, standing at the end of a street full of run-down buildings. "Keep an eye out for the building number."

They casually made their way down the desolate street. It was eerily quiet, as though the entire area was devoid of activity. It wasn't long before they came upon the last building at the end of the street.

Gerard sighed, crumpling the wrapping of his burger and tossing it onto the ground. "Good thing I skipped school with you guys for *this*…"

They stared at the decrepit wooden shack of a building for a few minutes. It looked as though a small gust of wind would knock the entire thing over. Where there wasn't a gaping hole, there were endless cracks.
A sign hung loosely above the wooden door. "Golden Leaf Tea Shoppe," Alexa read.

Gerard glanced at his friends. "This can't be right."

"Yeah." Mike added. "Seems sketchy — like we're going to be killed and have our organs harvested."

"Look, we came this far." Alexa shouted. "Let's just do it!"
She grabbed their wrists and pulled them up to the front door, knocking gently. To everyone's surprise, the door didn't collapse, but slowly swung open.

"Hello?" Her voice echoed as they made their way through a dark, narrow and musty corridor.

They stepped around several holes in the wooden floor, and ducked past more than one cobweb before reaching a second door. Once more Alexa knocked, only to find it slowly open, inviting the group further into the building.

Gerard started to pull against Alexa's grip. "We should just go…"

"Stop being such a baby," Alexa snubbed him.

He had never seen her like this; he was much more used to being in control. She was normally such a pushover — it was as if she was an entirely different person.

As they moved forward, the group stepped into a surprisingly well-lit, spacious room. The once pungent air had been replaced by an overwhelming floral scent. Stemming out from the entrance of the room was a systematic pattern: lamp, bookshelf, lamp. At the far side of the room, a hooded figure stood behind a raised wooden counter.

"Can I help you?" a deep voice, presumably from the figure, boomed through the air.

"We had heard there was supposed to be a game available here," Alexa inquired.

"Oh?" the figure responded, amused by her brash behavior.

"This is more than creepy," Mike whispered to Gerard.

"Ditch?" Gerard whispered back.

"You'd do that to your own girlfriend?" Mike stared in awe.

Gerard shrugged and mouthed, "First chance we get."

"You've come to the right place, young ones." the figure assured them. "I have what you are looking for right in the other room."

The bookshelf just to the right of the counter began to shake, slowly swinging open and revealing a hidden doorway.

"Just through here." The figure motioned, stepping out from behind the counter. "Follow me."

As Alexa stepped forward, she reached back, and once more, grabbed the boys firmly by their wrists. "Come on, assholes." She glared back at them. "Don't think I didn't hear your plan."

Mike scowled at Gerard as they were dragged into the back room. Inside, it was pitch black, save for a single ray of light illuminating a coffee table beside the hooded figure. Presented upon it were three different gems: a crescent shaped emerald, a round ruby, and a triangular topaz.

"Gems?" Alexa asked, perplexed.

"Very special gems." The figure's voice had become almost a whisper.

Suddenly Alexa stumbled as her temple throbbed in pain. She raised her hand to her head, rubbing it gently. "I can barely hear what you're saying, Gerard." She turned toward the boy in question.

Gerard hesitated. "I didn't say anything," he managed to respond. "Are you okay...?"

"Whatever!" Alexa exclaimed, dismissing him and turning back to the gems. "I'm fine."

"What does this have to do with the game?" Mike asked.

"These are the game," the figure sneered. "With these you can begin installation."

"...Okay," Gerard began skeptically, "but how, exactly? I mean, what system requires gems?"

"The greatest system in existence," the figure's voice boomed, filling the entire room. "Just watch!"

Suddenly, the entire area was filled with a bright light. The group moved to shield their eyes, and after a few moments, it became apparent how small the room was. Other than the table in the center, the room was empty; however, three of the walls were made of glass, revealing more rooms past them. Alexa, Mike and Gerard each made toward a wall. Alexa raised her hand to cover her gaping mouth, mesmerized by the scene unfolding before her.

A slim, pale-skinned girl wearing nothing but a pair of shredded jeans stood covered in bruises, cuts, and blood, glaring at a boy standing across from her. His shirt and jeans were untouched in contrast, flapping violently with strands of his blonde hair as though he was standing in front of a large fan. He closed the distance in an instant, grabbing the girl's exposed breasts and forcing her onto the ground.

"It's over," the boy sneered with a wide, toothy grin. "What happens next — well, I may seem a bit cruel. But as the man said before, this is the nature of the game. The strong survive, and the weak perish."

He lowered his head, pressing his lips against her bright pink nipple, and slowly kissed a path along her bony collar up to her neck. Without warning, he suddenly sunk his teeth deep into her skin. He pulled away, blood running down his chin as he chomped at the piece of loose flesh.

"Don't worry," he whispered. "You will — "

He was cut off as a pink light slashed through him. The boy's head spiraled through the air, landing several feet away from his body. The girl struggled to her feet, breathing heavily; her long, dark hair draped down the front of her body, partially covering her face and exposed flesh. From her right hand extended a pink beam of pure light.

On her stomach, four glowing pink lines of light formed a diamond around her belly button. It began to glow brighter and brighter as it drew in the blood from the headless corpse and her own body. The blood from the boy seemed to flow through the air like a ribbon, converging on the glowing symbol until all that remained was a withered corpse. As the blood stopped flowing, her entire body began to glow until she had become nothing but a beacon of pure light. And just as quickly as she was enveloped by the light, it shattered, and no trace of the girl remained.

Alexa stumbled backward, struggling to regain her composure. She turned to see that Gerard was on his knees, leaning over a puddle of vomit reflected in the left wall. Mike seemed to have fallen backwards, staring completely wide-eyed out the right window. Each scene, it appeared, was relatively the same.

"Wh…what the hell?" Alexa stammered.

"Is it not glorious?" the figure suddenly chimed in.

"This isn't a game!" Mike shouted, struggling to stand.

"No…no, I suppose it's not," the figure conceded. "It's something much, much greater: A chance to escape and begin anew."

Alexa paused for a moment, her gaze fixing on the figure more intently now.

"What does that mean?"

"Who cares what that means?!" Gerard finally seemed to regain his composure. "People just died! We need to get the police!"

Her eyes tepidly moved to meet Gerard's. She couldn't help but think of last night, and so many other similar nights; this man certainly left much to be desired. Not to mention the distance with her parents — there was so much she wished to run from. She closed her eyes as she felt a pull at her heart, tears beginning to swell. But he was right: this was crazy. This was not the answer she needed to pursue. She exhaled, opening her eyes and nodding frantically at the boys.

"Let's go!" she shouted, turning to run from the room.

However, as if she had no control, Alexa instinctively reached out and grasped the crescent emerald. Immediately, the gem began to glow, and a green aura flowed out from it, outlining her whole body. She felt amazing. Her heart raced, her skin tingled, and the hairs all over her body stood up on end. It was a rush greater than anything she had felt before, greater than anything she could have imagined. But then, the aura around her body faded and her right eye began to sting. It started as merely uncomfortable, but slowly intensified until pain consumed her. She screamed, and then suddenly she couldn't see from her right eye. It burned; blood ran down from the right side of her face and pooled onto the floor below her.

Gerard and Mike leapt forward, reaching out to grab her. As they closed the distance, they were suddenly held in place, unable to move.

"What?!" Gerard shouted before gritting his teeth.

The figure effortlessly glided across the floor, stopping before the two boys. It raised its fingers to their lips. "Hush now, little babies. The ordeal is nearly through."

Just like that, the two boys felt as though their voice had been taken right from their throats. Neither could make a sound.

Meanwhile, Alexa, covered in her own blood, was curled up on the ground. After what had felt like an eternity of pain, she went numb. Slowly, her body began to tremble, her breathing returning to normal. She raised her hand to her right eye and noticed that she could see once again. She felt normal, almost like nothing had even happened.

"What was that?" she managed to gasp out.

"Your rebirth," the figure said.

"Was that even real?" she whispered softly, turning to Gerard and Mike.

The two boys had regained their composure. As they came to their senses, they turned to Alexa, staring in awe.

"What's wrong?" Alexa stared at them, puzzled.

"Well —" Mike began.

"Your face..." Gerard blurted out.

"Yeah, it really hurt," Alexa stated. "I guess it was just a panic attack, though...?"

She turned to face the figure, noticing a large mirror on the far wall and seeing her reflection. She raised her hand to her mouth, tears pooling in her eyes. "Wh... what the...?"

An emerald-colored crescent ran through her right eye, starting at the center of her forehead and arching down through the center of her pupil until it curved back around, stopping at the center of her chin.

"Then, that pain..." She turned to the figure. "What is this!?"

"That is your mark," the figure stated. "Now you need just activate it in order to log in to the game."

"No game is worth begin scarred!" she shouted.

"Oh," the figure chimed in. "I think you will soon disagree with that statement. Now, who's next?"

Mike and Gerard took a step back.

Alexa's anger swelled. "You're going to leave me all alone here?!"

"Hey!" Gerard shouted back in defense. "It was your idea to do this! I didn't want to come!"

He took another step back. "This...this is too much," he said softly, before running out of the building.

Mike's head sank as he watched him go. "I'm...I'm sorry, Alexa."

He looked her in the eyes one last time before running after his friend.

The figure smirked, taking a step toward Alexa. "It's alright. This isn't a curse, but a gift," it said smoothly.

"No!" Alexa screamed.

As she did, a torrent of air shot outward from her body, filling the whole room. The curtain on the door waved violently, the mirror shattered, the table overturned, and the figure was blown back into the wall. Taken back by what had just happened, she darted out of the building and as far as she could, until she couldn't run any further, eventually stopping in the middle of the dark, moonlit street.

"What am I?" she asked softly, tears falling from her eyes as she slowly began making her way home.

Around midnight, she slid her key into the doorknob, sneaking inside and up to her room.

Exasperated, she fell onto her bed. "What am I supposed to do?"

Unexpectedly, she heard a voice answer her, echoing through her head. "You know what to do, child." She jolted up from her bed to look around — it was morning.

There was a sudden knock at her door.

"Breakfast," her mother shouted.

She got out of bed and walked over to her mirror. The mark was still there. Placing her hand over her eye, she sighed before changing her clothes and heading downstairs.

"Oh my god...honey!" Her mother exclaimed. "What did you do to your precious face?!"

"It's spirit week at school," Alexa murmured, lying.

Her mother's green eyes lingered over her; she seemed to accept her daughter's lie. "...Oh, okay, just face paint…You scared me."

Alexa began eating her cereal, keeping her head down the entire time.

Before long, her father came downstairs, dressed in his usual suit and tie. His dark hair was slicked back, and as soon as he sat at the table, he was already engrossed in his phone.

"Dear, did you know that Alex is participating in spirit week?" her mother said to her father.

"Oh? That's good," her father replied without looking up from his phone. "Are you going to be a cheerleader?"

She raised her head, lowering her brow and glaring at the man across from her.

"Foreign forces have successfully conquered the far continent, and are advancing east," her father methodically read aloud. "Things are going to start getting worse."

Alexa finished eating and excused herself from the table before going upstairs to grab her backpack. *Today is probably a good day to ditch class*, she thought.

She made her way toward school for the first couple of blocks, then changed directions, heading in the direction of a local drug store. She eventually found herself in the make-up aisle, a place she wasn't particularly acquainted with. She scanned the various powders and creams, exhaling.

"Need assistance?" asked a chubby woman with glasses, draped in a gaudy red vest.

"Uh...no." Alexa tilted her head away from the employee.

The woman simply smiled and stood next to her, scanning the selections. After a moment she reached out, taking a small container of cream, handing it to Alexa.

"This should help cover up that nasty bruise." The employee flashed a sincere smile as she walked away.

Alexa studied the container for a moment, reading the components and warning label.

She glanced up and down the aisle, sighing before pocketing the container and heading back to the entrance. She walked outside and toward an adjacent pizza place, making her way straight to the bathroom and making sure to lock the door before taking out the container. She dabbed her fingers into the cream and began to spread it over the mark. It seemed to be working — the mark began to fade under the cream. She smiled weakly, continuing to apply more until it was completely covered. Once she was satisfied, she pocketed the container and walked out to the lobby.

"Can I get—" she began, stopping once she noticed the bemused stare at the boy behind the counter.

"Uh... is something…?" She started to say before nervously averting her eyes.

"Your face," he responded. "What's up — parade?"

Taken back, she suddenly darted back to the bathroom, locking the door once again. She looked down into the sink, eyes shut tight, and then slowly lifted her head, opening her eyes. The mark had burned through the make-up, clear as ever on her pale face.

"Why?" She asked herself, tears welling in her eyes.

She lowered her head. *Cursed,* she thought.

Then, a familiar voice rang through her head. "Gift, not a curse."

She clenched her fist and looked up, only to step back in surprise. In the mirror she saw herself, but with white hair, grey, wrinkled skin, patches of black stained on her face, and gold, gleaming eyes. Then, her reflection spoke.

"Child," it said, "fear not. You have received a great gift."

Alexa took another step back, trembling against the door to the stall. "What...?"

Before she could continue, darkness enveloped the area, leaving only the mirror and her ghastly reflection visible.

"What is this!?" She screamed.

"The beginning," her reflection said. "You wanted this. Don't pretend you aren't excited to break free from the mundane. I have heard your heart cry out."

But not this way, she thought. "I just... not..."

"Enough!" Her reflection shouted. "Let me show you, then!"

The mirror's reflection disappeared, and a vast field appeared in its place. The lush, green meadow was stained with patches of crimson. *Blood*, Alexa realized. Two armies stood across from each other, one side lead by a woman clad in black, plated armor and equipped with a round shield and flail. Behind her were hundreds of humans and humanoid creatures equipped with various garments and weapons.

Across from them was a hoard of four legged beasts with black fur, bulging muscles, long claws, horns and fangs, wings and untamed manes.

As Alexa watched the scene unfold, she heard, "This world you see is the game you seek."

The female leader rushed forward, raising her shield to cover her upper body as she slammed her shield into a black beast. Without hesitation, she swung her flail, striking the beast's face. It was enough to stun the beast; it reeled back from the force of the blow. The woman turned her hand, still holding the flail, and extended her index finger. A beam of light, wrapped in sparks, suddenly erupted from the tip of her finger, piercing the beast's head. It wailed, then began to convulse before collapsing onto the ground. She continued on, trampling it effortlessly on her way to the next foe.

From behind her, figures holding staves and wands began volleying balls of flames into the masses of beasts. Most of the attacks only fizzled out against the beasts' thick skin.

"And, take a closer look, child," the voice whispered to Alexa. "That woman...is you."

"Change spells!" The woman shouted back at her group. "They are vulnerable to ice and wind damage!"

Battles waged all over the field, yet little by little, the woman was able to keep her forces moving forward, pushing the beasts back. The image faded, and Alexa's reflection reappeared in the familiar bathroom.

"This is your future. No... Your destiny," Alexa's reflection said. "It's not as though you fit into this world, so you can hardly call this running away. You're simply going to where you belong. "

There was a knock on the bathroom door, and suddenly the darkness had disappeared, her reflection her own. Covered in sweat and breathing heavily, she barely heard another sharp knock against the door.

"Excuse me!" a woman shouted. "Excuse me! You've been in there an awfully long time and my daughter desperately needs to use the restroom!"

Alexa shook her head, regaining her composure before turning to the door. She opened it to see the employee from the drug store, accompanied by two police officers. "That's the thief, officers!"

Shit, Alex thought to herself.

"Come with us, young lady," one of the officers said, reaching out to grab Alexa.

"N — no!" she screamed, raising her arms up to block her face. "No!"

A sudden, fierce current of air shot forward from her body, filling the small hallway. The sharp winds pulled and pushed against the woman and the officers until their bodies began to shred to pieces, blood wafting through the air as they screamed. Alexa lowered her arms to see the hallway stained red, littered with limbs and flesh.

"What... no," she gasped, her body trembling.

She heard the familiar voice. "Don't fret, child — this is your power. Embrace it. Cut through those who would stand before your destiny!"

The voice had become much louder than before. She raised her hand to her throbbing forehead.

"Now go!" the voice bellowed.

"Damn it," Alexa whispered, running through the bloody hallway. She didn't have much of a choice at this point.

She burst out of the restaurant, unsure of where she was going but determined to distance herself from the mess she'd made. Before long, she found herself at her school, through the front gate, into the familiar courtyard. She walked through here every day, arguing and laughing with Gerard and Mike. Why had she wanted to escape that? Was this really what she wanted?

She watched the students clustered together, eating lunch, socializing, trading the latest gossip while her life fell apart. Two days ago, she was in the library with Mike and Gerard. Now she was alone, hands stained with blood. Blankly she walked through the courtyard, staring straight ahead, unaware of the murmurs and stares.

"Is that blood on her shoes?" one of the girls whispered.

"What's up with her face?" another voice cried out.

Students stepped out of her path as she made her way to the double doors of the entrance. As she reached for the door handle, she noticed a familiar head of dark hair in the corner of her eye. She turned her head to see Gerard with his hand up a red-haired girl's shirt, kissing her neck.

It's too much, Gerard's voice rang through her head. It was the last thing he had said to her.

"It's too much..." Alexa said softly, to herself. "It's too much!?"

Her voice echoed through the courtyard. Gerard and the girl froze, turning to see Alexa, who had already closed the distance between them. Furiously she reached out, her hands clamping around each of their throats. The air grew dense, whirling around them with a defining howl. Gerard and the girl could only scream as small cuts opened up along their bodies. The air filled with blood as the cuts deepened, and one by one their limbs began to fall to the ground. The crescent scar on Alexa's face began to glow, brighter and brighter, as the blood began to swirl and flow into it. Then the winds calmed; she loosened her grip, and Gerard and his companion's severed heads fell atop a pile of withered flesh.

She stood over the remains, staring absently into the distance. It was as though she had just watched herself in a horror movie — *An Ordeal on Willow Street: Alexa's Ill Will*. However, the blood drenching her clothes proved otherwise. There was no turning back at this point.

"Freeze!"

Alexa slowly turned around to face a group of policemen, whose composure wavered as they took in the scene.

"Y-You're... you're under arrest," one of them stammered, shakily pointing a gun in her direction.

Alexa blinked, and the policeman's face began to fade. Starting with the mark on her face, her entire body began to glow green and then she suddenly shattered, green shards fading into the air. Hazily, she saw the earth disappear below her.

When she regained consciousness, she found herself lying on a grassy plain. She slowly came to her feet, raising her arm to block the aggressive light shining down over her.

"Baah," a creature to her left bellowed.

As her eyes adjusted, she looked over to see what appeared to be a sheep with purple wool, and a pair of curled horns and wings.

Alexa gazed in awe at the lush greenery surrounding her. "I guess... I made it."

I
Evan

In a small classroom at Oceanside Technical School, a boy sat at his desk, propping his head up with his hand. His messy, light brown hair fell just above his hazel eyes. He turned toward the adjacent window, staring outside at the bright blue sky, not focused on anything in particular, but envying the freedom. His teacher, slim and plain-looking, stood at the front of the classroom, textbook in hand. She pushed her square-framed, red glasses slightly up her nose as she spoke.

"Here, we can see where dropping the bomb on Hiroshima and Nagasaki ultimately stopped Japan's involvement in the war," she explained, her brown eyes locked onto the boy looking out the window.

"Mr. Farrant," her voice boomed.

The boy turned listlessly to see the teacher staring at him.

"Yeah," he responded apathetically.

"What resulted in Japan's surrender during World War II?" the teacher asked.

He shrugged. "I don't know."

"I literally just said it." She sighed. "You aren't paying attention again."

"Yeah." He nodded, turning his head to stare absently back out the window, simply wishing he could be away from the classroom.

The teacher shook her head and resumed the lesson.

Every second in the classroom edged along at a snail's pace. Evan spent his time moving his eyes between the window and the clock. Thirty minutes to go, then twenty-nine. He sighed. After what felt like an eternity, the bell rang and the boy stood up hastily, grabbing his bag.

"You don't get to leave, Mr. Farrant," the teacher told him, her brow furrowed. "Let's have a little chat."

He rolled his eyes, walking up to the front of the room. This wasn't the first time he had to stay after class. Lately, it seemed as though that was all that he did. As such, he found himself skipping days on a whim. What was the point in coming if his attendance wasn't appreciated?

"Evan, what is going on?" the teacher demanded, once all of the other students had left the room.

"What do you mean?" Evan replied.

"Don't do this," she groaned. "I know you're intelligent. You were able to breeze through your previous years at nearly the top of your class. Don't you want to graduate?"

"My grades are high enough that I will still graduate, even with a bad year." Evan shrugged.

"At the rate you skip school, I doubt that," the teacher said, shaking her head. "With your grades, you could have been summa cum laude. You're going to have a hard time getting into college."

"Don't waste your breath lecturing me," he spat, glaring at the teacher. "I showed up today; I'm not obligated to be your accomplishment."

"I don't think of my students like that," she replied tepidly. She wasn't used to being accused by her students. "You were so adamant. You challenged other students and teachers alike. I don't understand what changed. Help me to help you."

"My life isn't your problem," he said, staring coldly into her eyes.

"You used to talk about how you wanted to change the world," she continued, exasperated. "With the state of the world as it is now, it could use someone of your caliber. You could easily make a difference."

"What's the point?" he asked, annoyance becoming evident in his voice. "I don't give a damn about a pissing contest between countries. People don't want to live peacefully. They want to prove they're better than one another. People will always look out for themselves before others. There is no resolving that."
He pulled out a game cartridge from his pocket and held it up. "It's far more exciting to delve into fantasy worlds, where anything is actually possible."

The teacher wasn't sure what to say. They had had this conversation multiple times. Persistence wasn't working.

"I need to go now," he declared, turning to walk out of the classroom.

"Wait!" she called out.

He kept walking, his eyes staring off at the exit in the distance. All around him, students were gossiping and laughing amongst themselves. Each group he passed reminded him more and more of how isolated he was. He often felt that he no longer had anyone to confide in. As he opened the door to the courtyard, he remembered that he had work this afternoon.

Of course, he hadn't been in a hurry to get to work. Like school, he felt that he had just been showing up to get lectured. The only benefit of work, as opposed to school, was that he could earn some money. He walked slowly down the sidewalk, heading away from the school and deeper into the town, eyes unfocused and hazy.

He turned off the sidewalk and through a parking lot toward a mid-sized building. As he entered, he made his way to the back of the store, to the break room. The store was fairly small, but had a good selection of products: food, hardware, homeware, toys, and clothes. However, being a small operation, it certainly couldn't compete with larger, more specialized shops. He himself was only one of few employees, and, until recently, he had been employee of the month and on the fast track to a management position.

A sharp voice cut through the air. "Late again?"

Evan turned to see one of his co-workers, a girl of his age with short black hair and pale skin, sitting at a table in the middle of the break room on her phone. He almost never saw her without dark eyeliner and black nail polish. To add to the image of "rebellious teen," she bore a small stud pierced through her nose.

"So?" Evan responded lazily.

"I guess you're not so perfect after all." She smirked. "Up until the middle of summer, the other associates — me included — really didn't appreciate your exhausting work ethic. You give our generation a bad name."

Evan had made his way to a wall of cubed lockers. The combination lock on his clicked as it released. He pulled out a red apron, promptly tying it on over his clothes. He turned to face the girl. This is how it was, working hard got him resented, and the opposite got him scolded. Not that any of that mattered to him anymore.

"You must be so proud of me now, Eleanore."

"I told you not to call me that," she scoffed, glaring at him. "I know that you know its Elle."

"My bad." Evan smirked, making his way past her and towards the sales floor.

"Wait!" Elle called out.

He stopped in place, turning to face her once more.

"You have a good look in your eyes now," she said, stepping forward to close the distance between them. Face-to-face, she was just slightly shorter than Evan, and her own emerald green eyes stared into his. She moved her face closer to his own, whispering in his ear, "Empty, just like mine."

Evan watched her wearily as her gaze continued to edge ever so slowly toward his own. He hadn't exchanged many words with her before, but her whisper was curiously sad. However, it was short-lived as her voice reverted back to its usual sharp banter.

"If you ever want to hang out some time, that'd be cool," Elle added before pulling away and smilingly coyly.

Evan shook his head slightly. "You know I'm taken."

"Not that I really care about anything like that." Elle winked, retaking a seat at the nearby table to become completely absorbed in her phone.

Evan turned around and made his way out into the hall. On the walls between the break room and the sales floor hung various clipboards with printed lists attached. The first thing he always did when he got to work was check his assigned section, see if anything needed to be restocked, if anything was damaged, or if there was anything that looked untidy or unprofessional. The sections alternated depending on the week. Reading the clipboard, today it looked like he was assigned to clothes.

He made his way toward the clothing section, clipboard in hand. He moved mechanically through the various hangers and stands of clothes, barely checking, eyes moving listlessly from side to side. Everything seemed fine, at least by his standards. If he was nitpicking like he had been in the past, he may have adjusted and refolded some of the picked-through and wrinkled clothes. However, unable to bring himself to care, he continued down his checklist. As he turned around, he bumped into a shorter, bulgier woman with light curly hair flowing out from a modest hat.

"Excuse you!" She scoffed, scowling at him.

"Ah, sorry," Evan said softly.

"Oh?" The woman exclaimed. "You *work* here? I was beginning to think that no one did, it doesn't seem like there's anyone around. Don't blame *me* if anything gets stolen because the store isn't keeping an eye on anything."

"Okay…" Evan responded, thrown back by her comment. "Do you need any assistance?"

"Obviously," she spat back. "I know you have this shirt I want; I saw it the other day. I'm not seeing it now, so where are you keeping it?"

"Well, it could be sold out," Evan advised. "Do you know what it looks like? I can always help you search, or I can check in the back."

The woman hastily withdrew a small flyer. The shirt in question had been on sale the previous week, which had clearly been outlined at the top.

"Oh," Evan nodded. "That sale ended just the other day, and I believe we did actually sell out of this particular shirt."

"I was busy that day," the woman stated matter-of-factly. "But, I'm here now, and I have the flyer. You guys carry the shirt, and you need to honor this deal."

Evan stared in disbelief. This certainly wasn't the first time he had dealt with someone who was so obstinate, but lately it didn't take much for him to lose his temper. He attempted to conceal an exasperated sigh, but apparently, it did not go unnoticed by the woman.

"Look!" she shouted, raising his arms along with her voice. "You need to find this shirt now! Call a manager if you have to!"

Evan rubbed the back of his neck. "Sure. Just wait a moment while I go get them, and in the meantime, I'll double-check the back for you."

He gritted his teeth, making his way into the back room. As he made his way to the back room, he could feel the woman's indignant stare burning through the back of his company vest.

Evan ducked into a nearby corridor, knocking on a familiar wooden door that read "MANAGEMENT." Upon entering, he was greeted by an older man wearing a suit and tie, with straight, dark hair that he always wore combed-back.

"There is a customer who wants to speak with you," Evan alerted him. "It's in regard to the sale that has already ended; she's pretty adamant about getting what she wants. I'm going to double-check the back to see if we happen to have any."

The manager sighed, standing up. He turned, his gaze lingering over Evan for a moment. "Very well, and don't think I didn't notice you were late. We need to have a talk tonight before you leave."

Evan nodded before turning and heading into the stock room. *Great, more lectures*, he thought. The room was fairly small: a few shelves scattered with boxes. It was almost as though no one had ever attempted to organize it since the store had opened. He walked along the perimeter of the room, thinking that at this point, even if there was a shirt left, he would rather that woman leave upset than get what she wanted.

Luckily, they were legitimately out of the shirt. He smirked, making his way back onto the store floor to spot the manager still talking to the frantic woman.

"This has been a terrible experience!" The woman seemed to be ranting. "The staff is practically nonexistent, the one I did find rudely ran into me before telling me that you guys wouldn't honor your own sales."

This woman is exhausting, Evan thought before managing to get a word in. "I'm sorry to say, but as I feared, we don't have any more of that shirt left."

"Alright, go help out up front at the registers," the manager stated before turning his attention to the woman.

"I'm sorry ma'am, but that sale was specifically for those dates…" the manager's voice faded out as Evan left the area, walking up to see Elle manning the only open register to a long line of guests. He weaved through the line to the nearest register, motioning to the next guest and ringing up their merchandise.

Each customer seemed to be more annoyed than the last about the lack of staff and the extended wait times. By the end of his shift, the last thing Evan wanted to do was deal with the manager.

He knocked, opened the door and stepped into the office. The manager was at his desk, completely engrossed in his computer.

"I'm here," Evan announced, shifting impatiently from side to side.

The manager continued typing at his computer for a minute before looking up to see Evan. "Take a seat."

Evan did, watching as the manager continued to type frantically on his computer.

"So, what was it today?" The manager asked, somehow still typing.

"Sorry, I just --"

"That was more of a rhetorical question, Evan," the manager interrupted him. "By the way, where is your name tag?"

Shit, Evan thought as he raised his arm to touch the left side of his chest.

"I know things have been hard the past couple of months." The manager sighed, finally raising his eyes up to face Evan. "But this is getting ridiculous. I was expecting you to bounce back to how you were over time. Between lateness and poor work ethic, clearly it's only getting worse."

Evan could only nod in agreement; arguing back had become pointless as he never managed to make good on any of the changes he tried to promise.

"Go ahead and take off the next week," the manager stated, turning his complete attention to Evan now. "If, after that, this attitude persists, we are going to have to let you go. That's not a threat, it's just a fact."

Evan stood up slowly, turning away and heading to the door.

"Evan," the manager called out. "You're a good worker. Even today, you at least tried to put forth some effort with that ridiculous woman. Please, don't go down this path."

Evan said nothing, leaving the room and heading towards the entrance of the store. He made his way out into the parking lot where a girl with shoulder-length blonde hair and pale skin stood, waiting. Her light blue eyes fixated on Evan.

"You're late," she stated, although she was grinning.

"Sorry, Emma," Evan said softly. She was the one person he tried to avoid disappointing. "The manager kept me, *again*."

"And?" She sighed.

"Well, he gave me…like, a final warning," Evan explained. "They want me to take off this next week, and if I don't start going back to work mode, they're going to let me go."

Emma shook her head. "It's not like you want to work there anyway. Maybe you should really think about that during this week."

"Yeah." Evan lowered his eyes to the ground. "Anyway, are you ready? My aunt works late tonight, so we can go to my place."

"Okay." She smiled, glad to just be in his company. "Anyway, I certainly won't mind having more time with you this week."

They clasped hands, fingers lacing together, the brisk air whipping Emma's mid-length hair around her face as they walked down the side of the road. It was already autumn; the trees had transformed into a collage of browns, reds, and yellows.

"I'm glad summer is over," Evan breathed out.

Emma's face crinkled as she grumbled, "But now it's going to be cold."

"Still better than summer," Evan insisted, unable to keep the edge from his voice.

Emma always had to tread carefully around that subject. "I suppose." They continued onward in silence.

"Do you want to grab a pizza before we go to your place?" Emma asked suddenly.

"Uh, sure." Evan nodded.

They continued through the city, taking a detour once they reached a small park. Children played while their parents watched from the sidelines. The two sat down on an empty bench for a moment, Emma snuggling close to Evan.

He watched the carefree families in the park. "Strange how there's so much emphasis on the news about the current war, and yet there are people here who are completely carefree."

"I think it's important to maintain some sense of normalcy." Emma turned to stare at him. "Besides, you're one to talk. You do nothing but escape into fantasy worlds."

Evan smirked. "But, how can adults be so critical of our generation?" He sighed. "This current war isn't one that we started."

"Even if you place the burden on adults, you have to remember that we all breathe the same air," she pointed out. "We're all human. I highly doubt that enemy nations distinguish between generations. They probably intend to kill us all simply because we stand in their way. Besides, don't forget that we're officially adults too."

"I guess I just don't care," Evan said, and then, before he could stop himself, "Whether we live or die, it's all too cumbersome." He winced; this wasn't something he would have normally said to her.

Taken back, Emma let go of his hand, her light brown eyes reflected in his own. "What does that mean for us, then? Lest we forget, you begged me to give you a chance and professed your love for me."

Ashamed, Evan let his gaze fall. He always tried to avoid dragging Emma into his problems.

"I know what happened over the summer changed you," she continued gently. "I am trying to support you. Please don't forget that you still have me. Don't throw me away." She leaned in to kiss him.

He met her lips with his own. To him, she was a breath of fresh air in this suffocating world. He was honestly glad that at least, he had her. After a few moments, he felt a drop of rain hit his head.

"Ah. Let's go before we get caught in the rain." Emma pulled away, smiling at him. "We still have to pick up the pizza."

They got up holding hands and jogged hastily out of the park as the drops turned into a steady drizzle.

Outside the restaurant, an old man dressed in rags sat against the wall, next to the front door. In his hand was a dirty piece of cardboard with nonsense scribbled on it. He watched as the young couple made their way to the front door.

His grey eyes fixated on Evan, who didn't seem to notice.

Inside, a young girl with short, black hair glazed with pink highlights stood behind the counter. From behind her, the sounds of muffled arguing could be heard.

"What should we get?" Emma asked Evan.

"Anything is fine," Evan stated.

"Pineapple?" Emma grinned.

Evan grimaced, sticking his tongue out. "Fine, anything isn't fine. Let's just get pepperoni."

They stepped up to the counter.

"Large pepperoni pizza," Emma said to the employee.

"That'll be $8.00." The employee smiled weakly. "And it'll be about ten minutes."

Emma handed a few bills to the girl, and then she and Evan sat down on one of the available benches. The arguing in the back intensified, but the couple chose to ignore this, as Emma rested her head on Evan's shoulder.

"I love you," she whispered softly.

"I love you too," Evan replied.

Suddenly, a deafening scream echoed from the back of the restaurant. The young couple raised their heads, clinging tightly to one another before a teenage boy emerged from the back, his hands and uniform stained with red. He approached the girl behind the counter.

"Jessica, it's done," he sneered, his dark eyes illuminated with excitement.

"J… Jeff, what did you do?" Jessica stammered as she stepped away from him, her eyes focused on his dripping hands.

"I freed us from the tyranny of that asshole," his eyes wide with glee. "Now we can be together like we've always wanted. Whenever, wherever."

Horrified, Jessica continued to step backwards, casting her eyes away from Jeff's. "I told you. I don't even like you..."

"Don't be like that, baby. I'm the new boss, after all." Jeff sneered as he moved closer to her. "You don't want to be without a job, right?"

Evan continued to cling to Emma, who had already pulled out her phone and began to dial 9-1-1. However, noticing them out of his peripheral vision, Jeff turned to see the couple.

"...customers," he said softly to himself.

Emma froze, her finger hovering over the last 1.

Seeing the phone in her hand, Jeff raised his left arm, pointing his finger at her. A red star, tattooed on the back of his hand, began to glow as a small orb of flames swirled at his fingertip.

"Drop the phone," he said sternly.

She slowly placed the phone onto the floor, Jeff's eyes piercing through her like daggers.

"Kick it away from you," Jeff commanded.

Emma nudged it with her foot, causing it to slide into the middle of the room.

At once, the mass of flame shot forward like a bullet. It struck the phone, enveloping it in flames before exploding into fiery bits that scattered along the floor.

Jeff let out a cackle as everyone stared in shock.

"W… what the hell was that?" Jessica stammered.

"My power, baby," Jeff bragged, turning to face her.

"Do you think we can make a break for it?" Emma whispered to Evan.

He didn't respond, his body shaking and his eyes widening with fear. How did he get into this situation? He always tried to stay passive and go with the flow. He hadn't been standing out in any way. *Why can't I just live my life peacefully* he thought.

"Let's put on a show for our customers," Jeff said to Jessica, raising his hand up and groping her breasts. "Everyone loves dinner and a movie."

"Stop!" she cried out, backing away further only to hit the solid wall behind her. Tears began to flow down from her face as she realized she was trapped.

"I don't have to listen to that anymore." Jeff grinned, tightening his grip on her body. "I'm not just some third-rate pizza boy that you can look down on anymore."

He grabbed the collar of Jessica's uniform and with a single motion, tore it away, revealing a black, laced bra.

"I knew you weren't so pure." Jeff licked his lips. "Now let's see if they are as good as I imagined." He reached his hand hungrily toward her breasts. Jessica screamed, grabbing a nearby pen and impaling his oncoming hand. He groaned, blood spurting from the wound as he gritted his teeth.

"Now's our chance," Emma whispered to Evan, yanking him by the wrist out of the front door.

"You... bitch..." Jeff grunted, tearing the pen out with his free hand. His breathing became heavier as a gush of blood burst from the open wound and down his hand. He suddenly slapped Jessica, the force of the blow sending her to the ground.

"I thought you were the one. I would have taken such good care of you," Jeff roared, glaring down at her.

Jessica raised a hand to her throbbing cheek.

"You're just an asshole!" she screamed, before spitting at his face.

"I guess you aren't a very suitable girlfriend after all." Jeff wiped the saliva away somberly. "Girls are supposed to swallow."

He reached down with his left arm, tightening his hand around her neck. She clawed at his grip, gasping for air. The tattoo on the back of his hand began to glow bright red. She felt heat against her neck, building slowly from a warmth to an intense burning. Smoke rose from her neck as her skin melted away, flesh and blood running freely down the front of her body as she frantically tried to pull away.

Her eyes rolled back into her head as her body fell limp and her neck gave out, the skin and bone completely melted away. Her body fell to the ground while her head remained in Jeff's hand, blood oozing from her open throat. Jeff dropped her head next to her body, into a pool of crimson. Both Jessica's blood and Jeff's tattoo began to glow a bright red, resonating with one another. Her blood began flowing through the air like a ribbon, converging into the red star on Jeff's hand.

As the blood finished draining, Jeff turned toward the booths. "At least there's another girl waiting for me." But the store was empty. "Shit," he murmured.

Emma and Evan had made it to the street outside, where the rain had become a raging torrent. The two stumbled haphazardly, struggling to figure out which direction they were headed. *We're finally safe*, Evan thought, turning to see Emma looking around frantically.

Suddenly they heard a loud crash, and turned to see that the door to the pizza shop had been smashed down. Jeff was rushing towards them, the drops of rain seeming to evaporate into steam in his wake.

"No!" Evan shouted, taking a step back.

Emma glanced at him, smiling, before stepping forward to put herself between Jeff and Evan.

"Not so fast!" Jeff screamed, his voice echoing through the parking lot. He swung his left arm through the air. Flames erupted from the ground, running horizontally across the street from behind Emma and Evan.

Evan stared in disbelief. "What can we even do?" He had faced these situations numerous times in video games, but this wasn't a game. He didn't have a special power or tool to combat this lunatic.

"Don't worry." Emma smiled at him. "This is just like a video game, and no one has more experience in those than you. You'll think of something."

Evan's heart sunk as he listened to her. His face was white with fear, and he couldn't think of a single thing to do.

Noticing this, Emma nodded, kissing his forehead. "Then, I'll keep you safe."

Jeff had nearly reached them. "You aren't going anywhere!"

"Are you stupid!?" Emma screamed, exasperated. "Do you think it's smart to do this outside? A wall of fire?! Seriously!? You must want to attract the cops!"

"Let them come! They can't stop me!" he shouted back; his eyes lit up with joy. "I welcome a chance to let the world know of my strength! My whole life I've only been looked down on! Now, I will take my rightful place in society! I will be respected!"

Emma bit her lip, frustrated. The best she could hope to do was stall for time.

"First, I'll kill the boy, and then you and I can have some real fun!" Jeff cried out maniacally.

Finally finishing his trek across the parking lot, Jeff stood face to face with Emma and Evan. His long, dark hair was soaked by the rain and draped down in front of his face. He flicked it aside with his hand before reaching out to touch Emma's cheek. "I'll take real good care of you."

Then Evan snapped. Before Jeff's hand could reach her, he raised his arm, grabbing Jeff's wrist.

"Quiet this whole time." Jeff glared at Evan. "And all of a sudden you think you're a big boy now? You think you can just stand up to someone like me?!"

He pulled his wrist free and then raised his arm to slap Evan across the face.

Evan grunted, reeling backwards. He threw a punch at Jeff. As Evan's fist flew forward, Jeff's body began to glow red, the drops of rain becoming steam as they fell toward him. Before Evan could stop, his fist landed in Jeff's face. On contact, an intense heat seared Evan's knuckles. He withdrew his arm immediately, rubbing his burnt hand with his left.

Jeff smirked. "You can't even touch me, boy." Then, thrusting an arm forward at Evan, he shouted, "Die!"

Suddenly, Evan found himself on the ground. He groaned and looked up to see Emma, whose chest had been pierced by Jeff's bright red hand. Both Jeff and Evan stared in shock. Blood flowed from the hole in Emma, covering Jeff's hand as his tattoo began to glow brighter. He pulled his arm out from her body, and she collapsed. Evan leapt to his feet to grab her before she hit the ground. "No, not you too..." He began to cry as he pulled her closer.

His thoughts raced of all the times they had spent together. She had been his everything, nurturing and pushing him, always patient with his indifference and mistakes. She brought him more joy than anything or anyone else in this world, and she was all he had left. And yet, what had he ever done for her? Even today, he had told her he'd rather die. He felt horrible; the entire last few months he had simply taken her for granted. If he had known this was how it was going to end, then he would have made more of an effort so she wouldn't have had to babysit him so much. She didn't deserve this.

"It should have been me…" Evan gripped her tighter.

Emma stared up at him, smiling weakly with a single drop of blood running down from her lip.

"See... I knew... that... you cared," she managed to stammer as she coughed, splattering blood onto Evan's clothes.

It was too much. Tears poured from Evan's eyes as he closed them, gripping Emma tightly as her body went limp. He was now completely alone, and there was nothing he could do.

"Crying again?" Jeff said in disgust. "That bitch was more of a man than you can ever hope to be. If you had been a real man, you wouldn't have let her die for you. You've ruined my fun."

"I don't care," Evan sputtered softly. "Just hurry up and kill me too." Jeff glared at him.

"Well... you do act like a woman," he said softly. "No one would have to know. A hole is a hole... I'll just use you for some release and then kill you." Jeff reached down toward Evan when suddenly, everything around them froze. The drops of rain had stopped in motion, and the world seemed fuzzy. Despite it being night time, with looming dark clouds, the world seemed much brighter, almost grey.

A voice called out, echoing, "Do you want to live?"

Consumed by thoughts of Emma, Evan simply closed his eyes, the tears flowing more than ever.

The voice called out again. "Boy, do you want to live?"

Evan shook his head, "No! Just leave me alone already!"

He felt a warm touch on his shoulder, and opened his eyes, slowly looking up to see the old man from outside of the pizza shop. Despite his considerable number of wrinkles, Evan couldn't tear his gaze from the man's luminescent blue eyes.

"She gave her life for you. Would you waste that sacrifice?" the old man asked.

"I just don't have anything else to live for..." Evan cried, tears continuing to run down his face.

"You have a choice," the man said. "Don't be so hasty to choose death. Let me help you. I will give you the power to take revenge, as well as the opportunity to rebuild."

Evan looked up at him, unable to comprehend what this old man was getting at. He seemed to be treating it like it was a game. Evan looked down at Emma once more. "It's not like there's some spell I can learn to bring her back."
"Oh, ho ho…" The old man chuckled. "On the contrary, if you accept the power I offer, the same power that this boy wields, then you can travel to a world of magic. There, you can master powerful healing spells, even one that may be capable of reviving the dead."

Evan stared up at him in disbelief, the words barely registering.

The old man held out his hand. With a flash of light, a pale blue crystal in the shape of a flower sprouted out from his open palm. "You want your parents and your lover back, don't you?"

"How do you--" Evan began.

"Reach out and take it, if you wish to save Emma!" the old man's voice boomed.

Before he realized it, Evan had reached up and grabbed the crystal, shattering it. Energy erupted from the man's hand, pouring into Evan's and then flowing through his body. Suddenly, he cringed at a sting in the back of his right hand. He looked to see a blue line starting to etch a shape into his flesh. Once the pain subsided, Evan was left with a five-petaled, pale blue flower tattooed onto the thin skin of his right hand.

As Evan regained his wits, he looked to see the man was gone and time had begun to flow again. Instinctively, he reached up and grab his assailant's wrist. Jeff's bones began to creak and crack under the pressure of Evan's grip, until finally, a loud snap echoed throughout the empty parking lot.

Jeff howled, grabbing his wrist and stumbling backwards. "What the hell!? Where did that come from?!"

As though in a trance, Evan raised his right arm, carving a figure eight into the air. The drops of rain began to pull together, forming into several different orbs of water.

"How!?" Jeff screamed, a large mass of orange flames erupting from his body for just an instant. "Were you holding back this power this whole time!? Why let that girl die!?"

Jeff raised his left arm as flames began to flow freely from his open palm, creating a massive orb of fire.

Evan's body seemed to continue to move of its own accord. He steadied his hand just over the water orbs floating before him. Spreading his fingers apart, the orbs of water began to bend to his will, stretching out into cylinders.

"Damn you!" Jeff cried, throwing the orb of flame at Evan.

As the flame cut through the drops of rain, leaving a path of steam, Evan felt a sudden warmth in his free hand. He reached out, a pale aura shrouding his hand, and wrapped his fingers around the flames, clenching his grip and dissipating the flames with his bare hand.

"I...impossible!" Jeff stammered, taking a step back.

"How does it feel?" Evan smirked, suddenly aware of how powerful he felt. "How do you think that girl behind the counter felt?"

"W...what?" Jeff took another step back, his body trembling.

Evan's smile quickly turned to disdain. "How do you think Emma felt?"

"You're crazy!" Jeff turned his back to Evan, sprinting towards the distant pizza shack for cover.

Fueled by his rage, Evan clenched his hand into a fist and the cylinders of water suddenly froze over, becoming sharpened daggers of ice. They shot forward, piercing Jeff in the stomach, chest, and throat. Evan watched as Jeff tripped forward, collapsing onto the ground, the shards of ice protruding from his still body and oozing blood from underneath.

As though he had done so a thousand times before, Evan slowly made his way over to Jeff, kneeling and placing his right hand into the blood. The blood began to flow upward into the flower tattoo on Evan's hand. Now glowing a faint blue light, the tattoo began to soak up the blood, staining it a deep crimson. When all of the blood had been absorbed, Evan's tattoo returned to its usual light blue color. In turn, his entire body began to take on a similar pale blue hue. It felt as though his body was being tugged and pulled at.

His gaze moved over Jeff's impaled body before lingering on Emma's figure. He let out a weak exhale as fresh tears began to pool in his eyes.

"At least she looks peaceful," he whispered, the aura around his body growing heavier.

He shook his head furiously, wiping away his tears with his sleeve. *This wasn't the end*, he thought to himself.

"Emma! I will save you! I lo —" his voice cut off. His body had become completely consumed by blue light and he was shot upward, being pulled into the night sky before fading away as if a shooting star.

II
Amaryllis

As his body shattered, he felt his consciousness rise up. He looked down and was certain he saw the ground getting further and further away. The higher he went, the more his vision faded. It was as though he was floating in a sea of darkness. He wasn't sure how long it had been, but as time passed, his vision became more and more clear, eventually finding himself in a wide, open, white space. Lazily he turned his head, glancing at his surroundings.

This isn't so bad, he thought to himself. *I don't have to feel anything here.* However, just as he was resigning himself to his fate, everything came rushing back. He could once again feel the weight of his body, along with the sharp pain in his chest from losing Emma. The white space around him shattered, and he floated in space for a moment before, suddenly, he began to fall. He reached up, crying out as he fell toward a bottomless, deep darkness, tears flowing from his face. Then, just as quickly as he had begun to fall, he found himself planted in the center of a bustling town.

His clothes had mysteriously changed: he now wore a green, cloth tunic with black, cloth pants. He struggled to adjust, attempting to wipe his face with his arm while turning his head frantically to check his surroundings. To his immediate right was a large, white statue of a woman clad in armor and a scar around her left eye. The statue stood upon a pedestal, surrounded by a shallow pool of water. Extending from the statue were four paved, brick roads that lead north, south, east, and west. Several quaint, wooden houses with straw roofs were erected all around him, adjacent to the brick roads.

He exhaled, regaining his composure. Even so, his chest continued to throb with pain. He raised his arm, placing his hand over the pain in his heart. *Emma*, he thought. *That's right; I came here for a reason. I have no choice but to trust that old man and assume what I need to get her back is here.*

"Welcome to the town of Amaryllis," a voice suddenly called out.

Startled, Evan hastily spun around to see an old man. His long white beard and blue robes flowed behind him as he emerged from the other side of the nearby statue. Above the old man's head read, "Gil the Guide (NPC)." Evan straightened himself, exhaling and taking a step toward the wizard.

"I'm a Non-Playable Character — NPC for short — here to explain to you the basics of this game," Gil said cheerfully. "As an NPC, I cannot reactively speak with you; I can only present information that I have been previously programmed to. I will now begin my tutorial."

"Game?" Evan whispered to himself, suddenly realizing there were various bars and shapes within his field of vision.

"The game is essentially a role-playing game with a first-person view perspective," Gil explained. "You see everything with your eyes as if you were actually in this world. Since your body is the medium, anything you're subjected to will have some effect on you. You will need to eat and sleep in order to regulate bodily demands and functions. This is meant to provide a more realistic experience. A true escapist's paradise."

Evan pinched his own arm, noting the sensation of pain. *Pretty realistic indeed*, he thought before realizing that Gil had continued speaking.

"You can bring up a menu by voice command, or by clicking the small circle at the bottom corner of your view," Gil continued. "In the top left corner of your view is a display that shows your current health and magic. If your magic bar runs out, you won't be able to cast any spells, and if your health runs out, you will be removed from the game."

Evan looked up in the top left corner, where two bars, one red and one blue, ran parallel to one another.

"In the top right corner is a mini map that represents your immediate location, and depending on your dominate hand, the bottom corner has a menu interface for bringing up your inventory, stats, skill lists, etc.," Gil stated. "The system regulates all stat rolls, the amount of damage you deal and take, and whether or not you can hit your target. The easiest way to get used to it all will be to try it out."

Gil extended his arm, as if to invite Evan to see for himself.

Evan looked down at the bottom right corner; he extended his right arm out and pushed a small circle with the tip of his finger. A menu popped up, hovering in front of his body. With his finger, he clicked on a tab that said, "Party." Under the tab was a list of players in the immediate area. Most of the names were in a dark grey font, the only exception being Gil the Guide. "Go ahead and accept my party request and I'll walk you through killing monsters." Gil smiled.

A message popped up in Evan's view, reading: "Accept Party Request?" He hastily tapped the "yes" button. Then, the two made their way down the eastern road. To the right they passed by what appeared to be a marketplace, where several stands and booths were manned by NPCs and players alike.

"That is the marketplace," Gil told him. "You will learn more about that after this initial tutorial."

This was always the worst part about a game, Evan thought to himself. *Best to hurry along this tutorial. There's no way an NPC would be able to tell me what I need to know.*

Just opposite of the marketplace was a massive stone building with numerous steps that lead up multiple, ascending plateaus.

"That is the guild hall," Gil stated as they passed it. "You will learn more about that after this initial tutorial."

The two approached a large opening with walls extending out both right and left of it. They continued through, crossing a small bridge the led to a field. From here, Evan could see that the town was actually surrounded by towering walls, with a moat forming a circle the entire way around. He turned his eyes back to the vast greenery before him, where small, furry creatures hopped back and forth on all fours. They had long ears like rabbits, and a single horn extending from their foreheads.

"This is the weakest enemy," said Gil, pointing to one of the nearby creatures. "They are named jackalopes."

Evan stood before the creature. A sheathed, short sword suddenly appeared from thin air, hovering before him. He reached out, grasping the handle and unsheathing the blade, hooking the sheath to his belt and turning the blade toward the unsuspecting creature. Evan then lunged forward and the blade struck the beast's neck, severing it from its body. In red, the word "CRITICAL" rose up from the corpse. A window popped up in Evan's center view that read, "+10 experience, +5 gold."

"Good job," Gil said. "There is another bar at the bottom center of your view. It shows how much experience you've earned and how much more until you'll level up. Leveling up will give you a general boost to your base stats, as well as give you points to distribute as you see fit in order to learn skills."

Evan had noticed the long bar at the bottom center of his view, sectioned off at various points. Most were transparent, but the first bar had become filled with a deep blue. He grinned. *It won't be empty for long. This is my sort of thing, after all.*

"You can also improve a skill by using it," Gil added. "The more you use it, the more experience you'll get in that skill. For instance, swinging your sword improves your proficiency with a sword. For the most part, skills and spells are earned through leveling up, but some can be earned by doing quests or reading spell books and scrolls."

"Let's try a few more of these jackalopes," Gil continued.

Evan engaged another jackalope, thrusting his sword forward and piercing its face. The creature convulsed, sliding off the blade and falling limply to the ground.

"The system takes into account fatal and situational damage as well." Gil noted. "Piercing a monster's heart will deal a lot more damage than, say, cutting its leg. Similarly, when your health reaches zero, you don't appear at your last checkpoint. This is a one-chance opportunity. When you die in this game, you will be sent back to Earth, losing all knowledge and abilities that you have acquired here. Don't waste the gift you're given."

Evan nodded, gripping the sword more tightly now. This just meant that he only had one chance to bring Emma back, and he certainly had no intention of losing that.

"That being said, players can duel one another," Gil went on. "There are two options for a duel: you can either spar or fight to the death. Most towns are safe zones, where you can't be killed. However, this is not true for all towns. That's the overall basics of combat; you've officially completed your first quest. Please seek out other NPCs within the town in order to learn about other aspects of the game."

The party was suddenly disbanded, and Gil made his way back toward the statue.

A window popped up in front of Evan. It read, "Quest Completed." Underneath denoted additional experience and gold that had been gained.

"Finally," Evan murmured to himself. "I may not have ever played a game with my whole body, but it's not like I'm a noob. They could've given me a skip option..."

For the time being, Evan remained in the field, battling more jackalopes in order to build his experience. After what he considered to be a sufficient amount of leveling up, he made his way back into the marketplace he had passed earlier. As he moved deeper into the area, he heard a voice.

"Hey! Are you new?"

Evan turned to see a boy who, at first glance, appeared younger than himself. He had thick, teal hair that curved and curled around his head, clashing against his pale complexion.

Evan nodded, walking toward the wooden table the boy was standing behind.

"My name is Paul," the boy said, smiling. "I'm fairly new myself, probably only just a level or two above you. The gear I'm selling would probably be perfect for you!"

Evan looked down; hovering over the wooden table was a window with several tabs separating items, weapons, armor, accessories, and ingredients. Evan poked the armor tab, and a list of items appeared with a sidebar. He scrolled through the list.

"How'd you know I was new?" Evan asked as he scanned through the items.

"I saw you with the NPC," Paul gloated. "I'm pretty observant like that."

"Oh?" Evan appeased him. He generally tried to avoid people like Paul, but in this situation, he seemed to have little choice. Based on the surrounding vendors, Paul's area was by far the cheapest looking, and his prices certainly reflected that.

"So, how do you like it so far? A game that puts you into the world and lets you stay! So awesome," Paul rambled excitedly.

After a few moments of silence, Evan replied, "...I suppose," as he shifted uncomfortably and clicked over to the next tab.

"Is this your first time playing an MMORPG?" Paul inquired, confused by his lack of enthusiasm.

"No," Evan said abruptly. Shutting people out usually worked well for him, but Paul appeared to be an exceptionally persistent.

Paul squinted, studying Evan closely.

"Well, I played them like crazy back on Earth! My family was all on me about spending more time studying or hanging out with friends." Paul scoffed.

"Don't you think your parents are worried about you?" Evan asked, suddenly turning his gaze up to meet Paul's eyes.

"Who cares? I'm so done with them — and everyone else, for that matter," Paul declared with pride. "I'm on my own today, and forever."

"I see," Evan said softly, taking a step backward. "Well, I doubt any of this gear will be of much use. Generally, it's better to save money at lower levels and hold out for better gear once prices don't fluctuate so much from level to level."

Paul stared in awe.

"Y-yeah... I suppose," he stammered.

"See you," Evan said flatly, walking away without looking at him. He continued to brood as he moved deeper into the marketplace. *That kid is the worst kind of person — annoyingly persistent and ungrateful. At least he had people to come home to.*

Eventually, he came upon a booth with a sign reading, "One Stop Magic Emporium." Stepping up to the counter, he began to scroll through the options before attempting to speak to the vendor. "Excuse me."

Behind the counter was a tanned, older male with long, black hair and a bronze circlet fitted around his forehead. He sat in a fold-up chair and seemed extremely focused on the book he was reading.

"Yeah?" the clerk said unenthusiastically, his dark eyes never raising to greet Evan.

"Do you have any spell books?" Evan asked.

The man looked up from his book, staring at him incredulously. "Nothing for noobs," he scoffed, shaking his head before continuing to read.

Evan sighed as another customer approached the booth — an ebony-skinned boy around Evan's own age. He was clad in steel armor with a sword and shield crossed along his back. The vendor immediately laid his book down, catering his attention to the new player.

"Is there anything I can help you with today, sir?" The vendor asked, smiling broadly at the customer.

Evan glared at the vendor. "Look, can you just give me some information? I'm trying to find out about powerful healing spells."

"Look, kid," the vendor shouted, "Just get out of here!" He shooed Evan away with his hands.

Evan kept up his venomous glare as he reluctantly walked away. *Asshole*, he thought. From the corner of his eye, he couldn't help noticing that the boy in armor was watching him leave.

Evan sighed, once again standing in the field full of jackalopes. Whether he liked it or not, he was still low leveled. If there was a way to get what he wanted, he doubted it would be something attainable so early in the game. In his experience, games usually worked that way: the best skills were only accessible by the highest leveled players. He withdrew his short sword, looking at the blade before facing a nearby jackalope.

Aside from Evan were several other players scattered about the field. Everyone was sure to remain fairly spread out so that they had space to battle. Conveniently, there were plenty of enemies for everyone — nearly five jackalopes to a single player. Despite this, however, Evan moved quickly, taking down each more efficiently than the last. He learned from each battle, from each attack. Before he realized it, he had cleared out a significant area by himself. He had accumulated a good amount of experience and money. He turned his attention to the next, nearest jackalope. As he moved forward, a woman with fluffy green hair jumped ahead, striking the beast with a mace and killing it.

Evan took a step back, watching tepidly. She was coated in a thick, leather armor covering her entire body, including her hands. Apart from the mace, she held a small buckler in her other hand. The woman turned to face him, grinning.

"Sorry. I guess we both targeted the same creature." She laughed. "You've been making some big progress. If you hadn't noticed, a lot of the other players in this area have been keeping their eye on you."

Evan shrugged apathetically. "I don't think that's a problem."

The woman stood silent for a moment. "Maybe not. Are you new?"

"Yeah, I just got here," he told her.

"I'm fairly new myself," she declared proudly. "I only just got here a few days ago. My name is Leah."

"Evan," he responded.

"Would you be interested in partying with me?" she asked. "If enough of these jackalopes are killed, it'll spawn a boss. It might be hard to beat it with just us two, but if we form a party, we might be able to sway other players to join us as well."

Uninterested, Evan shook his head. "How hard can it be?"

Leah looked at him for a moment. "Um, are you familiar with super bosses?"

Evan smirked, thumbing his nose. "It's only the first area. Even if it's a super boss, I'm not concerned."

Leah frowned, confused. "What are you saying?"

"I can probably do it by myself."

Leah stared in disbelief. "Um, not that I don't appreciate your enthusiasm, but let's be honest. How high of a level could you possibly be after only a couple of hours? There's no way you could just come in and beat a super boss at such an early level."

Evan had been battling jackalopes for a while, and he had started to grasp some of the deeper components of the battle system. From what he could gauge, levels weren't everything. "Don't worry about me." He chuckled. "Good luck on your leveling."

Leah watched as he walked away, moving onto the nearest jackalope.

Evan continued to battle the monsters, moving at an increasingly aggressive pace as each beast went down with only one blow. His experience was increasing more and more slowly; he was finally reaching the point where beating these creatures was almost not worth the trouble. As he took down the next one, he turned to see something different.

Standing on its hind legs, just about as tall as Evan himself, was a furry, humanoid creature. Its body was quite muscular; instead of hands or feet, it had paws with protruding claws, and a swirling horn protruded from its forehead. It looked like a human-jackalope hybrid. Evan immediately dashed towards it, swinging his sword through the air. The beast jumped backwards quickly, avoiding the blow before leaping forward, swinging its arm downward and slashing towards Evan with its claws.

Evan raised his sword up, deflecting the oncoming claws. Leah and the other players in the area had stopped their battling to watch the scene unfolding in front of them.

It doesn't matter how strong the monster is, or the player is, for that matter, if the attacks don't connect, Evan thought. *Even the strongest monster can't take its heart or brain being pierced.*

The hybrid creature hopped forward, once more slashing its claws towards Evan.

He swung his sword upward, this time missing the beast's claws. They cut through the air, digging into Evan's left shoulder. He grunted in pain as blood flowed freely from the wound. His knees began to buckle, and his body trembled. It hurt much worse than he thought it would. It wasn't as though he had ever been in a fight, or cut by a weapon, for that matter. This was just on a whole other level. He felt his body grow heavier and noticed that his red health bar began to diminish rapidly.

From the distance, the players watching began to mock him.

"Dumbass noob," one player with leather armor sneered. "He has the most basic gear, with zero armor, and only a sword — not even a shield."

Another player with blonde hair shook his head. "He dug his own grave with his arrogance."

Leah clenched her fist tightly. "Are we really just going to stand here and let him die?"

"It's everyone for themselves," the player with leather armor stated.

Leah felt her body shake in indignation.

Evan gritted his teeth as the hybrid beast pulled its claws from his shoulder. Without warning it had swung its other arm forward to follow up with another slash. Evan stood in place, the claws sinking once more into his already wounded left shoulder. He shouted in agony, his eyes forcing themselves shut against the intense pain. His breathing had intensified and sweat had begun to pour out from his body.

"This pain is nothing!" His own voice echoed through the air as his eyes opened. A shimmering gold ring outlined each eye, and a deep purple aura began to surround his body.

He raised his left arm, gripping the beast's wrist. It howled as its bones snapped under Evan's grip. Leah, who had made a dash toward Evan, froze in place, watching in awe. It struggled, pulling at its arm to try and free itself. Simultaneously, Evan thrust his right arm forward, piercing his sword straight through the beast's heart. Its wail of agony echoed throughout the entire field, before its body went limp and slid off of the blade and to the ground. Evan glared down at the dead creature, while everyone else in the field had their eyes glued to Evan.

Evan exhaled, slowly regaining his composure. "I won't go down this quick." Now he felt more determined than ever before. More than a sense of responsibility or duty, he wanted with all of his heart to see Emma again.

After a moment, Evan noticed his audience — Leah, among the strangers who'd mocked him. The sea of faces conveyed various emotions, fear, jealousy, and even excitement.

Leah shook her head and jogged over to Evan. She placed her hand on his wounded shoulder.

"Shit!" Evan screamed in pain, his legs buckling.

He turned to see Leah's hand, now glowing, firmly placed on the open wound. Within moments, the pain in his shoulder began to fade, and his red health bar began to fill back up. He exhaled in relief.

"I can't believe how reckless you are," Leah scolded him.

Evan placed his right hand on his now healed shoulder, rubbing it. "Thanks, but you're not my mom. I don't need you to tell me how to live my life."

Leah shook her head. "I was just trying to be your friend. Why do you have to be such a dick?"

Evan's gaze lowered to the ground; despite this being his fight, she did reach out to him. Perhaps, he considered, one of the reasons he'd lost Emma was because he shut his heart off so tightly. Maybe it wasn't such a bad idea to open up once in a while. "I'm sorry."

"Still…" Leah smiled. "That was pretty awesome how you took that thing out."

"I told you I could take it by myself." Evan returned her smile, feeling more content than he ever had in his life.

III
Harpy

Evan swung his sword, slashing through air as a skeletal creature, covered in moss and mushrooms dashed backwards. *Fast*, Evan thought. The monster thrust its arm forward. Growing out of its palm was a mushroom, which twitched and wriggled as a mist of purple sprayed out from it and toward Evan.

"Barrier!"

The mist flowed around an invisible dome surrounding Evan.

"I got your back!" Leah's voice echoed. "Finish it!"

As the mist faded away, Evan dashed forward, thrusting his sword through the creature's skull.

The creature let out a wail of agony as it began to tremble and collapse into a pile of bones on the ground. Sprouting from the bones was a large, red mushroom.

Evan knelt down to touch it. A screen popped up reading, "ACQUIRED DEATH MUSHROOM x1."

"How many is that?" Evan turned, asking Leah.

"Ten," Leah counted, checking her inventory.

Evan stood up, walking towards Leah. "That's all we need, right?"

Leah nodded, smiling.

With that, a window popped up in front of Evan. "You've completed the Deadly Mushroom Quest." His rewarded experience and money were shown at the bottom of the pop-up.

"Great, I'm hungry." Evan raised his arms up, stretching as he moved towards Leah.

She smirked. "You're telling me."

The two started to make their way out of the forest.

"Hey," Evan stated. "What's up with these patches of black on the ground?"

Leah turned to him. "They are evidence of the super boss of this area, The Black Skeleton."

Evan nodded, studying the ground intently.

Leah gritted her teeth, narrowing her eyes at him. "Hey," she growled. "Don't go thinking just because you beat the Jackalope Prince that you can go around tackling every super boss on your own."

He chuckled. "Wouldn't dream of it."

"Really?" Leah seemed unconvinced.

"I promise," Evan said.

Leah watched him cautiously. "…Okay." After a moment, she added, "And don't go thinking you can take on any super boss you want. If you plan to fight a boss, come get me!"

Evan simply nodded as the two made their way out of the forest, through the field and toward the town of Amaryllis. Once there, the two bade good night and parted ways.

Evan headed for the cheap hotel nearby where he'd rented a room. It wasn't much — small and square, with a bed and a desk — but it gave him a place to rest between grinding.

He had been training with Leah for almost a full day. Once he'd unlocked the door, he made a beeline straight for the bed. He fell asleep almost instantly.

Evan sat in the backseat of his parents' car as he and his family drove down a dark mountain pass, headed home. They had spent the past day hiking, exploring, and taking in the fresh mountain air. Evan really couldn't see the appeal. He sighed, glancing at his phone: 9:21 p.m., and still no reception. As a result, he hadn't heard from Emma all day. He stared out his window, watching as they descended toward the brightly lit city at the base of the mountain, the only beacon in an otherwise dimly lit stretch of road. To him, they couldn't get home fast enough.

"Wasn't that fun?" Evan's dad exclaimed with enthusiasm.

Evan shifted his eyes, glancing and avoiding his father's gaze through the rearview mirror. After a few moments of awkward silence, his dad turned his eyes back to the road. Evan pulled out his phone. 9:24 p.m. Still no signal. I wonder what she's doing, he thought, turning his attention back to the window.

"Any more stops?" Evan's mom asked, glancing at her husband. "The night is still young." She turned in her seat to turn to her son for an answer.

Evan always felt more inclined to respond to his mother; he couldn't help but feel as though she took great care to avoid harsh tones and stares. It was as though she feared that doing so would physically harm him. He closed his eyes before turning to face her. Aside from her green eyes, Evan shared the majority of his physical features with her, although he was far paler.

"Let's just go home," Evan insisted. "It's late."

His mother smiled at him and turned away, and once more the family sat in silence, continuing down the mountain road.

After a few minutes, the radio suddenly clicked on. A man with a thick southern accent seemed to be nearing the end of a rant about the state of the country. Society had progressed too far, and people should re-access their roots, he was saying. Evan had, of course, immediately turned his attention to his phone — 9:30 p.m., but now with a single bar of signal. He began typing frantically, eager to reconnect with Emma: "On our way back now, let's catch up tonight." By the time the message had sent, he realized the car had filled with the twangs of country music.

Evan's dad turned the volume up on the radio. "You just don't hear good music like this anymore."

Evan shook his head; he'd never understood the appeal of country music. Meanwhile, his phone lit up, vibrating frantically; several messages had come through at once from all times of the day. He started to read through them; "9:31am – Miss you already! –Emma", "12:01pm – Eating at our favorite restaurant for lunch! Hope you aren't stuck eating a raccoon! –Emma", "4:25pm – <3 –Emma." However, his content was cut short.

A sudden screech echoed through the car, and two headlights appeared around the upcoming corner. Evan looked up, his heart pounding rapidly as he watched the oncoming lights. Time seemed to stand still as he gripped his cell phone. All of his recent memories of Emma flooded into his mind: eating together at school, spending time together after school, and texting each other constantly.

He recalled the first time they'd met — Evan was sitting in the library after school, playing a hand-held gaming device. He spent most of his free time playing games rather than studying these days.

"You know," said a gentle voice in his ear, "it's more effective if you utilize type advantage."

Evan had turned to see a pale-skinned girl with shoulder-length blonde hair hovering over his shoulder. He immediately moved his chair away from her, distancing himself on instinct. Despite this, she'd taken a seat right next to him, her eyes fixated on the game screen.

Wanting to get back to the game in peace, he figured indulging her would make her leave. "I'm doing this on purpose to challenge myself. I don't need help."

"Oh? You must be a pretty serious gamer then." The girl smiled. "My name is Emma."

Suddenly, Evan felt his body jerk; his family's car had come to a complete halt, narrowly avoiding a collision with the oncoming car.

"Damn drunk drivers..." Evan's dad exhaled. "Is everyone okay?"

"Y...yeah," Evan stammered, breathing heavily, his grip as tight as ever on his phone.

His mother remained silent.

After taking a few moments to regain themselves, the car started back up and they slowly made their way down the mountain pass. Evan glanced down at his phone, reading Emma's most recent response: "Sure, let me know when you get home." He smiled, more eager than ever to talk to her. He responded, "Will do. I miss you; it's been a rough day." With that, he closed his eyes and leaned his head against the cushion of the car seat.

Before he could fall asleep, Evan's eyes snapped open to another screech. I just want to get home, he thought. This is ridiculous. He twisted his body, trying to see behind the car.

"Shit," Evan's dad cursed, pressing hit foot further down on the gas pedal. "Not again..."

The car began to speed up, but the faster they went, the louder the screeching seemed to get. Around the next bend, the road widened, and adjacent to it was a large section of dirt and gravel that loomed over the city below. Evan's dad pulled off to the side. The screeching intensified until two headlights appeared in the distance from behind the family's car, barreling down the road at breakneck speed. However, rather than drive past the family, the car came to a sudden halt, parking behind theirs.

Evan's mom stared at her husband intently. He turned to her, smiling and leaned in to give her a kiss.

"It'll be okay," he whispered, before opening his door and stepping out of the car.

As he did, the driver's side door of the other car opened and a skinny man in a tank top with torn jeans stumbled out of the car. The smell of alcohol wafted through the air.

"Do you need a ride or something?" Evan's dad called out to the man. "We're trying to get back to the city, so if you need to get there, we can help."

The drunken man smirked; he had a scruffy, unkempt goatee, and his black eyes were glazed over. As he swung his right arm through the air, a gash spread across Evan's dad's neck and blood began to pour out from the open wound. He collapsed to the ground, blood pooling beneath his body. The drunken man laughed maniacally, while Evan's mom screamed in horror. The man turned toward the sound, a disturbing look of interest crossing his face briefly as he shuffled his way over to the car.

"Looky here," the drunken man slurred. "I can have me sum real fun with you, 'fore it's time ta go."

He crawled into the vehicle, looming over Evan's mom, the stench of alcohol filled the air. On the side of the man's neck, Evan noticed a black, x-shaped tattoo.

Everything felt surreal; how could an inconvenient family outing turn into something like this? Evan's body had gone numb. All he could do was watch in horror. The man's poorly shaven face closed in on his mother.

"Evan, run!" his mother screamed, slamming her knee up into the man's stomach.

The man groaned, reeling backwards. Before he could regain his composure, he was met with a swift kick, forcing him out of the open driver's side door. Evan's mom opened her own door and got out of the car, noticing that Evan remained in the back seat. She quickly opened his door and grabbed his arm. "Come on!"

She pulled him out and along with her as she ran from the vehicles. However, the two didn't get far before a sudden gust of wind enveloped them from behind. The two fell face first into the pavement. Evan's mom, without missing a beat, took to her feet immediately, pulling her son up with her. She wouldn't let him die. They struggled to run forward as the drunken man made his way closer toward the two.

"Ya can't escape!" He shouted, swinging his arm through the air wildly.

The air grew heavier around Evan and his mother as their movement began to slow.

"You need to run!" Evan's mother yelled, staring into her son's eyes.

Evan had halted in place. "Emma," he said methodically. "Where is Emma?"

His mother stared in awe at her son, who was clearly cracking from the shock. How could she protect him? He wasn't even able to listen to her. She bit her lip, looking around frantically.

However, it was too late. A whistling sound echoed through the area. Evan's mom turned to see a focused, spiraling cone of air rushing at her and her son. She grabbed her son's collar, and with a swift motion threw him off to the side. The sharp cone of wind billowed toward her, digging into her chest and forcing her backwards onto the ground.

"Damn kid ruined my fun!" the drunken man shouted. "Made me hit the wrong one!"

The man turned to see Evan lying motionless on the ground near his mother.

"Well... least I didn't make no orphans." The drunken man sneered. "Good job."

The tattoo on his neck began to glow as his body swayed. The blood from

Evan's mother and father began to gravitate toward the tattoo, seeping into it, until the bodies were completely drained. The drunken man's body was enveloped in a bright light, which shattered without a trace.

Evan lifted his body, turning his head to see his mother's and father's shriveled bodies in the distance. *A nightmare*, he thought. *This must be a nightmare.*

At that moment, he shot up, awake in his rented room. An all too real nightmare from his past.

"I wouldn't call that fair," he said softly, wiping tears from his eyes.

He was sitting up in a small bed at an inn in Amaryllis.

"It's not like I need to be reminded," he said to himself. "That's why I'm here; to get back what was lost."

He exhaled, rolled out of bed, and began to get dressed. His adventuring with Leah had paid off; he now had hard, leather garments as well as a longsword, and a small round shield. After equipping his gear, he left his room for the day, waving at the usual attendants. Everyone here seemed nice; it would be easy to simply stay in Amaryllis and start anew. He could certainly see the appeal of escaping from Earth to here. However, for him, it wasn't so easy to forget what had happened.

He made his way up the stone steps of the guild hall, where all of the guilds, major and minor, had set up recruiting stations. Evan walked by as the usual recruiters called out and attempted to wave him over. He smirked, shaking his head as he continued toward the center of the hall. He had quickly risen in level and status, his progress garnering him significant attention from others.

He eventually came upon a large bulletin board with several flyers pinned up. He touched the board, causing a menu to pop up in front of him. "'Raid Boss: Free the town from the tyranny of the mythical winged beast,'" Evan murmured, reading aloud to himself. "'Villagers are beseeching a powerful group of warriors to defeat Hollyhead the Harpy Queen.' This looks like the final quest for this area. If I complete it, I'll finally be able to move on."

He clicked "Accept" before turning from the board. *Sorry Leah — I lied*, he thought, before heading for the exit.

Evan made his way down the steps and across the paved road, heading into the marketplace. He sighed in relief, grateful that Paul wasn't manning his booth. Just about every day, that boy had tried talking to him and selling him goods. Evan all-around disliked him.

Evan stepped up to the Magic Emporium, scrolling through the menu. The man behind the counter glanced around his book at Evan, chuckling. "Kid, you've come here damn near every day to look through my inventory."

"Seems like he's grown considerably within a short time though," the ebony-skinned boy in armor said, stepping up beside Evan. "Put his purchase on my tab today." He paused, turning to face Evan. "Care to take a walk with me?"

Evan glanced over at the boy without acknowledging him. Promptly he purchased four vials of blue liquid and four vials of red, reluctantly allowing the boy to pay.

"I suppose I owe you as much now," Evan said, scrolling through his equipment menu to equip the potions to his belt, for easy access.

The boy smiled. "My name is Mike."

"Evan."

Mike turned, walking toward the guild hall. Begrudgingly, Evan followed him. *Here it comes*, he thought with a sigh.

"Evan," Mike began, intently focused on the boy in question, "have you ever considered joining a guild?"

"Not particularly," Evan replied. "I play better alone."

"Yes, I can see that," Mike chuckled. "Still, I represent the most powerful guild in the game. We are always looking for players with extreme potential or skill, and I think you have both."

"Are you recruiting me for a guild?" Evan glared at Mike. "Or asking me out on a date?"

Mike smiled, unfazed. "Would you be willing to, at least, come and meet with our leader?"

Evan paused, facing Mike. "I really don't have time to waste getting caught up in guild politics. I have my own agenda."

"Of course. However, there is no doubt that being in a guild, especially the most powerful one, has its…" Mike paused, withdrawing a scroll from his inventory and extending it out to Evan. "Privileges."

Evan eyed the scroll suspiciously before taking it. He stared at Mike for a moment, then hesitantly unrolled the scroll. It was labeled, "Resurrection Spell."

"This…" Evan's head shot up, his expression darkening. "How did you know about this?"

"I was there the day you first came to that man's shop," Mike said simply. "I heard what you said about needing powerful healing spells." He smirked. "I assume this is what you wanted? The ability to resurrect the dead."

"So, now what?" Evan asked, clinging tightly to the scroll.

"Don't worry — I'm not going to take it from you," Mike assured him. "Consider it... a gift." He smiled, although Evan still wasn't convinced. "All I request is that you just come to meet our leader. You don't even have to commit to joining."

Evan stared at Mike, considering for a moment before realizing he had little choice if he wanted the scroll.

"Fine, but I need to finish the final quest in this town," he stated. "Can you agree to meet me first thing tomorrow morning?"

Mike nodded. "Of course. See you then."

Evan watched as Mike ascended the stone steps, heading into the guild hall. He looked down at the scroll once again before stashing it into his inventory, wondering how long Mike had been observing him. He had a bad feeling about this.

"Damn that Mike..." He sighed, making his way to the center of town. As he approached, Evan noticed several people huddled together around the familiar female statue.

"Join us!" A boy shouted, waving at pedestrians. A girl from the group noticed as Evan made his way up to the statue; she strolled over toward him.

Evan turned to face her. Her hair was golden, reaching past her shoulders, and her body was wrapped in soft leather adornments.

"Hey, are you trying to do this quest too?" she asked, pointing at the statue.

"Yeah," he said flatly, uninterested and wondering what she wanted from him.

"My name is Diane. Why not join our team?" She pointed at two boys who were waving down other passing players. "Harpies are supposed to be incredibly ferocious spirits of wind. Although, it's a raid boss, so regardless of the monster, you'd have to be at an impossibly high level to win alone."

"I'm fine." Evan turned to face the statue. She was right, and her offer was appealing, but he felt as though this was something he had to do alone.

Diane groaned. "Don't be like that." Her voice softened as she stepped closer to him. Evan felt her press her breasts against his side. "MMORPGs are all about making new friends," she whispered in his ear. "If you help us, I'll help you."

Evan turned his head, glaring at her.

"You think this is all just a game?" he said, struggling to contain his voice to a whisper.

"Yeah, a fun one." She giggled, brushing her cheek against his.

Roughly, he pushed her away, forcing her to stumble and fall to the ground. Her friends quickly took notice, running over to the two.

"What's the meaning of this!?" shouted a boy with spiky red hair.

The other boy knelt down to help Diane up. Upon seeing his teal, curly hair, Evan recognized him as Paul.

Before Evan could defend himself, Diane cut him off.

"Oh, Mark…" She spoke softly again, leaning heavily on Paul for support. "I was just asking if he would help, and then all of a sudden he attacked me," she whined.

"What the hell, man!" Mark shouted, stepping toward Evan. "There's no need to be an asshole."

Others walking by had stopped, watching the drama unfold.

Evan glanced around at the crowd before turning his eyes to Diane. "Is that so? I think your group should re-evaluate its priorities." He glared pointedly at Paul, who remained silent.

"What does that mean!?" Mark shouted, glancing back at his friends and then back to Evan.

"It's easier to survive if you use a sword instead of breasts," Evan stated.

Diane's jaw dropped, and she shot Evan a look of faux disgust.

"Just because I wouldn't let you feel me up, you have to attack me?!" she shouted, covering her chest with her arm.

Evan sighed; this was more than he'd bargained for. He hadn't even instigated the girl, and yet, he'd somehow gotten pulled into her drama. He could probably force them to leave him alone, but he'd rather avoid that.

"You wanted a piece of my girlfriend, huh!?" Mark bellowed, getting closer to Evan and drawing his sword.

"This is getting out of hand…" Evan groaned.

"It'll be over soon enough," Mark sneered. "I demand you duel me!"

"I don't have time for that," Evan said, turning away.

"Well, you shouldn't go around being an asshole then!" Mark shouted.

Evan turned back, glaring at Mark. "I hate to break it to you, but your girlfriend is a whore and you're an idiot." Evan faced the statue again, placing a hand on it. The statue began glowing.

"You coward!" Mark cried, dashing forward to stab Evan.

Suddenly, Evan was enveloped in a blue light, and then he vanished as Mark's blade pierced through nothing but air.

Mark gripped his blade, glaring at the empty spot where Evan had been.

Diane edged closer to Mark, wrapping her arms around him.

"Don't worry, baby — that raid boss will kill him," she whispered into his ear.

"He'd better hope so," Mark growled, sheathing his sword.

Evan found himself at the base of a small hill; his heart was still racing from his previous confrontation. He exhaled, making his way up a trail that had been carved out of its side. Why people liked that existed, he would never understand. He hadn't done anything wrong; all he wanted to do was play this game and get Emma back. It seemed like he was always being forced into situations against his will.

"Why can't I just exist without having to answer to someone or something all the time?" He spoke to himself, venting his frustration. "If there is a God, then he must be out to get me."

As he made his way up the hill, he met no resistance from enemies, which Evan found odd. Usually various monsters would block the path, but this area was conveniently — and suspiciously — empty. He sighed; a bit disappointed in the lack of monsters. After his encounter with Diane, he could use something to take out his stress on. It was only a short distance to the top, where a harpy floated in the air, glaring intimidatingly. The harpy was slender; her limbs were more bone than skin, which was pale blue, and covered in strange markings. Red stripes ran down the length of each leg and arm, which was wrapped in leather belts up to her plate mail. Crimson feathers protruded from her elbows, knees, feet, hands, and grew out from her back into two large wings. Despite all of this, she had the face of a beautiful, young woman. Above her head in plain text read, "Hollyhead the Harpy Queen."

The creature screeched, and suddenly dashed toward him. As she reached Evan, she swiped her claws. Evan easily met them with his blade. They clashed, pushing against one another in a deadlock. He rolled the blade, parrying her claw upward, and then lunged forward, thrusting his sword into her left shoulder. She wailed, reeling backwards. The blade tore out of her shoulder as she did, blood splattering the ground, running down her shoulder, and covering his sword.

Evan quickly rushed forward, swinging his blade toward her. The harpy reached out, grabbing the blade with her claw. She tightened her grip, allowing the blade to dig into her hand and drawing a fresh stream of blood. Evan pulled back, but the harpy quickly snapped the top of the blade off, tossing the loose tip at him like a dagger. It grazed his cheek, and blood flowed freely from the cut.

Evan jumped back just in time to avoid another swipe of her claw, raising his broken sword up in defense.

The harpy cried out, shooting toward him with her claw poised to slash.

As Evan gripped the blade with both hands, a blue aura formed around his body, which climbed up the length of the sword solidifying around it so that the blade had become encased in jagged ice. The harpy screeched and her nails lengthened, stretching out further and further from the base of her claw. Evan stood his ground, slashing his blade diagonally through the air as the harpy came within reach. The blade struck her neck, severing her head from her body. As the harpy's head soared off to the side, her body fell limp next to Evan.

Evan exhaled as a window popped up in his center view, displaying his rewards. He dismissed the window as the ice melted off his sword, and suddenly he was enveloped in the same blue light that had brought him here, teleporting back to the town.

IV
Corruption

Evan suddenly appeared back in the town square with a flash of blue light. The crowd began murmuring, staring at him in disbelief.

"Did he kill that boss... alone?"

"That's impossible..."

"He would need to be at least level 20..."

Mark, Paul, and Diane stared at Evan, shocked.

"Must have been luck," Mark murmured through his teeth.

Evan turned away from the crowd, walking east toward the marketplace. The battle had been fierce, but just about every battle he had been in during his stay in this place had been. Even if he barely got by after each battle, that was fine. If he couldn't survive to the end and save Emma, then he had nothing left to live for anyway.

"Let's keep an eye on him," Mark whispered to the other two. "If he leaves the town, we'll kill him."

Diane furrowed her brow.

Evan turned into the marketplace, walking toward a familiar booth.

"Hey Leah," Evan greeted the familiar green-haired woman. "My sword broke. Can you repair it?" He placed the blade down onto her booth.

Leah sighed, gazing down reproachfully at the blade.

"If you're going to keep breaking swords, why not just invest in a magic sword skill?"

Evan shrugged. "Well, I made do this time."

"You always say that." Leah shook her head. "You fight like you don't care if you live or die."

Her brown eyes focused intently on him, glazed with concern. Evan could only stare blankly at her. She closed her eyes, taking the sword and placing it onto the anvil next to her booth. She took a seat in front of it, picked up a nearby hammer and began to strike the blade to sharpen it.

"Listen, I'm serious." Her eyes focused on the blade. "I am going to stop servicing your gear if you don't stop being so reckless."

"Well, you won't have to worry about me much longer," Evan replied as he watched her. "I just beat the Harpy Queen, which marks the end of all my quests in this area."

Her hammer stopped in midair at his words.

"…oh," she said softly, the hammer falling toward the blade once more. "Who'd you party with for that? You know...I could have helped…"

"I did it alone, of course," Evan stated simply.

Leah sighed as a final strike echoed through the air, fully restoring Evan's sword.

She let the hammer slide out of her hand, hitting the ground with a *clank*. Taking the mended weapon in her hand, she stood up and faced Evan.

"At least come visit sometime," she breathed out softly.

"We'll see," he told her blankly. "I don't do all this for the fun of it. I've got something I need to do."

"I see." Leah's eyes lowered. "Something important enough to risk your life for?"

"Yeah." Evan reached out taking the blade from her. "Now, all that's left is the Black Skeleton."

Her eyes shot up, her gaze drilling into him.

"Wait," she shouted frantically at his declaration. "You promised me!"

Evan smiled weakly at her.

"Why are you being so reckless!?" she shouted. "It's one thing to have a goal to work toward; it's another thing to just run into danger for no reason at all!"

Evan shook his head. "It can't be helped."

"At least let me come with you!" she pleaded, walking out from behind her booth.

"Sorry, Leah." He turned, walking away from her. This was something he intended to do alone — he didn't need to risk anyone else's life but his own.

As she watched him head out of town, she noticed three figures following him, a fourth close behind. Immediately she returned to her booth, quickly packing away her wares.

Once in the field, Evan made his way to the adjacent forest. He stepped through the threshold of the trees and onto a dirt path that extended forward into the forest. The night sky was mostly blocked by a canopy of branches and leaves, moonlight bleeding through what space was available.

Not far behind him; Mark smirked. "Alright, let's go in after him."

"I'm going to stay here," Diane said obstinately.

Mark spun around, glaring at Diane. "What!? This is our chance!"

"Nah, I'm not a forest type of girl. You two go on ahead if you want." She turned her attention to a nearby jackalope, kneeling down and watching it hop back and forth.

Mark stared at her in disbelief before turning to Paul.

"Well, it's not like that forest leads anywhere," Paul said. "We can always ambush him from this entrance once he emerges, weakened and tired."

Mark sighed. "Fine..."

As Evan moved deeper into the forest, he noticed his surroundings seeming to decay. The lush green leaves had fallen off the trees, now brown and tattered along the ground. The trees themselves had grayed; the bark rotted off the bases.

Eventually he came around a small bend, and then he saw it: an ebony skeleton, limply holding a curved sword by its side. It wasn't massive, but it was tall — about two feet taller than Evan. A tattered leather buckler hung from its bony, decayed waist, and a faint purple aura radiated from the undead creature. Evan noted that the ground beneath it had rotted far further than the rest of the surrounding area.

Cautiously Evan drew his longsword and readied his own buckler. Although he'd tried to conceal himself in the trees, he seemed to catch the skeleton's empty eyes, as it prepared its weapons to attack.

His cover blown, Evan dashed forward, swinging his sword toward the undead warrior. The skeleton raised its buckler, halting Evan's blade. The closer he came to the enemy, the heavier the air became, until Evan found himself gasping for breath. Dimly, he realized that his red health bar was slowly depleting. Before he could counter it, the skeleton had swung its own sword down toward him. Evan raised his shield to guard against the attack, but to no avail; a sharp pain pulsed through his forearm as he watched his shield shatter to pieces. The force of the blow pushed him back; Evan planted his boots firmly into the rotten earth, but the attack forced him several feet back. A large gash now lined his forearm, spilling a thick trail of blood. Incredibly, his health had dropped a whole quarter from the encounter. He took a slight breath as his blue tattoo began to glow, and his left forearm became wrapped in a blue aura. Gradually, the wound closed, and his health began to rise.

Sword in hand, the skeleton rushed at him. Evan swung his blade forward in response, but then the skeleton shifted, charging with its shield drawn. With an echoing clang, Evan's attack was met by the oncoming shield, and swiftly, the two leapt back from one another. Evan glanced at his sword, noticing a crack in in the metal from the impact. "What the hell?"

Again, the skeleton lunged forward. Evan immediately took a step back, spinning his body to the left so that he simultaneously evaded the attack while moving closer to the hellion. From there, Evan made his own stab into the creature's side; however, his weapon shattered on contact. He could only stare in awe as the skeleton countered, turning and slashing the boy. Evan groaned; his leather armor had torn vertically down the center. He reeled back as the skeleton immediately followed up with another attack. Breathing heavily, Evan quickly raised his shattered sword, preparing to block as much as he could, but as the skeleton's blade cut through the air toward the boy, a blue aura shot out from the hilt of his broken blade. The aura weaved itself into a blade of ice, easily halting the skeleton's attack.

Evan rolled his wrist, parrying the skeleton's blade with his icy weapon. Then, he quickly stabbed forward into the fiend's left shoulder. The creature howled, and a patch of ice began to spread out from the point of impact. Evan knew he had to act fast; his magic was draining with every second he maintained the ice. Promptly he lunged forward, slashing at the skeleton again. It tried to raise its buckler, but the patch of ice had locked the skeleton's arm in place. Evan's blade struck the fiend and he followed through, rapidly slashing the skeleton's body and greatly reducing its health. Finally, the skeleton let out a wail of agony, and its dark bones crumbled to dust into the earth below.

Evan exhaled as the blade of ice melted into a puddle on the ground, his magic nearly spent. A window popped up providing his experience and reward: a unique buckler. More importantly, he could finally finish this quest and leave Amaryllis. Now, his real quest could begin; he wouldn't let anyone stop him from getting Emma back.

After dismissing the pop-up, he withdrew two small glass bottles from his inventory: one filled with a deep red liquid, and another filled with a shimmering blue liquid. He downed them both in seconds as his health and magic bar slowly filled back to their maximum values. Once healed, he made his way out of the woods, only to hear a sharp voice echo through the air.

"Stay where you are!"

Evan turned to find Mark, Paul and Diane blocking the exit, weapons at the ready.

Mark smirked. "Nowhere to run to now. Perhaps you can convince us to

spare you. Drop all your gear, items, and money, and get on your knees and beg."
Evan shook his head. "I'm afraid I can't do that."

Mark nodded at Paul, who shot an arrow from his crossbow, piercing Evan in the stomach. He gritted his teeth as the pain shot through his body and his health bar took a slight dip.

"You never learn!" Diane shouted. "You mess with us, and you'll die!"

"You guys are such assholes," Evan groaned as he pulled the arrow from his gut. He then brought up his inventory and equipped the buckler he had just received. He raised it up, covering the center of his body.

"What a pathetic shield!" Diane laughed. "It suits you."

Mark's eyes widened as he took a step backwards.

"I see one of you isn't as dumb as they appear," Evan said softly.

"What…?" Diane looked back at Mark.

A faint purple aura had spread out from the buckler and surrounded Evan.

"W…why would you equip something that's cursed?" Mark stammered.

"You didn't leave me with much choice." Evan stood his ground, glaring at the trio.

"I'm not afraid!" Paul shouted as he shot a barrage of arrows at Evan.

Evan shifted the buckler to meet the trajectory of the arrows, each crumbling to dust upon impact.

"What the hell?!" Paul stumbled back; his eyes wide with disbelief. "They should have at least damaged such a puny shield!"

"This is the Unholy Buckler," Evan stated matter-of-factly as he slowly edged closer to the group.

"There's no way someone as low a level as you beat the Black Skeleton!" Diane screamed, throwing her arms up in a fit.

"Levels are just numbers," Evan flashed a quick smirk.

Suddenly, he rushed forward, bashing the buckler against Diane's armor and cracking it as she reeled back from the blow.

"Sh-shit," she stammered, coughing and stumbling backwards.

Evan immediately bashed her armor again, shattering it to pieces. Her cheeks became flushed, her body only covered by the game's default bra and panties. Gazing over her body, Evan noticed a pink diamond tattooed on her left inner thigh. She quickly raised her arms to cover herself, slinking back behind Mark and Paul.

"Do something!" she screamed.

Mark and Paul stood, awestruck, watching as Evan held his ground.

"You idiots are useless!" Diane screeched from behind them.

A spear suddenly appeared in her hands, the head erupting with a pink aura. She phased forward, appearing suddenly in front of Evan and thrusting the spear toward him. He blocked with his buckler, splintering the spear in half. He withdrew his broken sword and in an instant, ice had formed into a blade from the hilt. He slashed the girl's exposed stomach and she fell backwards, blood gushing from the wound and onto the grass. Evan loomed over her as her health began to drop.

"Wait!" Mark cried out. "We're sorry! We surrender!!"

Evan looked up at Mark, nodding. "Very well. If you leave and never show yourself in front of me again, I will spare you."

Suddenly, the trees behind them rustled, and Evan turned to see Mike jump down from a nearby branch.

"Don't be naïve," he said. "If you don't kill them now, they will likely come after you again — just as they have already done twice now."

Evan rolled his eyes. "What're you doing here?"

"I saw these three follow you out of town earlier and decided to follow them," Mike said. "You shouldn't take your eyes off of your opponent."

Evan turned to see that Diane had gotten to her feet, a knife in her hand, and somehow, she had already closed in on him. Evan grunted as the knife punctured his stomach. He couldn't believe how stubborn she was being. Pain and anger bubbling within him, he struck her face with his buckler, forcing her back onto the ground. He then pulled the knife from his gut and tossed it off into the brush.

"NO!" Mark screamed. "What're you doing!? Don't antagonize him!"

Diane scoffed, slowly making her way to her feet. She wiped the blood from her lips, breathing heavily. "Shut up, Mark, you always were a coward."

"It's over," Evan said flatly, struggling to hold back his feelings of contempt. She had been out for him since day one, and he'd love nothing more than to put her in his place. But he knew all too well that killing wouldn't solve anything.

Mike moved his eyes from Evan to Diane, who only glared.

"Shut up, asshole!" she cried. "Your friend is right. If you don't kill me now, then I, at least, will pursue you until I kill you myself."

Evan sighed. "What is your problem?"

"This world is kill or be killed," she said.

"Why? That makes no sense." Evan shook his head.

"You're pathetically naïve," she said, spitting blood at his feet. "You killed someone to get here — we all did. That is the only way to enter this realm. Everyone here is a murderer."

Evan blinked. "That was…"

"Different?" She finished his sentence. "Murder is murder. Grow up! Do you know why the pain here is real? These bodies are our real bodies. So, what do you think happens when your health hits zero?"

Evan looked down at the ground. It was becoming more and more clear that she couldn't be reasoned with.

"You *die*," she continued. "We are all murderers here, regardless of the circumstances. We killed to get here, and killing others is the easiest way to stay here. Why do you think that killing another player provides such high bonuses? There is no room for morality in this world."

Mike placed a hand on Evan's shoulder. "The girl speaks the truth. Your hands were sullied the moment you entered this world." Mike pointed to Evan's hand. "That tattoo is evidence."

Evan closed his eyes. "It's my choice, isn't it?" He opened his eyes to look at Diane. "I'm willing to risk you coming back. It'll be good motivation to stay strong."

"Dumbass," she sneered.

Another barrage of arrows approached Evan's left. He reacted late, raising his buckler to fend off a few, but taking a couple of arrows in his side. He groaned in pain as Mike distanced himself from the boy.

Immediately after their surprise attack, Mark and Paul took the opportunity to flank him.

Mark dashed toward Evan. He gripped his sword with both hands, swinging the blade to attempt to cleave off Evan's head. However, Evan raised his buckler and the blade struck it instead, cracking, but sending Evan to the ground.

Again, Evan heard a slew of arrows rushing toward him. He raised his buckler, blocking what bolts he could, groaning as more plunged into his body and his health slowly dwindled. Mike continued to only watch from the distance.

While Evan attempted to stand, Mark took opportunity to swing his blade at him. Evan stepped toward Mark, avoiding the slash and stabbing Mark's stomach with his blade of ice. Mark groaned, blood spilling out from his gut as the blade was withdrawn. Following through, Evan swung his blade again, this time slicing Mark's upper body. Blood splattered onto Evan's body and face. Paul aimed from a distance, ready to fire again.

"Is this what you really want?" Evan asked softly.

"How...dare you!" Mark screamed. "You're pathetic! You nearly killed my girlfriend! You think we'd really just let all that go!?"

He let out a roar of fury, bringing his sword down upon Evan. Without hesitation, Evan raised his buckler, and Mark's weapon broke to pieces against it. Relentless, Mark began to swing his arms wildly. Evan could see the desperation in his eyes as he stepped back out of Mark's reach.

"Very well…" Evan sighed.

As Mark lunged forward, Evan took one last, hard look at the boy's face. He then thrust his sword forward, piercing Mark's chest. Mark gasped, blood trickling down his lips. Evan pulled his sword away, allowing Mark's body to fall limply onto the ground. He looked down at the corpse, its blood beginning to pool, as he burned the details into his memory. If he was going to become a murderer, then the least he could do is remember what he had done.

Mike smirked.

"No!" Diane screamed.

A flurry of arrows flew toward Evan once more. He rolled out of the way, quickly springing to his feet. He rushed toward Paul, swinging his sword upward and cutting him from his hip up through his shoulder. Paul gasped; blood spilled from his mouth and the large gash that Evan had just created. Paul fell backward, his eyes closing softly as he hit the ground. Evan turned to see Diane, barely able to stand, holding her broken spear.

Evan slowly made his way to her, staring intently. As he came within her reach, she snarled, thrusting the splintered wood at him. He raised his buckler, stopping the attack. The purple aura flowed from the buckler, seeping into the wood. It began rotting, and quickly crumbled in her hands.

He hesitated.

Her eye twitched, and she began to scream. "Now what!? Still going to spare me!? After all of this!?"

He lowered his eyes.

"You had no problem slaying my boyfriend and his friend in cold blood! Oh, don't tell me it's because I'm a girl! Can't hurt girls? Or, are you just some pervert who wants to use me as a sex slave?!" She spat at his face. "You disgust

—"

A red line spread across her neck; the skin opened, and blood poured from the gash. She fell to her knees, and her body collapsed onto the ground. Evan lowered his arm, the blade of ice melting away. His gaze lingered over her sprawled out body. He couldn't bring himself to feel sorry for her; he had tried so many times to spare her. Ultimately, his goal was more important than their lives.

The battle having ended, the fallen trio's bodies began to shimmer with light. Blood from their bodies, the ground, and what had spilled onto Evan began to glow as the skin on his hand absorbed it. The bodies soon became nothing but shriveled bags of bones.

A window popped up, providing his rewards. "4x multiplier," he read.

Mike casually walked over to Evan. "Yes. Remember what the girl said. Defeating another player is the fastest way to gain experience, and level up. This is why many players share her attitude, and, to her point, we all did have to murder to get here anyway."

Evan looked down at the ground, feeling emptier than ever. Is this really what he would have to become in order to get Emma back? How many more people would he have to kill? How many more people would he choose to kill? *Will I even be the same person at the end of all of this?* He thought.

Suddenly Leah's voice called out, "What's going on here!?"

"A friend of yours?" Mike asked, watching the girl make her way toward them.

Evan looked up at her, broken sword in hand, his armor torn, and his body covered in grime, blood, and wounds. She grimaced as she reached him.

"Why?" she demanded. "Why did you just murder three people!?"

Evan stared at her. "I had no choice."

"It seems like you never have a choice," Leah scolded.

"What are you even doing here, Leah?" he yelled.

"I was worried!" she retorted. "How can I not be?! Look at yourself!"

Evan glared at her. "I don't know what you want me to say."

"Say you'll stop being so reckless!" Leah demanded. "Say you're not a murderer! Say you're sorry! Say you'll just stay here, where it's safe! Say anything..."

Mike stared expectantly at Evan.

"I can't do that," Evan exhaled. "I have something I must do."

"Something so important that you'd become a murderer!?"

"If I must murder to become strong...strong enough to get what I desire," Evan said coldly, "then I will. Besides, we're all already murderers..."

"I see," Leah said, taking a step backwards. Tears formed in her eyes as she continued. "I can't follow you down that path. I know we did bad things to get here, but I never thought you could indulge in that behavior. I guess I was wrong about you."

Evan smiled weakly. "I guess you were."

Leah glowered at him. "You jerk! People can live here without having to spill one another's blood, you know! There's no reason why we can't be civil, like we were before...on Earth."

"This isn't Earth," Mike intervened. "People came here to escape from what Earth provided. So, there aren't a whole lot of people who will accept living here the way they lived there."

Leah scoffed, turning to Evan. "Fine. Don't bother asking me for help anymore."

"I won't," Evan retorted.

Leah lowered her eyes, turning away from the two and running back to the town.

"Not much of a ladies man, I see," Mike chuckled.

"Pretty sure I already said I'm not much of a team player," Evan stated, annoyed. "Besides, I have my own reason for being here."

"We all do," Mike said. "But that doesn't mean you should shut everyone out of your life. It's easier to survive in groups."

"I don't want to waste time goofing off." Evan glanced at Mike. "I have something I must do, and it takes priority. Can you guarantee that your guild won't stop me from moving freely?"

"No, but just because you'll be expected to take part in missions doesn't mean you won't get free time," Mike explained. "Besides, all the resources available to you will make your quest much easier."

Evan looked up at the night sky. He already accepted the scroll from Mike. At this point, he had an obligation to meet Mike's leader. "Well, let's get this over with."

V
Alexgrad

Evan and Mike appeared before a large gate, with two soldiers standing on either side.

"Good day," one addressed Mike.

Mike nodded, leading Evan through the gate. The initial stretch from the gate to the city was a vast trench, with thick walls extending on either side of them and funneling into a confined pathway.

"Did you know that certain cities were built by the players?" Mike asked.

"Of all of them, this is by far the grandest. We call it... Alexgrad." They stepped out from the trench's path and into an open area. In the distance was a large, stone castle sitting well above the ground, reaching endlessly into the sky.

Directly in front of them was another gated barricade, although the soldiers immediately allowed them passage. Past the second gate was a large grassy field. Several soldiers were fighting one another while one walked back and forth, apparently leading the group.

"This city is the base of operations for our guild," Mike said, he and Evan looking out at the training soldiers. "If you join, you will have free access to this city and the resources within it. You could live quite comfortably here. Although, if you enjoy danger, there are always combat missions available."

Evan scanned the field before turning to Mike with a smirk. "This is the whole city?"

"Er, no..." Mike cleared his throat. "Our Guild is more like its own self-sufficient society. Not all of the roles are combat roles. We need people to forge gear, farm the land, provide food, mine for resources, medics, and anything we can get, really. This first area is set up for optimal military functionality. If we get attacked, we'd rather have our soldiers take the brunt of the force, rather than the civilians. However, most of our citizens have some basic combat ability."

Evan nodded as they continued to walk; he couldn't deny the benefits of such a large guild. It would beat scavenging in the field by himself every day. Halfway through the field, several soldiers were practicing magic. The two stopped and watched as a soldier shot a ball of fire at a distant target, incinerating it.

"We have a master in each field of combat to help teach and progress our soldiers," Mike said. "Beyond this field are barracks, specialty shops, and classrooms set up specifically for our military, and beyond that is the civilian city, which is more like the city you started in."

Evan began to feel as though joining them might not be such a bad idea. If nothing else, he would be able to develop his skills exponentially. *I can always leave when I've reached a level I'm satisfied with*, he thought to himself.

Eventually they reached the other side of the field, passing through another gate. Inside this area was a more conservative cityscape: paved roads with square, stone buildings lining the street. Several soldiers, fully equipped in steel armor, were marching in three perfectly straight lines.

"Our teams are given the best gear," Mike stated. "We issue it based on rank and level. It's a bit of an incentive to get promoted, making it much easier than grinding."

"Given the setup, I doubt many soldiers get the opportunity to spend late nights grinding anyway," Evan remarked softly.

"I suppose not." Mike scoffed. "We have special teams that grind gear specifically for issue and anything that is exceptionally rare is stored in our supply storage. Items like that get evaluated and eventually issued to exceptional soldiers. You could easily get into a position like that if you joined us."

The two continued through the streets, passing several groups of carefree soldiers.

"Although this is a military, it's still more lax than, say, the Marines or anything like that from Earth," Mike continued. "Education and combat standards are what are most important. We don't want to compromise anyone's individuality."

"That's good," Evan chuckled. "I've never been good with strict regulations."

"Lucky you — our only uniform requirement is an emblem that can be placed anywhere on your body as long as it's visible," Mike mentioned before continuing onward, heading deeper into the city. They passed through a large, stone archway, and continued along through a wide street. Apartments lined either side, all the way up to a large gate in the distance. Now they walked beneath an overpass and came upon a large, open market. Shops, booths, and tables spread out in all directions.

"All of the best gear comes through here," Mike gloated.

Most of the shops were open, with various gear, food, and items on display. Merchants eagerly approached pedestrians, brandishing shimmering jewelry, armor, and weapons. It was far busier than the marketplace in Amaryllis, and far livelier.

"This is pretty much the soul of our city," Mike said.

"I can see that." Evan scanned the marketplace. Everyone seemed so natural, as though they had lived here their whole lives. As though they didn't have to worry for their own safety at all. He paused, unable to put out of his mind what had just happened with Paul and his friends. Taking notice, Mike continued his dialogue.

"Perhaps you'd like to stop and get some gear?" Mike asked, glancing over at Evan's torn and ragged armor. "That last battle seemed a bit rough, after all."

Evan stared at him, unamused. *Says the guy who stood there and watched me almost die*, he thought to himself. They approached a stone building, with a large shield and a helmet mounted atop it hanging above its entrance. As they entered, Evan's eye was drawn by the various colored armors. Full sets were dressed onto several mannequins spread throughout the main lobby. "I leveled up quite a bit since all that happened," he told Mike. "I'm not sure where I am with gear anymore."

"Heh, you might be one of the few people who care about leveling consistently." Mike chuckled. "Most players are happy with being boosted as high as possible and getting whatever is available. At your level, you probably can't quite get any heavy armor yet, anyway. The best you could hope to upgrade to is thicker leather, or maybe some light chain mail."

"That's fine," Evan said, scrolling through the options. "I tend to utilize magic mostly anyway, so I don't need to be, like, a tank."

Evan purchased several enchanted pieces of armor, including a new thicker, leather tunic and pants, a chain mail undershirt, and chained boots and gloves.

"Mind if we check out weapons and accessories?"

"No problem at all." Mike smiled. "We still have time before the scheduled meeting. Let's see a healer as well and see if we can't get that cursed buckler removed."

Not far down the street was yet another stone building with a thick, broad sword stretched horizontally above the door. Embroidered along the blade read, "Bellum." As with the previous store, several swords were on display right in the lobby, with a wider assortment of weapons mounted on the walls and behind the main counter.

"Isn't your sword broken?" Mike asked.

"Yeah, so what?" Evan snapped back defensively.

"You used it as a base and cast magic through it to create a frozen sword," Mike explained.

"Yeah, I know how my own spell works," Evan said bluntly. It seemed as though all Mike did was condescend him.

Mike smirked. "Aren't you planning on just being able to create swords from nothing with that type of spell? Why waste money on expensive swords, when you could just buy a wand that will help boost your magic damage? It would be the same thing, having it as the base and creating a sword of ice."

Saving money isn't necessarily a bad thing, he thought. Although, when it came to games, he was no stranger to having more than he ever needed. In the end, whatever made his skills more effective was the best bet. Despite this, conceding to Mike wasn't something he really wanted to do. He paused for a moment more before reluctantly responding, "Yeah, I guess."

"It just seems like it'd be more efficient, and you'd get more out of it," Mike suggested.

The two left the weapon shop, making their way over to a nearby stall, draped in purple cloth. Evan glanced through various books, accessories, and staves before ultimately buying a wand that provided, among other things, a boost to ice damage. In addition, he purchased a couple of plain silver earrings, one socketed with a blue orb, as well as a leather-bound book which contained several basics for manipulating ice.

"Alright, let's get that buckler off you and see the fruits of your purchases." Mike smiled.

He led Evan to a nearby large, white building. Hanging down from the roof over the entrance was a piece of cloth with a red cross etched into it. Inside, there were several rows of chairs, many of which were filled with people. Mike waved his arm, catching the attention of a nearby woman dressed in a white robe. She immediately came over, leading the two into a small room filled with various charts and posters depicting the human body. The woman immediately began examining the buckler.

"What about the people in the lobby?" Evan inquired.

"Don't worry about them," she retorted without hesitation. Her hand began to radiate a white light, and just as she moved it over the buckler, it slid off Evan's arm, falling to the ground with an echoing *clang*.

"Think someone would buy it in the marketplace?" Evan asked Mike.

"Probably." Mike knelt down, scooping up the shield before handing it over to Evan.

"I'll buy it from you right now," the woman in white intervened. "By breaking that item down we can study the properties of the curse and perhaps find a way to break curses more easily."

"Sure," Evan said, bringing up a trade window and exchanging the item for gold. "Can I use a room to equip my new stuff?"

The woman in white nodded. "You can use this room."

"I'll wait for you outside then," Mike stated as he and the woman both left the room, closing the door behind them. Evan promptly brought up his inventory window, removing his damaged and outdated gear with a couple of clicks. "I doubt anyone would buy this crap at this point."

Items in the inventory had a few options available: they could be equipped, thrown away, or broken down. By breaking the items down, they would become base materials that could be used for crafting other armor and weapons. This is what Evan opted to do before equipping his new gear. He stepped out of the room with fresh armor, two silver rings attached to his upper left ear, and one hanging off his right earlobe. He turned to see Mike leaning against the wall.

"Do I have time to sell off some stuff?" Evan asked.

Mike nodded but said nothing. Considering his usual banter, Evan noted that he had been uncharacteristically quiet this whole time.

Upon leaving the medical building, the two headed back to the marketplace, where Evan proceeded to pawn off his excess materials before continuing north with Mike to a small domesticated village area.

"This is where non-military inhabitants live," Mike pointed out.

The area was based atop a large field, much different from the city itself. Houses sat on patches of grass with trees and brushes lining the paved streets. At the center of it all was a large basin filled with water, with a tall pillar of marble reaching up into the sky. Mike had picked up the pace, and they moved hastily through the village. Eventually, reaching yet another gate.

"Beyond here is the castle," Mike announced.

The two passed unceremoniously through the gate, following steps up toward the elevated castle. At the entrance, two guards nodded in acknowledgement to Mike before they walked by. Past them was a large circular room, at the center of which was a statue of a woman standing tall within a fountain of water. She held a flail in one hand, while a small shield was attached to her other. A crescent shape was etched into the right side of her face, curving around her right eye.

"That's our leader, Queen Alexa." Mike smiled proudly, his eyes lingering over the statue as they passed it.

Outside the circular room was a hallway leading up to an ornate set of wooden doors. Mike pushed them open to reveal what appeared to be a throne room. The throne itself, sturdy and marble, sat at the opposite side at the end of a long, velvet strip of carpet. A woman dressed in a steel corset sat upon it, her eyes focused intently on the two as they approached.

"Is this the boy?" she asked Mike as they came within speaking distance.

Evan immediately noticed the green crescent scar carved in the skin around her eye, unmistakably matching the statue.

Mike kneeled before answering, "Of course, my Queen."

"Don't be ridiculous," she snapped. "Just take your place by my side."

Mike smirked, standing up and making his way to her side.

"Must you always be so goofy?" she sighed before focusing on Evan. "Well, Mike informs me that you resist joining us. Not a lot of players do that, so, why is it that you've come here today?" Her eyes were stern, matching those carved in her statue.

Evan shifted, uncomfortable beneath her gaze; it felt awkward to be looked down on.

"Well," he began, "I'm not much of a follower. Like I told Mike, I have my own agenda. So, if I'm to be attached to a guild, I would want one where I would be allotted a degree of freedom and would need to have a thorough understanding of the guild's own goals."

"You can't be serious," she scoffed. "Information is on a need-to-know basis. At your level, you'd need to just follow orders. Leaders aren't good leaders if they have unorganized troops. I'm not providing special treatment to a foot soldier. There are plenty of benefits, and chances to get what you want out of this guild. You can't just —"

"Wait, I know you," Evan interrupted, staring in awe. "You were the one who murdered that boy at school a year ago."

Mike turned from Evan to Alexa, meeting her gaze. Clearly perturbed, Mike stared wide-eyed at his queen, practically begging for a response. Alexa's auburn hair swayed through the air as she shook her head, before turning her attention back to Evan.

"You…went to that school?" Alexa asked, her eyes narrowing. "What's your name?"

"That information is on a need-to-know basis." Evan smirked.

Alexa chuckled. "Fine. Despite looking familiar, I can't say I know you anyway,"

Mike's eyes lingered on Evan.

"You can't expect me to spill my guts to you," Alexa said simply. "It's your decision to join or not. If you want what we have to offer, then you must bear our name and follow our orders. If you perform well, you'll eventually be in a position where you'll know more and have more freedom."

Evan sighed. "I don't have any intention of just doing what I'm told."

"Then, it sounds like you already made up your mind." Alexa shrugged. "So, why come here at all?"

"Despite only being here for a short time, I've actually heard of you — and this guild — through many other players," Evan told her. "I figured coming here directly would let me get a better understanding for how this guild worked. Also, now that I know who you are, I'm starting to wonder about this whole 'game' situation. What are you trying to do?"

Alexa smirked. "The same thing you are."

Evan glared at her. "I highly doubt that."

Alexa returned his stare. "Very well; at this point, we're just spinning our wheels. I am running an organization after all."

She brought up a window and began pressing a few buttons. "Please be on your way."

Mike bowed to her and led Evan out of the throne room, out of the castle, and all the way to the entrance of the city in complete silence.

After what seemed like ages, Mike, said, "I do hope you'll at least consider us in the future." He smiled, but Evan could tell that it was forced.

"We'll see," Evan replied, turning his back on Mike and the city. This had been enough of a detour. *I don't have time to mess around with some escapist woman*, he thought to himself.

With that over with, Evan made his way away from the city. Within moments, a window appeared in front Mike bearing the message, "Keep an eye on the boy. –Alexa."

Evan sighed, unsure of where he was. He hadn't managed to get too far, remaining just outside of the city checking his quest list and map. "I probably should have at least asked for directions. This was probably part of that guy's plan."

On his map, a beacon had lit up to the south of his position. As he clicked on it, a small window reading, "Quest: Holy Herb" popped up.

"I guess this is the only thing I can do at the moment," Evan murmured to himself. "No choice but to head towards that."

Meanwhile, three women watched from atop the city wall.

"There's the target," said a muscular woman. She was encased in a metallic plate and had short, red hair.

A slender woman with long, flowing blonde hair and wrapped in leather garments watched him intently. "Keep our distance, but let's trail him."

A petite, white-clothed woman with blue hair nodded, and all at once the three became transparent, following behind the boy at a distance.

As Evan made his way south across the plain, he noticed many new monsters. One was especially aggressive: a large beast that charged on all fours with white fur, black stripes, and sharp, jagged teeth and claws. Before it could reach him, Evan extended his wand and a bolt of ice shot forward, striking the beast's face. Its nose, mouth, and whiskers became covered in a patch of ice. A sharp cone of ice extended from the tip of the wand, and Evan dashed forward. Swinging the wand downward like a sword, he slashed through the beast's face. It collapsed, dying as Evan's rewards were displayed.

Despite the strength of the monsters he met in the area, his new gear — and several enchantments and bonuses that came with it — provided him with more than enough strength to easily defeat them. He continued to take on various monsters as he made his way south, occasionally checking his map to make sure he was still in route to the nearest city.

Half a day went by. Evan's hair was matted and sweat ran freely down his face. He breathed heavily as he trudged over a hill to get a better view. In the distance, he could see a large wooden barricade. *Finally, a reprieve*, he thought to himself. He continued down the hill and through the plains toward his destination.

The sun bore down on him as he continued to move forward. Monsters freely roamed the plains, although their aggression had subsided from earlier.

Evan sighed, thankful that they no longer initiated fights. Because of this, he approached the barricade with relative ease. Around the outpost, several large, sharpened wooden posts stuck into the ground to create a perimeter. Directly right of the outpost was a large, endlessly expanding forest.

Two soldiers, clad in steel garments, stood atop a platform just behind the wooden posts. Between them was a sign hanging over an archway read, 'Slayers.' The men stared down at Evan.

"What do you want?" one of them shouted down.

Evan looked up, shielding his eyes from the sun. "Am I able to find lodging and food here?"

The soldier sneered. "If you have money. But this is a mercenary outpost, not an official town. Don't expect much."

Evan nodded, slowly making his way through the entrance. He wasn't expecting much, but at this point anything was better than sleeping out in the field with a bunch of monsters.

As he walked inside, he noticed that about two thirds of the camp was a grassy field. Several men dressed in plated armor were fighting one another. Evan turned to his right to face a gap in the wall, which led directly into the adjacent forest. To his immediate left was a towering building. Assuming it to be the main building, he made his way toward it.

Once inside, he found an expansive hall. The bottom floor appeared to be a tavern; it held a long bar against the far wall with numerous tables scattered throughout the area. Just about all of the tables were filled with men, clad in plated armor and leather adornments. There were much fewer women, all of whom were dressed in short skirts and bustier as they walked from table to table. As Evan stepped into the hall the room hushed, everyone turned to look at him.

"What the hell do you want!?" a large man from behind the bar shouted.

Evan hastily made his way over to the bar, glancing down at the floor to avoid everyone's gaze. The last thing he wanted was to make a big deal out of this; he was hoping to stay low. "I'm just a traveler. I was told I could rent a room here?"

The bartender looked Evan over. "1,000 gold…per hour."

Evan sighed. "Could I just order some food then?"

A large man clad in thick, steel plated armor, stepped up from behind Evan and slammed his massive hand on the bar. "We don't take kindly to outsiders. Especially weak little things like you."

The hall suddenly filled with an uproar of laughter. The large man turned to face his peers, smirking.

"I suggest," he said slowly, the smell of alcohol filling Evan's nostrils, "you leave."

Evan glared at the man, staring into his deep blue eyes. Several deep scars ran across his face, one that seemed to cut through his left eye, and long, blonde hair draped over his shoulders. *A village of nothing but players,* Evan thought, *making up all of their own rules. This is inconvenient.*

"This is the only town for quite a way; surely you could offer me some pity?" Evan appealed.

The man snorted, laughing uncontrollably, the rest of the hall following in his lead. "The weak die and the strong survive. If you're too weak to survive on your own, you don't deserve to live."

"Then why are you in a guild?" Evan asked.

The room went silent.

The man glared at Evan, stepping closer so that his monstrous shadow loomed over the boy. "Everyone in this guild carries their own weight; if they can't, then they are left behind."

Evan shook his head. "Still, you're compensating for weaknesses in other fields. Even just sharing information, providing goods and services, you're providing access to information and supplies that would be normally inaccessible to solo players."

The men within the room, clearly confused, had begun murmuring to themselves.

"You talk big with your fancy words, kid," the man scoffed.

"Fine, let's make it simpler." Evan smirked. "A test of strength: if I win, you let me buy some food and a room to stay for the night."

"Now we're talking." The man grinned, bearing a jagged, dull set of teeth. "But I'll do you one better. If you win, you can eat to your fill and sleep here for the night, free of charge. I'll acknowledge your strength. But if you lose, I will kill you with my own hands."

Evan nodded. "A duel, then?"

The man snorted. "You couldn't possibly hope to win against me in a straight duel."

The hall filled with roars of laughter once more.

"There's no fun in watching someone die in one blow," the man continued, "so, there is a monster you can kill as proof."

"Fine," Evan replied.

The man motioned toward the door with his head, before exiting the building. Evan accompanied him, the entire hall following suit. The man took Evan just outside of the outpost, into the field from where Evan had just traveled from. Many of the men stood high up, behind the wooden posts where the soldiers were, and several leaned against the outer wall, looking out into the field. All of the women had draped themselves onto select men.

"Every day, a certain monster spawns in these fields." The man smiled mischievously at Evan. "Only a handful of our men can take it out. But we need the daily materials it drops to forge weapons and armor. Kill it by yourself or die trying."

Evan sighed. "I guess I don't have much of a choice."

The man took a few steps back, standing just ahead of the group that had now gathered in the field. After a few moments, the ground in front of Evan began to crack open. A large paw reached up, and the beast slowly pulled himself up onto the field.

The beast was covered in fur, with a bushy mane, sharp fangs, and deep red eyes. From its backside an armored tail extended upward, curling through the air. At the end of the tail was a large stinger, much like a scorpions. The creature stood on all fours, talons protruding from the joints on its legs, and two black wings extended out from its back. It roared at the onlookers before patrolling back and forth along a set path.

"You can forfeit now if you want!" the man shouted. "If you beg, maybe we can find a position suitable for you — a barmaid, perhaps?"

The group of men exploded into laughter.

Evan stared at the monster as he walked toward it, realizing that he was surprisingly calm. Of course, this wasn't the first time he had fought a strong enemy on his own.

From the adjacent forest, the three women from Alexgrad watched, still invisible. "I'll bet the kid pisses himself," the red-haired woman said to her cohorts.

Within a few feet of the beast, Evan clapped his hands together. A blue aura surrounded his body, and an icy mist began to swirl around him rapidly. Shards of ice and snow mixed in with the mist, creating a miniature snowstorm around him.

The large man stared intently at Evan, murmuring to himself. "Perhaps this kid isn't such a noob after all."

Evan cupped his right hand, and several glowing blue shards gathered into it. He stepped forward, thrusting his right arm forward and sending a blast of frigid air at the beast. Upon impact, it snarled as patches of ice began to envelope its face.

Frantically, the beast swiped its claws forward. Evan leapt backwards, narrowly avoiding the slash. He immediately withdrew his wand and, holding it in his right hand, he pointed it toward the beast. A blue orb formed at the tip, and with a flick of his wrist, the orb shot forward and struck the beast's face. It roared, furious as a new coat of ice began to bridge between the established patches.

As the beast let out another wail of agony, Evan quickly shot himself forward. Hearing another loud roar, he turned his head, expecting another beast. Instead the men had begun cheering. He smirked, turning back just in time to see a burst of flames spreading through the air toward him. He planted himself onto the ground, extending his left arm. As he did, the mist around his body began to flow toward his left shoulder and then up his arm, ultimately swirling around his hand. The flames began to disperse and freeze over as Evan's hand sunk into them.

The ice spread across the flames, toward the beast and moving into its mouth, coating the inside with ice. The beast began coughing, quickly clamping down with its jaw and cutting off the flow of flames. The flames that had been frozen in midair shattered, and shards of ice fell to the ground.

The men from behind shouted in excitement, and the large man that had led them smirked, whispering to himself, "Impressive."

Evan ran forward, pointing the tip of his wand at the beast. As he closed in, the beast suddenly lunged forward, clamping his teeth into Evan's right shoulder. Evan let out a howl of pain as his wand fell to the ground, and blood began to run freely down his arm and into the beast's mouth. The crowd of men went silent. Suddenly, the beast let up, pulling its mouth back. Its tail had stretched up, coming down and piercing Evan's open wound. He let out another scream, and then suddenly a horrible, stinging pain began spreading through his body from his shoulder.

He quickly leapt backwards, cringing as he placed his good hand over the wound. His hand glowed bright blue, and light began to flow into his shoulder. The pain slowly subsided and his health began to rise. Meanwhile, the monster had taken to the sky, hovering slightly before diving toward Evan.

"Too bad," the large man whispered to himself.

Evan gritted his teeth as the icy air around him intensified, swirling even more rapidly. As the beast closed in, Evan shouted, and the remainder of the icy air around him began to condense into shards of ice. The ice continued gathering until the mist had turned into several icy spires that hovered around his body. All at once they shot forward, piercing the beast's face, neck, body, limbs, and wings. The creature halted in the air, letting out a final wail of agony before falling straight to the ground, lying limp.

A window popped up in front of Evan, displaying his experience, gold, and loot. The men behind him stared in awe.

From the distance, the red-haired woman scoffed. "Lucky."

"Perhaps, perhaps not." The blonde woman smirked. "Let's fall back for now. We'll just keep an eye on the outpost until he leaves."

The three women from Alexgard moved back, retreating into the cover of the forest.

Evan exhaled as he turned and walked back toward the outpost. The men had begun cheering even more than before. *Jeez, these people are exhausting*, Evan thought to himself. When he reached the large man, he brought up a trade window, offering the materials he had just earned. The man sneered, accepting the trade. "Well, that was a surprise."

Evan smiled weakly.

"Come on, let's get you something to eat," the man said. "You can sit at my table; we have the best of everything there."

Evan followed the man back into the guild hall. Several men congratulating him as he walked past them.

In the center of the hall, Evan sat alone with the large man at a round table.

"My name is Royce," the man's voice boomed. "Leader of this guild. Who're you?"

"Evan," Evan replied thickly, biting into some sort of drumstick that was laid out before him.

Royce grinned, watching Evan eagerly eat the food, and then motioning to some nearby women.

"What's your preference?" Royce asked Evan.

Evan looked up, staring at Royce for a moment before noticing a variety of women had joined them. He swallowed his mouthful of food and turned to Royce. "Oh, I don't have one…"

Royce chuckled, not noticing Evan's affliction. "Like em' all, eh? A ladies man? I can appreciate that."

Royce pointed to the girl with shoulder-length blonde hair. "Take care of our guest."

She sat next to Evan, and then a girl with black hair and another with red took their positions on either side of Royce, the fourth girl wandering off to a different table.

Evan glanced at the girl, smiling awkwardly. She forced a smile, placing her hands on his shoulders and pushing her body against his. Evan shifted uncomfortably.

Suddenly, a skinny man, clad in an assortment of steel armor walked up, standing to Royce's side. His dark hair was trimmed short, and he maintained a well-kept goatee. He leaned down, cupping his hand along the side of his mouth, whispering into the man's ear. Royce nodded, and shooed the man away, motioning his hand lazily through the air. The thinner man sneered, and glanced over to see Evan. His eyes lingered on the boy for a moment before he turned and took his leave. Evan felt as though he had seen him somewhere before.

"Don't mind Gavin," Royce said, noticing the exchange between the two. "So, where are you from?"

"I walked from Alexgrad," Evan bit into a fresh piece of meat.

"Walked?" Royce and the girls stared at the boy in disbelief.

"Well, I think they were mad because I refused to join their guild." Evan shrugged, gnawing at the remainder of the meat on the bone.

Royce chuckled. "I think I may have severely misjudged you. Well then, how about joining our guild?"

Evan looked up at Royce, the girls clamoring over him. The blonde had already begun rubbing Evan's shoulders and arms. "Thanks, but no thanks. My quest cursor brought me here, but now it's centered on that forest out there. I think that's where I'm meant to go."

"Forest?" Royce considered, his eyes glancing from one spot to another on the table. "Oh…you mean the Illusionary Forest…"

Evan stopped eating for a moment, looking up at Royce.

"I suppose you *were* able to take out that manticore," Royce murmured, staring at table. He looked up at Evan. "If you're sure, I will lend you two scouts to accompany you to the center of the forest. Without experienced hunters, you'd easily get lost and go mad in that place."

Evan nodded. "I won't decline help at this point."

"Very well. Will you be leaving first thing in the morning?"

"Yeah. That wouldn't be such a bad idea. I could use some rest." Evan stood up, stretching his arms up and breaking free from the blonde.

"Show him to his room," Royce said to the blonde girl.

She nodded, standing up and hooking her arm around his. They walked to the nearby stairwell, arm in arm. The room cheered as they ascended the stairs. At the top of the stairs Evan broke free from the blonde's grasp. "Sorry, I can walk myself."

She simply nodded. Eventually the girl stopped in front of a wooden door, opening it and leading Evan inside and to the bed. Her eyes remained glued to the floor as she slowly began to remove her clothes. Her breasts bounced out from underneath her robe as it fell around her ankles. There was a noticeable bush of hair protruding from between her legs as she stepped closer to him, wrapping her arms around his waist.

Evan took a step back. "Um…?"

"This is what I'm for." Her voice was barely a whisper as her eyes slowly rose up. When her eyes met his, she flinched, shutting them quickly. "I'm sorry."

He couldn't believe how timid she was. She was the one who was making all the moves, and yet she was the one who was afraid. Worst of all, it was as though she was apologizing for trying to do what she had been told to do. Clearly there was more to this guild than Evan initially realized.

"What the hell is going on?" Evan murmured to himself. "Sorry, I'm not sure what you're for or what you think I want…but I need to be alone."

She looked at him, her eyes widened in surprise. Clearly relieved, she nodded frantically, redressing herself before turning and leaving the room. Evan collapsed onto the bed. That had been the first naked woman he had seen in a long time…since Emma. They used to spend almost every night together. A tear ran down his right cheek.

"Emma...I miss you." He exhaled, closing his eyes and falling asleep almost immediately.

Evan was awoken by a loud, muffled noise. His eyes were fixated on the ceiling, and he was breathing heavily. After a few moments, he remembered where he was, but his room was empty. Then, he heard it again: undeniably a scream, followed by muffled voices and laughter. Rolling out of bed, he made his way to the window of the room to see a group of people standing in the center of the town. As he opened the window, another scream filled the air; the voices were much clearer now.

"Alright men, we have a new crop tonight," snarled a clean-shaven man. In the center of the crowd were three naked women, sprawled out on the ground. "You know the rules; we each take turns with them. Once everyone is satisfied, we leave them here. If they are still alive by the morning, we keep them around." The man grinned. "You can do whatever you want to them, but nothing fatal until everyone has had a go at each of them."

The men laughed and grinned, moving closer to the girls. Their naked bodies trembled, and tears poured down each of their faces as they looked up at the men looming over them.

Suddenly, Evan dropped down from the sky, landing in the center of the crowd. His body seemed to be moving of its own accord. He glared at the man who had been talking.

"Oh, if it isn't the little hero," the man scoffed. "Was the blonde not to your liking? We can arrange for another go, but this little ritual is off limits to non-clan members."

Evan glanced down at the trembling girls, lying on the cold ground in what had to be a puddle mixed of their own sweat, tears, and urine. He returned his glare toward the man.

"I see now," Evan said softly.

"Eh?" the man said, placing his hand behind his ear. "Speak up."

"Were all the women in this guild given this little... initiation?" Evan asked.

"Of course. This is how we do things. Didn't you hear Royce? If you aren't strong enough to survive on your own, then you don't deserve to live. This is all women are good for after all, but even so, we have no use for weak women. Well, even though it's frowned upon, I suppose we could let you join, just this once. Perhaps that'll help change your —"

The man's head spiraled through the air before landing some distance away, and his body crumpled limply to the ground. Evan stood before the group; wand held tightly in his right hand. A beam of black energy extended from the tip like a sword. His eyes gleamed gold and black mist had begun to rise from his body. He turned, focusing intently on the next target, he gritted his teeth. Before the group could tell what had happened, Evan lunged forward, slashing another man, blood staining the ground and Evan's clothes. He felt better than he ever had before; his body surged with energy.

The women screamed at the sight of the growing pool of blood, and the men quickly began to withdraw their own weapons. However, Evan moved efficiently, taking down each man with the least possible effort. By the time any of the men had been able to get a hold on their weapon, they were dead. Evan stood before the three women, covered in blood. He raised his right arm in the air. All the blood in the area — on his clothes, the ground, and from the men's bodies — began to converge into the tattoo on the back of his hand.

Royce stood from a distance, watching as the corpses of his brethren withered away.

Once all the blood had been absorbed, Evan turned to face the women. *Take them*, a voice ran through his head.

"What…" Evan murmured.

Take them, they're your reward. "N…no…" He held his hand to his head as the black mist rising from his body intensified. A stinging pain shot through his entire body.

"R…run!" he stammered, shouting at the women.

They remained grounded, frozen in fear as he slowly stepped toward them. A smirk spread across his face. Never before had he desired to force himself upon someone, but now, it was all he could think of. His mind clouded, as his anger and frustration seemed to peak. He hadn't been with Emma for quite some time. He needed some kind of release. As Evan edged closer, a voice boomed through the air.

"This is how you repay me!?" Royce shouted at Evan.

Evan turned to face Royce; his golden eyes wide with madness. Surprised, Royce took a step backwards, "What the…"

Evan screamed, mist erupted from his body and the beam of black energy extending from his wand strengthened; his wand began to crack. He pushed himself off the ground, rushing toward Royce like a bullet. The beam of black energy sliced through the air; Royce raised his left arm, meeting the beam with his gauntlet. The beam of energy sliced through the armor with ease. Royce gritted his teeth, his body flinching as blood poured from his severed forearm.

"You're not Evan. Who are you?" Royce coughed.

Evan sneered, raising the beam of energy straight into the air. He swung his arm down, cleaving through Royce's left shoulder and out through his right side. Royce's body split, collapsing onto the ground, and his blood joined his brethren's inside of Evan's tattoo. Several soldiers stood just outside of the hall, watching as Evan cleaved their leader in half. Once finished absorbing the blood, he turned his blade of energy onto the other men.

Evan dashed forward, swinging the blade through the air toward his next victim. As the blade reached the man's body, the wand in Evan's hand shattered, and the energy dispersed. Taking advantage of this, the man swung his knee up into Evan's stomach. Evan fell to his own knee, blood spilling out of his mouth as he coughed. He raised his head as a large metal fist crashed into his cheek, forcing him onto the ground. The men cheered, drawing their weapons.

Time to run, the voice rang through Evan's head. He slowly stood to his feet; a deep blue bruise spread across his cheek. The men loomed over him; weapons ready. Evan smirked, darting off toward the entrance to the woods. Not expecting him to take off so quickly, the men idled for a moment before someone finally shouted, "After him!"

The forest had no beaten path, but Evan moved swiftly, leaping over brush and logs. *Just continue straight*, the voice in his head rang. His head ached; he had no time or energy to question the voice. As he leapt out into a clearing, a monstrous, grotesque mushroom with stubby arms, legs, and a mouth, baring fangs, stood before him. Evan halted in place, but the monster had already noticed him; a spray of purple mist spewed out of the mushroom's mouth and closed in on Evan.

Evan instinctively raised his right arm, his opened palm facing the monster. A black, glass-like orb formed in his hand. It suddenly shot forward, cutting through the mist, dispersing it, and flying toward the monster. Upon impact, the orb shattered, and numerous black spires shot out in all directions, several piercing the monster. At the points of impact, a black sheet spread out, coating the monster. Just as quickly as the monster became coated in ice, it shattered, pieces of black fragments littering the ground

"There he is!" A voice came from behind him.

Evan turned to see two gruff men dressed in leather standing at the edge of the clearing.

"What's up with his face?" one of the men said.

Only Evan's left eye remained gold; the other had returned to its normal hue. The black mist around his body had also receded. *Not much time left*, the voice rang. Evan's right arm instinctively rose up once again, his palming facing the men. The men sneered, charging forward, each holding a large axe. The black, glass-like orb formed in Evan's palm once more, shooting forward toward the men. It exploded just in front of them, the bulk of the spires piercing their bodies and face. The men hit the ground instantly, still in pools of their own blood.

The blood of the men, like so many others from tonight, flowed into Evan's tattoo. Once the processed finished, his left eye returned to normal. A window popped up showing the combined experience of the monster and all the men he had slain. Evan's head felt fuzzy; he took a moment to breathe. His body was heavy, and he felt more exhausted than he ever had in his life. "What's going on?"

He heard voices echoing through the woods around him. *No time*, he thought, turning to where the monster had been and running forward, deeper into the woods.

VI
Alicia & Rose

Evan had been wandering through the forest, fighting enraged guild members and monsters alike for three days now. His supplies were low; he hadn't seen guild members in some time, but monster spawns remained frequent. He had taken to moving cautiously, taking the path of least resistance and avoiding as many encounters as possible. When forced to battle, he would have to take extended stops to heal, wait for his mana to restore, and heal again until he was fit enough to continue. And yet, despite his health and mana being full, his body felt fatigued.

He had no idea where he was headed, and he lost track of where he had come from after the first day. At this rate, he was bound to die before finding his destination. His location on his map seemed to be unreliable, as his cursor would jump from spot to spot without warning. Meanwhile, his destination hadn't moved an inch from the map.

Tepidly, he sat down at the base of a nearby tree. He exhaled, looking out at the sea of trees before him. Fresh sweat rolled down the side of his head, and his breathing was labored. It had been awhile since he had last rested. His eyes fluttered open and shut, as he struggled to stay awake. He was sure that if he passed out here, he wouldn't wake up. In his delirium, he swore he heard a raspy voice call out; "Straight ahead." His head sank down as he felt himself begin to slip into sleep.

A sudden snapping sound caused him to dart his head upward, looking around frantically. He remained quiet, holding his breath to the best of his ability. After a few moments, silence.

"It must've been nothing," he exhaled.

With that, he stood up, instinctively heading straight ahead.

Eventually, he came upon a large sign in the distance. Sore, sweaty, and extremely tired, he dashed into the town for reprieve. Pausing to take in his surroundings, he realized that the city was built into the forest. Aside from the open area, the buildings all appeared to be tree houses.

"Not my first choice," he said to himself, breathing heavily. "Guess I'm not in a position to complain, though."

As he searched for an inn, the hairs on the back of his neck stood up. He shifted uncomfortably, glancing around at the numerous stares he'd garnered. He wasn't used to being the center of attention.

Thankfully, he soon found a large tree towards the center of town. At the very top was an equally large house with the word "Inn" inscribed on it. At the base of the tree, a spiral staircase of wood extended out from the bark. As Evan made his way up the staircase, he could see how truly massive the building was.

The tree must have extended at least fifty feet into the air, the building following suit.

He walked inside, entering a lobby furnished with several couches and tables as well as a reception desk opposite the front door. As he made his way towards it, a pointed-eared, suited man with combed silver hair greeted him.

"Good afternoon, sir."

"Uh, hey," Evan breathed out. "Yeah, so, do you have any available rooms?"

"Of course," the receptionist responded; his bright blue eyes focused intently on the boy. "The fee is one hundred gold per night. We need fifty gold up front, and any other debts accrued will be collected at checkout."

Evan opened his inventory, summoning up fifty gold. He was exhausted; it was all he could to place the gold onto the finished counter.

"Very good, sir," the receptionist said, taking the gold and retrieving a key from cabinets behind him. "Each room has a bed as well as access to the famous healing waters. It can be accessed through your shower, or extra-large bath, if you'd prefer." The receptionist placed the key in Evan's hand. "Room service is available if you desire. If you go into the nearby elevator, your room is up three floors and down to your left — room 310."

Evan nodded, before heading for the elevator and stepping inside it. As the doors closed, he propped himself against the rail, grateful for the chance to relax. His body ached, and he was drenched in sweat. As the elevator started to rise, his eyes fluttered shut.

At the next floor, a loud *ding* jarred him awake. The door opened and two elven girls stepped in.

The first girl was the same height as Evan, with flowing blonde hair and pointed ears. Her pale, slender body was draped in a white robe.

The second girl, slightly shorter than the first, had wavy, long pink hair with similar ears and complexion to her companion. Her green eyes immediately focused onto the boy in front of them.

"Oh…a human," the blonde said softly.

The two were now staring at Evan.

The shorter of the two smiled. "How rare."

"Rare…?" Evan asked, struggling to stand up straight.

"Yes," the blonde responded. "I don't know how you got here, but this is a hidden location on the map. The requirements for initiating the starting quest within this town are unknown. You've got to be pretty lucky."

"Requirements?" Evan was completely oblivious. "Do you mean that quest lines aren't the same for every player?"

"Indeed," the pink-haired girl said. "No one is aware of the specifics. However, after the first town, it seems as though quests deviate from player to player."

Suddenly, the elevator stopped. The elves stepped out, followed by Evan. He stood in the hall, consumed in thought over quest requirements. *I thought I was making all my decisions up until now, but if I was being led here, what exactly is this world?*

The elves watched curiously.

"If these are our real bodies, could quests come from real desires…?" He murmured gently.

"Pretty sharp," the blonde girl smirked.

"…what… oh… right." Evan stammered, surprised by the sudden intrusion. "Elves have better hearing than humans."

"Bingo." The smaller girl grinned. "That theory has been bouncing around for a while, but I doubt it's possible to prove it. What's the name of the quest that brought you here?"

Evan pulled up his quest log. "Hmm... *Inquire About Holy Herb.*"

The elves exchanged a wide-eyed glance.

"Well, isn't that interesting," the blonde whispered softly. "What's your name?"

"Evan. Yours?"

"Rose," she stated.

"I'm Alicia!" The pink-haired girl exclaimed exuberantly.

"If you need a party, don't hesitate to call us." She offered cloyingly.

Evan suddenly received two friend requests. "Uh, sure… thanks."

He accepted hesitantly. Normally he would have declined such an offer from complete strangers, but he could feel them pressuring him, and mostly, he just wanted to go to bed. He turned his head to look down the hall toward his room. Alicia glanced at Rose, smirking and stepping closer to Evan.

"We don't mind if you want to form a party now," Alicia whispered into his ear. "You already have a room, right?"

Evan took a step backward before responding. "I'm pretty tired. I walked all the way from Alexgrad and got chased through that crazy forest."

"Aww, don't be like that." Rose took a step toward Evan as well. "The water in this inn relaxes and refreshes the body, while replenishing health and magic."

"If we get tired, we can just move to the shower or hot tub." Alicia insisted.

The two were practically on top of Evan now; he stepped back until he was pressed against the wall. He had dealt with a lot of different people at this point, but he'd never felt so inconvenienced.

"Just give it some thought?" Rose smiled. "We're in room 333 if you change your mind."

The two turned, walking in the opposite direction. Evan sighed in relief as he made his way to his room. Once inside, he shut the door, locked it and unequipped all of his gear. After an immensely relaxing shower, he collapsed onto his bed. It was incredibly soft; he sank into the cushion and fell asleep almost instantly.

One hour later, Rose and Alicia stood outside of his room.

"Are you sure you saw him go in here?" Rose looked at Alicia skeptically.

"Of course! Have I ever been wrong before?" asked Alicia with confidence.

"Yeah, a lot actually," Rose stated monotonously.

"Well…shut up." Alicia scowled, glaring at Rose.

"Just open the door already then," Rose sighed.

Alicia's hand shined with white light as it turned the doorknob. The door opened to reveal Evan; sound asleep on the bed. Two girls, dressed in steel corsets, loomed over the bed while a third hovered a sword over Evan's exposed neck.

"What's going on?" Rose demanded.

The two elves stepped closer to the would-be assassins. Surprised to see that they weren't the only intruders, the tallest of the assassins threw down an orb, and a bright light filled the room. Rose and Alicia quickly shielded their eyes. When the light faded, the girls were gone.

Rose began blinking rapidly, trying to adjust her eyes. "What the hell?"

Alicia squinted. "Did you see their insignia?"

"Yeah, Queen Alexa's troops. Just who is this boy?" Rose asked, the blurry masses around her coming into focus once again.

"I believe he's the one we're meant to find," Alicia speculated. Once acclimated, Rose took a seat, brushing through windows of her inventory, while Alicia made her way over to Evan's bed. She pulled the covers up to check underneath.

Rose rolled her eyes. "Really, though?"

"Might as well check." Alicia smirked. "It's not like he'll ever show us." She crawled into the bed, cuddling up against Evan's body.

Rose shook her head, smirking. "That's just too mean."

The elves remained in the room and after a few hours passed, Evan began to stir awake. As his eyes slowly opened, he noticed an unfamiliar warmth against his body. Looking down, he recognized the elf from earlier, Alicia, wearing only undergarments.

"You were great," Alicia breathed out, slowly reaching her hand up to brush his face.

Evan stared at her, and then looked up to see Rose watching.

"My turn." Rose made her way over to the bed.

Evan raised a hand to his head. "Did you drug me?" He felt like he was always being pulled into inconvenient situations. *It's not like I agreed to team up with them,* he thought indignantly. *What's the value in being so aggressive?*

"You're fine," Rose smirked.

"Calm down, you baby." Alicia rolled her eyes.

"Yeah, so what are you doing in my room?" Evan sighed.

"Well —" Rose began.

"We came in to see if you had changed your mind and we found three would-be assassins hovering over you," Alicia interjected.

"You broke into my room?" Evan exclaimed, rubbing his forehead with his free hand. *These women are even worse than I thought.*

"That's what you're worried about?" Alicia exclaimed. "We would have made you cum! It's not like you wouldn't have enjoyed it."

"That… aside…" Rose sighed, struggling to regain control of the conversation. "We stayed to make sure you didn't die in your sleep. Surely that counts for something?"

I guess they did save my life, he thought. "Did you recognize them?"

"No, but they had Queen Alexa's insignia," Alicia said.

"Damn that Alexa," Evan grumbled. "She must really not trust me."

"What's your relation to her?" Rose asked.

"There is none," Evan replied. "Other than…we apparently went to the same school before this." He hesitated. "She also tried to recruit me."

"Personally?" Rose asked anxiously. "That's not a common occurrence…"

"Well, I met with her," Evan said.

"Most people don't," Alicia chimed in. "But she has probably tried to recruit every single person who has entered this game."

"The fact that there were people sent to kill you can only mean she doesn't trust you," Rose pointed out. "Did you deny recruitment?"

"Yeah," Evan stated. "I didn't see much point. I have my own goals, after all."

"That was probably a bad idea." Rose shook her head.

"Yeah, from what I hear, Alexa doesn't appreciate rejection," Alicia nodded.

"Seems like a recurring theme in this game." Evan glared at Alicia, who returned the look emphatically.

Rose cleared her throat. "Well, it certainly wouldn't hurt if you had two beautiful elves at your side to protect you."

"Most men would be envious of this situation." Alicia smiled. "Two girls wanting to cater to their every need and keep them from harm."

"Right..." Evan shifted uncomfortably.

"We want to join you for a while," Rose said.

"I'm really not much of a team player," Evan protested.

"You'll learn as you go," Alicia insisted.

"I'm not going to drag other people into my problems!" Evan shouted; his eyes wider than they had ever been before. "I won't let other people die because of my selfish choices!"

"Don't kid yourself," Alicia snapped. "We aren't that weak. Lest you forget, we saved your life just a little while ago."

"You've been lucky until now," Rose interjected. "You can't rush into every situation headfirst and expect the best scenario. If you don't start thinking about your goals seriously, then there's no way you'll achieve them."

Evan narrowed his eyes. There was some truth in what they said. *I've already taken numerous lives,* he reminded himself. *Am I really willing to go down this path? Can I risk another two lives?*

"Accept," Rose stated, a window popping up, inviting him to join a party.

He stared at the two, shaking his head. *It's likely they won't leave until I accept.* "Not much of a choice." He tapped the accept button.

"So, what is your plan now that you've rested?" Alicia asked.

"I guess I'll just follow my quest-line," Evan said flatly. "If quests are based on desires, then following my quests should tell me more about the revival ritual."

"What?!" Rose stared at Evan intently.

"Yeah, I came here because I was promised I could find a way to revive someone who has died," Evan explained. "I've already got a list of the necessary ingredients."

"Let me see that list." Rose extended her hand out.

Evan summoned it from his inventory and handed it to Rose. Alicia and Rose sat next to each other, reading down the list.

"The first item listed is Holy Herb..." Alicia murmured.

"Yeah..." Rose affirmed as she handed it back to Evan.

"Is something wrong?" Evan asked.

"No..." Rose smiled. "I just think we've made the right choice in teaming up."

"So, how about that turn?" Alicia moved closer to Evan.

"Err, look, no offense," Evan exhaled, raising his hand up to stop her advance. "I'm sure a lot of guys dream about this situation. But I'm trying to revive my girlfriend. Doing anything with someone else would feel like cheating on her."

"But...she's dead," Alicia stated bluntly.

Rose stroked her chin. "Not sure if she's lucky, or you're just stupid."

"I think most boyfriends would get it while they could," Alicia considered. "A dead girlfriend can't hold grudges."

"Alicia!" Rose scolded.

Evan glared at her. "What would be the point in me doing all of this work if I was just going to fuck someone else?"

"That's... true..." Alicia said softly. "I'm sorry."

Evan exhaled. "It's fine."

Rose smiled. "Well, I think that counts for our first group bonding exercise. Shall we get something to eat then?"

"Yeah, I'm starving," Alicia said.

"Alright." Evan nodded, getting up and gathering his gear.

"Try not to wander off." Rose addressed Evan. "The city of Alchemilla isn't the most welcoming for humans."

Alicia whispered to Evan, "Alchemilla is the name of the city."

"I got it..." Evan replied, already regretting his decision to team up with them.

The group left the inn, heading into the city. Evan following the two elves lead.

"Where should we go?" Alicia asked.

"Let's just go to Moonlight," Rose said.

"We always go there," Alicia complained.

"So? You like it there. Just yesterday you said it was your favorite place in the whole city."

"Yeah, it is." Alicia nodded.

Rose shook her head.

The group made their way through the city, as they did, other elves stopped to stare at Evan. They passed several tree houses until they reached a tree with a crescent moon carved into the bark. Rose stepped up to the tree, bringing up her inventory. "Get close to me."

Alicia and Evan stepped closer as a silver crescent moon appeared in Rose's hand. She aligned up the shape with the carving, pushing it in. Almost immediately, a silver light engulfed Rose, Alicia, and Evan.

The group appeared inside a small café. The ceiling was dark blue with what appeared to be scattered stars splattered across it. This provided the only source of light in the place. All around the perimeter of the room were booths with pale yellow cushions and black marble tables. About every other booth housed a group of elves. Adjacent from where they appeared was a bar with several stools placed around it. Behind the bar was a female elf with shoulder-length purple hair and pale blue eyes.

"Welcome back!" she shouted, waving at the group.

"Long time no see, Phoebe!" Alicia waved back, smiling.
The group walked up to the bar.
"Newcomer? Human?" Phoebe stared at Evan intently.
"He's alright," Rose said.
"I see. Well, nice to meetcha then," Phoebe smiled.
"Thanks," Evan returned her smile weakly.
"We'll seat ourselves in the corner; we have a bit to talk about," Rose said.
"Let me know when you're ready to order," Phoebe told them.
The group made their way to an empty booth.
"What is this place?" Evan asked. "I know this is an elven village, but I figured the tree houses would be the extent of the quirks."
Alicia sneered. "Silly humans, always assuming."
Evan stared at her for a moment. "Uh, right." He turned to Rose.
"The tree from outside just suddenly appeared one day," Rose explained. "Along with a notice that everyone within the town had received a silver crescent moon stone; no one was really sure what it was. Eventually someone figured out that you could fit the crescent shaped stone into the slot and that made them disappear. So, everyone was eager to try it for themselves. Of course, the stone wasn't an indestructible item. Once used, it was gone from your inventory. So, you —"
"So, it turned out the items were gifted by the owner of the establishment," Alicia interrupted. "Every week they hide various stashes of the stones throughout the surrounding area and post hints about where you can find them. So, it's like a game within a game, plus the food is really good."
Rose nodded.
"I see," Evan said, picking up a nearby menu.
As he attempted to glance through the menu, Evan's shoulder slumped; the whole thing seemed to be in what he assumed was elven language.
"I already know what I want," Alicia said, as if gloating about a prize she had won.
"Well, you do get the same thing every time," Rose stated plainly.
"Hey," Alicia snapped at her. "Shut up."
"I can't read this," Evan grumbled miserably.
Alicia and Rose turned from each other's gaze and stared at him blankly before saying in unison, "Oh…yeah…"
"Well, what do you like?" Rose asked, getting up and moving next to Evan. She pressed her body up against him, looking at the menu from over his shoulder.
"Err… do they have coffee, or maybe some kind of sandwich?" he asked, edging closer to the wall opposite of Rose. He wasn't used to such aggressive displays.
"No coffee, just various teas. I believe there may be a variation that would have similar effects and taste, though." Rose pointed to a single phrase on the menu. "What kind of sandwich?" She turned, moving her face closer to his.
"Hey!" Alicia exclaimed, crawling under the table.
She popped up on the other side of the booth, next to Rose and Evan. He became sandwiched by the two, as the three squished together in the small space.

"There's not room for all three of us!" Evan's voice was drowned out by the two sister's quarreling.

"You three look like you're having fun." Phoebe smirked, standing at the edge of the table. "You're causing a ruckus and disturbing the other customers."

The rest of the elves in the room had all turned to see what was happening.

"Sorry…" Evan murmured.

Rose and Alicia carefully removed themselves from Evan's side and went back to the adjacent one.

"Now, what will you have?" Phoebe asked.

"I want the strawberry deluxe cup!" Alicia exclaimed, smiling.

"I actually wasn't asking you," Phoebe said, sticking her tongue out. Alicia glared at her.

"Let's do the Celestia Tea and the Mini Shrimp Wraps," Rose said. "And he'll have Scorian Tea with the Leaf Herb Beef Wrap."

Phoebe nodded as she jotted down their orders, her white skirt swaying as she sauntered away from them.

"That bitch didn't take my order," Alicia scoffed.

Rose rolled her eyes. "You get the same thing every time; I'm sure that's why."

"Not the point," Alicia said.

"Strange how this place has essentially become its own self-sustaining society," Evan said. "There's available food and jobs. It's almost like we never left Earth; we're just doing the same thing over in a new environment."

"I think that's just the nature of humans." Rose turned to look at him.

"Even though these people didn't fit in on Earth, that doesn't make them degenerates or anything. They just needed a place of their own to fit in."

"Don't make it sound too utopian," Alicia rolled her eyes. "There are plenty of dangers. The worst of which would be rude waitresses…"

"Get over yourself," Rose sighed.

Evan was lost in his own thoughts. *First Paul, who was so eager to be away from his family, and then that band of mercenaries. People who couldn't fit into society are doing quite well here.*

"Well, for a lot of people, I'm sure this place is utopian," Evan said softly.

Alicia glanced at Rose.

"Well, anyway, do either of you have any idea on where to start with this quest line?" Evan asked, changing the subject. "You seem to know more about this Holy Herb than I do."

Rose nodded.

"It's a rare herb that is used in most medicines," Alicia said. "It's the primary source of revenue for this city."

"It's located somewhere in the surrounding forest," Rose added. "Only the royalty within the city knows the exact location."

"And you said this place is near impossible to find," Evan recalled. "So, it's likely the forest itself that serves as the maze." He sighed. "Any chance of getting some directly from the ruler of this city?"

"Doubtful," Alicia responded. "It's so rare that any vendors would be hard-pressed to give up any they happened to have. The ones who farm for it are paid well enough by the rulers that they wouldn't need to sell on the side."

"You might be able to buy some, but you would probably be charged an outrageous cost, especially since you're human," Rose said.

"Not to mention, your recipe calls for two herbs total," Alicia added.

Phoebe returned, placing everyone's orders in front of them.

"Anything else?" the waitress asked sweetly.

Alicia glared at her order. There were several large strawberries mixed in with various other berries and fruits.

"You got lucky," she grumbled under her breath.

Phoebe flashed a smile, then turned and left.

"You guys make it seem like buying it or finding it is impossible," Evan stated. "My best option may be stealing some."

Rose nodded but said nothing.

"Won't that put you both in bad standings with this city?" Evan asked. "Isn't this your home? Are you sure you want to come along with me?"

"This place has gotten rather boring anyway," Alicia told him. "Although I'll miss this café." She popped a strawberry into her mouth.

"Besides, you're far more interesting," Rose said. "I think something good will happen if we come along with you." She sipped her tea thoughtfully.

"I see." Evan looked down at his food.

He picked up his cup of tea, sipping it cautiously. Despite the light color, it was surprisingly bold.

"Tasty?" Rose asked, staring at him.

Evan nodded, turning his eyes to the wrap in front of him. Similar to a burrito on Earth, the wrap contained some kind of meat with a thick green leaf securing it snugly. He picked it up and took a bite.

"Delicious," he declared, continuing ravenously.

Alicia chuckled, still picking at her bowl of various fruits.

"Well then, how about telling me about what types of skills you've invested in to?" Evan asked. "We can assess each other's abilities and try to come up with a plan of action."

Alicia and Rose both brought up their skill windows, flicking the edge so that it spun around to face Evan. Before leaning in to look at them, he brought up his own skill window and dragged it through the air with his finger, positioning it in front of them.

"Well, we should probably do some scouting and then head back to the inn to formulate a real plan," Rose said, picking up a piece of shrimp wrapped tightly in a green leaf and eating it.

"Sounds good," Alicia said.

The group continued eating before resuming casual conversation.

"So, why did you guys pick the elven race?" Evan asked.

Alicia locked her eyes onto her food, clenching her fist.

Rose placed her hand on Alicia's shoulder. "Well, in previous games we always chose spell-casters and support roles."

"We…?" Evan looked at Alicia. "You two know each other in real life?"

"We're sisters," Alicia managed to say.

"I'm the older one, obviously." Rose smiled.

"Only by two years!" Alicia exclaimed.

Evan chuckled. "I see. At least you get to be here with someone you know."

"Yeah..." Alicia smiled.

"Still, it's weird that you would want to have a threesome together," Evan said.

Alicia glared at him. "It's not weird!"

Rose shrugged. "Kind of weird."

"Pretty weird." Evan nodded.

"Whatever!" Alicia pouted. "Sisters experiment all the time! I guess it's only okay as long as nobody talks about it! We aren't even on Earth anymore. Stop judging me by standards of a place we don't even live in."

Rose looked at Evan sympathetically. He smirked in response.

Once they had finished their meals, Rose placed some gold on the table, and they made their way to the front of the café.

"So, how do we get out? There doesn't seem to be a door," Evan said, looking at the two.

"Allow me." Alicia stepped forward. "Thank you for the meal!"

The three were engulfed in light, and when the light faded, and everything became clear they had appeared outside of the tree they had entered from.

"They made it so that you can't leave if you're too much of an asshole or anything," Alicia said. "You have to sincerely express your gratitude for their hospitality. Something that is lost on Earth I might add. Planet Incest doesn't look so bad after all, eh?"

Evan snickered, shaking his head. "So, split up?"

"Do you even know where you're going?" Rose asked.

"Err, I suppose not," Evan admitted.

"I'll go —" Rose began.

"I'll go with Evan!" Alicia cut her off.

Rose grinned. "Alright, let's meet back up in the room in one hour."

Alicia nodded.

Rose turned from the two and walked off into the distance.

"Let's keep an eye on the local vendors then — see if we can identify any deliverers from the palace." Alicia latched onto Evan's arm, her breasts pressing against his body.

"Really though?" Evan squirmed in frustration, attempting to pull away from her grasp.

"It'll look less suspicious if we're a couple." Alicia grinned.

Evan sighed.

The two ventured into the heart of the city. As they walked, onlookers stared at the two with disgusts.

"I thought we were supposed to avoid attention," Evan complained. "Why are they staring at us?"

"Because we're a mixed couple? Duh." Alicia rolled her eyes.

"Wasn't the point to not stand out?" Evan sighed. "Seriously... the cuddling really didn't serve any purpose did it?"

Alicia ignored him. "Shhh, we're here."

They came upon a large tree and ascended the wooden staircase spiraling up to the top.

"Oh, honey, I just don't know that we can afford it," Alicia said with an elevated affliction.

At this point Evan decided to simply go with the flow, nodding weakly at Alicia's exuberant actions.

A few elves coming down the stairs stared at them, shaking their heads. At the top of the steps was a small, wooden building. As the two walked inside, Evan breathed in a strong blend of aromas. The store itself was stocked with herbs, flowers, and potions.

"This is the premium shop for alchemy," Alicia whispered. "They're sure to get regular deliveries daily."

They stood in front of a box, filled with assorted flowers of red, blue, and yellow.

"Aren't they beautiful?" She swooned over Evan.

"Yeah?" He pulled away from her but failed to break from her grasp.

An elf dressed in casual clothes walked into the store holding a large box. He placed it on the countertop, in front of the store's associate.

"Sign here," he said, handing a piece of parchment to the vendor.

"Buy me some flowers, honey," Alicia suddenly said, loudly enough that everyone in the store could hear.

"Err —" Evan began.

Before he could say anything, Alicia interrupted.

"What!? You can afford liquor and whores, but I can't get one flower!?" She shouted, slapping him across the face before storming out of the store.

Evan's cheek throbbed. He stood, confused, unsure of what had just happened.

The employee behind the counter chuckled. "Tough luck, kid. Maybe you should stick to your own race after all."

The deliverer snickered, leaving the box and making his way out of the shop. Evan followed shortly after, groaning. "What the hell just happened?"

Outside the store, he watched the elf reach the bottom of the stairs and head toward the palace. He made his way down the stairs as well. At the bottom, Alicia dropped down from a nearby branch, landing next to him.

"Does your boo-boo hurt?" She said sweetly, moving her body up against his and planting her breasts firmly against him. His heart raced. She whispered softly, "I'll make it up to you if you want."

"What even was all that?" Evan asked, taking a step back.

"That guy at the counter," Alicia explained. "He was delivering supplies from the palace. That was just a distraction. On my way out the door I was able to place a tracker onto his body and I've memorized his screen name."

"Did you have to hit me?" Evan asked.

"Calm down, you baby — I said I'd make it up to you." Alicia rolled her eyes.

Evan sighed. "Let's just go back and tell Rose what we found."

Alicia nodded, and the two made their way back to the inn. She remained wrapped around Evan's arm the entire time.

In Evan's room, Rose sat at the coffee table, reading a pamphlet and waiting. She turned her head when the door opened. "I just got in as well. Find anything out?"

"Yeah, I tagged one of the deliverers from the palace, and I got his screen name," Alicia informed her. "So, we should be able to see where he comes and goes from."

"Good," Rose responded. "The palace is pretty heavily guarded. Our best bet is to keep our distance and see if that guy you tagged shows us a convenient way in. Once we find where they're processing the Holy Herb, we should be able to pinpoint where it's coming in from."

"I suggest we rest, then." Evan said. "If this place is as heavily guarded as you say, we'll need full strength and clear minds. We should also make sure our gear is good and we've got a stock of potions. If Holy Herb is so valuable, it must be a 24-hour operation; nighttime is probably our best bet. We'll get the benefit of the shadows to help cover us."

"Sounds like a plan," Rose agreed, casually beginning to strip away her armor.

"Wh-what are you doing?" Evan stammered, rushing to place his hand over his eyes.

"Shower time," Rose stated simply.

"Yay!" Alicia exclaimed, removing her gear as well.

"You're welcome to join us." Rose smirked.

"I thought we went over this…" Evan sighed.

Rose shrugged. "What you're doing is nice and all, but it's still naïve."

Evan clenched his fist. His eyes fixated on the ground, avoiding Rose entirely. He was growing increasingly aggravated by the elves' advances.

Rose was fully nude now. "There's no guarantee you'll live to see your quest line finished. There's no sense in making yourself suffer. I doubt your girlfriend would want to see you killing yourself over this."

She stepped directly in front of Evan, her bare feet within his line of sight. He turned to look at an empty spot on the floor.

"Look at yourself." Alicia shook her head, naked as well.

Alicia stepped into Evan's line of vision. He gritted his teeth at her bare feet, quickly shutting his eyes he shouted, "Stop doing this!"

"You can't even bring yourself to look at another woman's naked body," Alicia scoffed, disgusted. "Like even seeing a nipple will taint you and you won't be perfect anymore."

Evan's head shot up, glaring at her.

"Sca-ry," Rose elongated before stepping forward and embracing him. "No one here, no one at all — it's perfect. You have to embrace your imperfections if you want to be really happy."

"We don't mean to make you feel bad," Alicia began. "We joined you because we see you're hurting. We just want to help you."

Evan's body trembled. He raised his arms up, returning Rose's embrace. Tears began to flow freely from his eyes, all the weight he had felt in his chest began to ease up, and he felt lighter. He had spent the whole time pushing forward, effectively ignoring his own feelings. This was the first chance he had a chance to stop and feel. He exhaled, stepping away from Rose and wiping his eyes.

"Thank you." Evan smiled weakly before walking over to the bed.

As Rose made her way to the shower, Alicia walked over to Evan. She placed her hand on his shoulder. When he turned to face her, she brought her hand to his neck, pulling his head toward her own and pressing her lips against his. His heart raced; his body began to feel hot. He found himself sinking into the kiss, his body beginning to move on his own. He placed his hand on her hip. It had been so long. He raised his other hand to her breast. She exhaled, moaning heavily, and suddenly his eyes shot open and he pulled away.

"That's disappointing..." Alicia closed her eyes, turning from him and heading into the bathroom.

Evan fell backwards onto the bed as tears began to flow down his face once again. He couldn't believe what he had almost done. He didn't realize how much he had craved physical release until just now. The worst part was that it seemed as though he was willing to take it from anyone, even someone he just met.

"That hurts the most." His eyes clamped shut as exhaustion began to take over. "Does Emma mean that little to me?"

VII
Confrontation

Half an hour later, the sun had begun to set, and the sky was now blanketed in orange and red. Evan's eyes stung as he looked up at the ceiling, the sound of running water still in the distance. Suddenly the water stopped; Rose came out first, exhaling in relief. "That was nice."

Still naked, but drying off with a towel, she looked over to see Evan staring at the ceiling and rolled her eyes. "Are you really going to pout every time we come on to you? If so, this will be a long journey."

Evan sighed, pulling himself up and to his feet, his eyes scanning her tepidly. Her skin was consistently pale aside from the occasional mole scattered throughout her body. A tuft of blonde hair sat just beneath her stomach. As his eyes moved up her figure, he noticed a purple flower tattooed over her left breast. It was easy to forget that everyone had been scarred to get here. Evan instinctively placed his left hand over the flower tattoo carved into his right hand, reminded of his own ordeal in getting to this place.

"Look," he said softly, "I know that this whole thing might all just be bullshit. Maybe I'll die — maybe the potion won't even work. However, I want to believe I'll be reunited with her. I can't let myself believe otherwise if I hope to see her again."

He took a moment to avert his eyes from Rose, only to turn to see Alicia walking out from the bathroom.

"Everyone wants to believe death isn't permanent," Alicia added. Her body was just as pale as her sister's, although with hardly any moles or blemishes to speak of. A pink patch sprouted out from between her legs and as if to match her sister, she had a deep red, eight-pointed star tattooed over her right breast.

"It's important that you realize that even though miracles are possible in this world, curses and tragedies are as well," Alicia stated bluntly. "That's why most people just take what they can get."

"I suppose." Evan turned his eyes to the floor as he let out a breath.

"You already know that in this world, these bodies are our real bodies." Rose reached for his wrist, bringing his hand up to her exposed breast. Evan's eyes widened; try as he might to resist, Rose's determined grip kept his palm cupped perfectly over her nipple.

Alicia shook her head at Evan's reluctance before continuing somberly. "However, the elves here aren't really elves. They are humans who look like elves."

"Our bodies were transformed with magic and we've been permanently changed into this form," Rose said, her eyes lowering as she released her grip on Evan and allowing his hand to escape.

"What?" Evan exclaimed.

"Of course, that isn't public information," Alicia continued for her sister. "Everyone who chose races other than human simply thought this was a game. It's fun to be different in games; usually the most popular races are non-human. However, now we're all stuck like this. Even if we go back to Earth, we really wouldn't belong, would we?"

Rose nodded, her eyes rising to meet Evan's gaze. "We'd be lucky to not get captured and experimented on."

For the first time, Evan felt as though Alicia and Rose were genuinely depressed. He turned his gaze to his own tattoo. This world was filled with much more tragedy than he had been expecting. What was the point of it all? Why did this world even exist in the first place? Even if he did succeed in reviving Emma, what would he have to lose along the way? Was it all really worth it? He lowered his hand, turning his eyes back to Alicia and Rose. "I'm sorry…"

"Don't be." Rose flashed a weak smile. "A lot of people don't have a home to return to now, even if they wanted to. We just wanted you to know that you aren't alone."

Alicia turned to her sister, smiling and reaching out to hold her hand. "All we have right now is each other."

Rose pulled her sister closer to her, fully embracing her. The two seemed to blend into one another. Evan hastily flicked a falling tear from the pit of his eye, moved, not by their circumstances, but by the bond that they had. They were certainly making the most of a bad situation. *Can I say I'm doing the same?* He thought.

"I see," Evan said. "That explains a lot about your current relationship."

The sisters, pulling apart, returned their stares to Evan, lingering for a moment before Rose began. "So… how about now?"

"Would you be willing to take us now?" Alicia echoed as she and her sister moved even closer to Evan.

Each had taken a side; he could feel their breath on his neck. His body trembled with excitement. As much as he wanted to resist, perhaps this wasn't such a bad idea after all. Since getting here, he had more or less been alone, swimming through a sea of blood and death. Having someone to lean on would certainly ease his suffering. Then his mind wandered to Emma. Suddenly a tear ran down his cheek. "Ah… I'm… going to take a shower…"

He quickly moved passed the girls, wiping the tear away and fleeing into the bathroom.

The two sisters smiled weakly at one another.

Once inside, he positioned himself in front of the sink, gripping it tightly with both hands. He felt a sharp pain deep within his chest. His eyes trembled, and his breathing wavered. Up until this point, he had felt more or less numb, but finally making a connection with someone seemed to bring him back to reality.

He lingered in front of the sink for a moment, inhaling and exhaling heavily. After a few minutes, he removed his gear and made his way into the shower. He turned on the faucets, freeing the stream of hot water, and began to relax. Of course, this was short-lived as a familiar voice made him jump.

"Isn't the water great?" Alicia asked, pushing her breasts up against his back and wrapping her arms around his body. "It's mixed with Holy Herb."

The embrace proved too much. He could feel the tears begin to pour down his face as though a floodgate had opened. He sank to his knees; Alicia sank with him, remaining in the embrace, leaning her head against his back.

"It's okay," she said as she gently kissed his back. "You're not alone."

The shower continued without incident.

Once Evan and Alicia had exited the bathroom, Alicia brought up a large-scale projected map of the city. A red dot flashed on the right side of the map, near what was labeled as the palace.

"This is the deliverer," she stated, pointing at the dot. "Right now, it seems he's back at the palace, presumably finding out about his next job."

"Once he begins to move, it would probably help to try and tail him," Rose chimed in.

Alicia nodded. "Yeah, I suppose the best scenario would be that we jump him while he's in an isolated area."

Rose agreed.

Evan watched in silence. If he hadn't already vowed to do whatever it took to achieve his goal, this would not have sounded like the best solution. *They're pretty violent individuals*, he thought to himself.

Suddenly, the dot began to move away from the palace. "Nice," Alicia snickered.

They watched as the dot went directly along the main strip of the city, passing several buildings before reaching the edge of town and moving into the surrounding forest.

"We couldn't ask for a better situation!" Alicia exclaimed, closing the map and jumping up with enthusiasm.

Rose and Evan nodded, standing up and making their way out of the room.

Once the group entered the forest, Alicia reopened the map. The dot had stopped about halfway through the area, now between the city and the rest of the world.

"Must be a drop-off," Rose said. "If we're lucky, maybe we can get there before they meet whoever their supposed to be meeting."

Evan exhaled in relief.

"What?" Alicia asked.

"Ah, nothing." Evan smiled uncomfortably. "Just, the last time I was in this forest I was running for my life. Bad memories."

"Heh," Alicia chuckled. "Well, we'll protect you from any scary monsters. No need to worry."

Evan snickered as Alicia closed the map, and the group began running in the direction of where the dot had stopped.

Before long, light flooded through the widening gaps between the trees, and up ahead, the group could see a clearing. They slowed their pace, positioning themselves within the brush.

"Damn, we're late," Alicia cursed through her teeth.

The deliverer, along with two other elves clad in armor, was talking to three burly men. Apparently wounded, the three men were covered in scrapes and bruises. Between them was a small wooden box.

"If you would be so kind as to check, you'll find every herb is accounted for." The deliverer extended his arm, presenting the box.

One of the men stepped forward, Evan recognized his dark hair and trimmed goatee – it was Gavin. He lifted the lid of the box, peering in but closing it just as quickly. "It looks all accounted for," he grumbled.

"Very good." The deliverer smiled. "So, I will need to collect our payment then."

The largest of the men stepped forward, extending a brown burlap bag to the elves. The deliverer accepted it, and immediately poured the contents onto the ground. The man who had handed it to him glared at the elf in disdain. The deliverer carefully counted out each piece, before returning them back to the bag and then stashing it within his clothes.

"Excellent," the deliverer exclaimed. "I do hope you will think of us again."

With that, the three elves turned and made their way back towards the city from which they came.

The burly men began to speak quietly amongst themselves.

"We shouldn't have to rely on inferior creatures," the largest man growled.

The final man, shorter than the other two, and with shaggy brown hair, shook his head. "None of us liked having to do this, but we had little choice after what happened the other day."

"We're without a leader, and our manpower is drastically low," Gavin added. "We have to think about what we need to do in order to survive."

"We don't deserve to survive if we have to rely on others," the largest man boomed.

The rest of the group shifted, glancing away from the man.

"Let's just go," Gavin pressed. "We can figure out what to do next once we're back in the village."

Suddenly, a large ball of fire shot out from the forest towards the group of men.

"Get out of the way!" Gavin shouted.

However, the ground beneath the men began to crack and shake, as they scrambled to move out of the path of the attack.

"We're under attack!" The largest man shouted, drawing a large axe from his back.

Gavin immediately thought of the herbs, and ran to cover the box with his body, watching as the largest man simply dashed forward toward the ball of flame. As he moved, the air around his body began to swirl violently. A loud whistling echoed through the area as the head of his axe became engulfed in a small, violent concentration of swirling air. Once he had come closer to the ball of fire, he swung his axe through the flame. The ball split in half, and with a loud boom, the swell of air surrounding his axe and body exploded, forcing all of the flames outward as they dissipated.

"Come out, you cowards!" the man yelled, standing his ground and staring into the forest in front of him.

Evan dashed forward, Rose and Alicia on his heels. Ice and air swirled around his body, forming several daggers of ice that gravitated around him.

"You!" the large man bellowed. The air around him began to swirl violently once more before he darted toward Evan.

As they approached one another, the daggers of ice around Evan shot forward. The large man, moving at breakneck speed, easily avoided each blade. Before Evan knew it, the man was within reach, swinging his axe down to cleave through him.

As the blade came within inches of Evan's head, the man was halted in place by a large spire of earth that had rapidly — and unnaturally — began protruding from the ground, piercing through his chest.

Evan took a step back, turning to see Rose kneeling with both of her palms flat on the ground. Alicia smirked, slowly walking forward to take her place beside Evan. "I told you we'd protect you."

Evan exhaled, chuckling.

"God...damn...you..." The large man coughed up blood. "You'll...pay...for...this..."

His eyes shut, and his body went limp. The blood from his body began to move through the air toward Rose, slipping under her robe and flowing into her tattoo.

"Shit, the others are already gone," Alicia cursed in frustration as she stared out at an empty clearing.

"They were from that mercenary outpost on the outskirts of the forest," Rose said as she took to her feet. "We'll just have to go there, I guess. The real question is, why did he rush straight for Evan?"

Evan turned to face Rose. "I was at that outpost a few days ago, resting."

Rose and Alicia both turned their full attention toward Evan.

"They really are brutes," Evan sighed. "I woke up in the middle of the night to find a sadistic ritual. They were enslaving and raping women. I felt something come over me, and I began attacking them indiscriminately. The next thing I really remember is fleeing through the forest."

Alicia stared in disbelief. "What the shit..."

"I see," Rose said, turning her attention back to Evan. "That is pretty horrible, and that would explain why those men sought the Holy Herb, to try and heal their wounds."

Evan nodded. "I'm mostly just surprised that I'm still alive. I had to risk my life proving my strength just to get them to let me stay the night."

"The fact that you're alive is almost unbelievable," Alicia exclaimed. "Rumors are that these men are incredibly strong — apparently as much so as they are disgusting."

"It's hard to explain." Evan rubbed the back of his neck. "Once I snapped, I felt a surge of power, and I heard a voice guiding me. It was more like I was watching my body move on its own…in ways I couldn't hope to."

Alicia and Rose exchanged glances.

"Well," Rose began, turning back to Evan. "If you have all that power, it should be no problem to infiltrate that place and steal some holy herb."

"Rose!" Alicia blurted out.

Rose only smirked, shaking her head. "It's fine."

Evan watched, confused.

"Um?" he started. "What's wrong?"

"Nothing," Rose said dismissively. "Nothing has changed. Let's regroup and head towards that outpost."

Rose stepped past the dead man and took the lead. Alicia sighed, following her sister reluctantly, with Evan close behind. The group made their way into the woods once more, heading towards the mercenary outpost.

"Wait," Rose called back, stopping suddenly. The ground ahead seemed littered with patches of shiny, black sheets. Rose cautiously approached one as Alicia and Evan stared from a distance.

"Don't!" Evan called out instinctively.

Alicia took a short step forward, her eyes fixated on her sister.

Rose raised an arm, dismissing them as she came within reach of the closest patch. She kneeled, looking at it for a moment before glancing back at Evan.

"I'm guessing this isn't a trap. Leftovers?"

Evan nodded.

Alicia immediately turned her attention to Evan, looking bewildered.

Rose turned toward the sheet of black ice. She hovered her hand over it; despite the timeframe, she never would have guessed that this had been here for over a day. The cold radiating from the patch felt harsh enough to freeze her hand in place.

"Alright," Rose finally said, stepping back from the ice. "Let's be careful moving around these patches."

Alicia and Evan nodded, moving around the frozen, dark shapes as they continued forward.

It wasn't long before the group came upon the looming wooden pillars erected around the perimeter of the outpost. They stopped short, remaining in the cover of the forest.

"It's pretty quiet, all things considered," Rose observed.

Evan remained fixated on the area in front of him; he was hoping to never have to come back here. Watching those men prepare to rape those women was unlike anything he'd ever seen. His hands certainly weren't clean: Mark, Paul, and Diane were all murdered by him. He didn't want to forget that. However, these brutes weren't being threatened by these women. They didn't have to do terrible things.

Before coming to this world, he really hadn't felt any sort of adrenaline high. He never reveled in competitive sports. He barely even played any video games that pitted players against one another. He simply didn't care about being the very best. The past few months alone, he struggled with simply getting by day to day. Not everything needed to be a competition. Yet, so many people loved to feel as though they were better off than others.

Unfortunately, it seemed this world brought out the primal aggression in players. Perhaps they had been like he was on Earth: tepid wallflowers who had no real presence. Now granted with these incredible powers, they didn't have to simply endure being bullied anymore. They could do whatever they wanted, and even worse, there were no laws to keep them in check.

“I couldn't just stand there and watch those girls be raped,” Evan said quietly. "I just wanted to save them.”

Rose sighed, "Unfortunately, by fleeing from the scene, it's likely that the girls were subject to much worse things."

Evan quickly turned towards Rose, surprised by her accusation.

"She's right..." Alicia spoke softly. "If they couldn't catch you, do you think they would come back and learn their lesson? They probably let out all their frustration and anger on the very women you set out to save."

Rose nodded. "If you were going to save them, then you should have brought them with you. Or, at the very least, completely removed the threat of the men."

Evan hadn't really thought about it, but it made sense. Anything that may have happened to them after was a result of his actions. To make matters worse, he simply ran away, choosing self-preservation. *What was I even trying to prove?* He thought to himself.

"Damn it..." Evan cursed softly, clenching his fist.

Rose chuckled. "You're a weird guy. Isn't our focus the herb?"

"I suppose," Evan replied somberly. "I just feel bad."

"It is what it is," Alicia stated simply. "Everyone in this world has the potential to fight and become strong. Those girls may not have chosen to be captured and used, but they're choosing to remain captives."

"Alicia!" Rose scolded. "Don't be a jerk."

Alicia shrugged. "Are we going to do anything or just sit here and talk about it?"

"Alright," Rose sighed. "This place isn't very big. I guess the best thing is to split up and check each area."

"To be honest," Evan intervened. "It's probably in the main building. They use that bar as their base of operations, so to speak. Everyone is likely held up in there, using the herb as necessary. They don't seem smart enough to hide it or lock it up."

"Alright!" Alicia exclaimed. "Then let's go!"

Rose shook her head. "Calm down. If you go in blasting fireballs again, you might end up burning up the herb. Be mindful, Alicia."

Alicia stuck her tongue out and raised her middle finger.

"Cute." Rose smirked.

Evan chuckled; the two *did* seem to suit one another.

They slowly made their way around the perimeter of the outpost, remaining in the forest as long as they could before coming up to the backside of the bar. Rose checked a nearby door, pushing against it. "Lock."

She placed her palm on the door, and before long, the wood began to crumble away. She stepped through the archway, with Alicia and Evan close behind. They moved quietly through a poorly lit, wide corridor, hearing chattering voices just up ahead. As they reached the end, the room opened into the large bar area that Evan recognized from before. The room wasn't much emptier than his first visit. And, across the room, atop the bar, was the chest with the herb.

The three stood with their backs against the wall, remaining quiet.

"What's the plan?" Evan whispered.

"Rose and I will create a distraction," Alicia murmured. "Stay here, and we'll draw them outside. While we're doing that, you need to grab some of the herb and head back to the forest. We'll rendezvous there."

Alicia motioned to Rose, and the two quickly left the way they had come. Evan stood awkwardly against the wall, reminded of any number of school dances in which he was too shy to ask any girl for a dance. Luckily, he was good at blending in with his surroundings. *Being a wallflower is finally going to pay off*, he thought.

Before long, he heard a sudden crash. Then, a *whoosh* and a wave of heat; he turned his head to catch a glimpse of a large ball of fire that had come barreling through the main hall. It carved a path along the ground and ripped a hole in the back wall. There was a mix of screams and groans. He peeked around the corner to see numerous women flat on the floor, and all of the men rushing to squeeze through a hole where the front door had been. He shook his head and made his way into the main area, taking the time to check that each woman he passed was still breathing as he made his way to the bar.

Meanwhile, outside, Rose and Alicia stood in the middle of the open area of the outpost, back-to-back with their hands placed together and close to their chests. They were surrounded by a wide ring of flames, which kept the men at bay.

"Surround them!" One of the men shouted, directing them to take positions all the way around the girls. "We'll combine our skills when everyone is in position!"

The men got into position around the two girls and each withdrew a weapon. Within moments, the sound of whipping wind tore through the air. Each man's weapon seemed to have its own mini hurricane billowing around it.

"Wind," Alicia murmured. "It won't work like they hope."

Rose chuckled, "Let's do *that* technique. Draw them in."

"Fine."

The men all swung their weapons against the wall of flame, dispersing and blowing away bits of fire throughout the area. The ring of flame reeled back, seeming to have shrunken, now much closer to the girls.

"It worked!" One man shouted. "Keep it up!"

The men cheered, making their way up to the wall once more, preparing their weapons as they advanced. Again, they attacked, pushing the ring surrounding the girls further inward, now within ten feet of the girls.

"This should be the last time!" A man shouted. "Then, we'll get to have some real fun!"

"As if I'm going to just roll over and take it like these assholes are used to." Alicia scowled.

As the men advanced yet again, the ground beneath them began to crack and shake. Several of them took a step forward, only to have their feet sink into the earth. Shards of rock began to rise from the ground, creating holes in the ground that was steadily becoming uneven.

"Be careful!" A voice boomed throughout the air. "Work to keep your footing and balance!"

The men struggled to do so. Some, more thoughtful than others, made use of their ability to manipulate wind, wrapping gusts around their feet to hover slightly off the ground. It was they who noticed first: hovering above the two girls were numerous boulders of concentrated earth. The flames that were once a perimeter around the girls were now flowing upward, wrapping around the individual rocks.

"Shit!" A man shouted, pointing to the sky. "Watch out for above!"

"Too late," Rose stated simply.

Alicia and Rose simultaneously dropped to their knees, pressing their palms against the earth. The orbs, meanwhile, began to rapidly fall from the sky. Alicia and Rose watched as they crashed into men and ground alike.

The earth charred and sank; even an indirect hit proved fatal for the men. Before long, all of them had been caught in the burning ground, and all that remained were corpses. Alicia and Rose took to their feet, standing in the only untouched area, within a small perimeter around them. Blood rapidly flowed into the two girls' tattoos from the ground around them.

Alicia reached her arm through the air. As she closed her eyes and exhaled, the remaining flames smoldered at her command. In the meantime, Rose, mimicking her sister's movements, began to shift the earth, shuffling charred ground. Before long, a safe path had been created for them to tread upon.

"Let's go," Rose said, taking the lead.

Back inside the bar, after the shaking had subsided, Evan made his way to the chest and began to fill his inventory with several pieces of the herb.

"Alright," Evan said to himself. He turned to see that many of the women had taken to their feet but remained in the general area.

"Everyone is free to go!" Evan projected his voice. "We've taken care of all the dangerous men here!"

The women shifted uncomfortably, looking around at one another.

"Nothing is even left here for you anymore," Evan pressed.

"I wouldn't be so sure," a voice hissed from behind.

Evan turned to see two knives flying towards him. *Too fast.* The first sunk into his left thigh, and the next dug into his left shoulder. Evan gritted his teeth as the pain pulsated through his shoulder. He immediately fell to a knee, looking up to see the man with the goatee, clad in steel armor and standing atop the bar. In one hand he held a girl, and in the other, a knife.

"Gavin," Evan breathed.

"Evan!" Alicia shouted, as she and her sister came into the bar.

"Stay put!" Gavin screamed, pressing the edge of his knife a little deeper against the women's neck. "If you move, I'll murder this girl!"

Alicia stared at him for a moment, then stepped toward Evan. A casualty or two wasn't a big deal to her; they had just wiped out a large group of men outside. Her priority was Evan.

"Alicia!" Rose shouted, grabbing her sister by the shoulder.

"Stay back," Evan reaffirmed.

"I won't let him die." Alicia's gaze moved from Gavin to the captive girl. "Keep that in mind."

Gavin, thrown off guard for a moment, quickly regained his composure.

"What do you want?" Evan called out.

"For you to leave," Gavin stated. "You got what you came for, didn't you? Then just go, this place is none of your business!"

Evan stared at him for a moment, and then turned to see the other women in the room. They seemed equally as terrified as the woman held hostage.

Alicia took the liberty to answer. "Fine by us!"

"No!" Evan darted his attention to Alicia, glaring at her, before returning his gaze back to Gavin. "The only way I can leave is if you free all these women and let them come with me."

"Greedy, aren't you?" Gavin grimaced. "I could let you have your favorite one, if that will satisfy you. I should really be thanking you anyway; you gave me a wonderful gift. With Royce gone, I can assume control of this operation, and rebuild things how I want!"

Evan sighed. "I can't —"

"Evan, shut up." Alicia glared at him before addressing Gavin. "Look, all of your followers are dead — just stains on the ground outside. If I really wanted to, I don't mind sacrificing that girl to stop your ambitions. But, even at this point, if the rest of these girls banded together, even *they* could overthrow you."

The women standing around glanced at one another before turning their attention back to the situation.

"If you really wanted to start over, then you should have run away instead of confronting us," Rose added.

Gavin took half a step back, looking around the room frantically, and strengthening his hold on his hostage. "Shut up! What do you whores know!?"

Feeling a grip on his ankle, Gavin looked down to see what appeared to be a branch, protruding from the bar counter, curling up his leg. "What the hell?!"

With Gavin distracted, Evan grabbed the knives in his shoulder and thigh and began to pull. He groaned as wave after wave of pain flew through his body. He gritted his teeth, and the knives tore out of his wounds, with spurts of blood beginning to flow freely. He breathed slowly as his right hand began to glow with a pale blue light and placed it first over his shoulder wound. Skin began to regrow as the opening slowly closed. Then, he moved his glowing hand to his thigh. With both wounds mended, his health bar filled back up significantly.

Taking this as her opportunity, the girl being held thrust her elbow into Gavin's stomach. He groaned, reeling backwards and losing his grip on her. She stumbled forward, frantically making her way to the rest of the women.

"Shit!" Gavin cursed. That was the least of his worries as, before he'd realized, a large orb of flame was barreling toward him. He struggled in panic, pulling at the leg that the branch held in place.

Everyone watched as the flame engulfed his body. A sudden shockwave erupted from him, toppling the tables and knocking everyone off their feet. The flames had now dispersed completely, and a steady, violent wind whipped around Gavin's body. The bar lay in ruins, with broken glass and spilled liquor littering the floor.

"I'm not the leader for nothing!" Gavin screamed.

"He's right," Rose said, struggling to get to her feet. "Even from this distance, there's a strong pull and push from the residual wind. He's on a different level compared to those from before."

Alicia groaned, standing slowly. "Yeah, but he put himself in a terrible position. With all that alcohol there, all I'd have to do would be launch another fireball and he'd be done."

"We'll have to try to create an opening, then," Evan stated, standing up carefully and still slightly woozy. He glanced over to see that all the women had been forced against the back wall, presumably from the shockwave, and were unconscious.

The tattoo on the back of his hand shined, and ice slowly encased his hand before growing out into a long spire. *Cold,* he thought. *I probably shouldn't waste too much time. Maintaining this weapon might end up backfiring.* He tried running forward, feeling the force of the wind push against him. The closer he got, the harder it was to advance. Gavin watched in contentment.

"Fool," he sneered, reaching out his arm out and focusing the wind in front of his body.

The wind built up rapidly and then suddenly exploded, sending a massive gust toward Evan. The gust enveloped him, forcing him backward against the adjacent wall. Upon impact, part of the spire had shattered, leaving only his hand encased in a now jagged block of ice. In addition, all over his body were shallow cuts. He slowly got to his feet, turning his attention to a smug Gavin. The barrier of wind had returned to billowing around only the user's body.

"Good job," Alicia called out to Evan as she approached him.

She placed her hand over his, a faint light shimmering from her palm as the ice began to slowly melt away, freeing Evan's trembling, discolored hand. He slowly flexed his fingers, hoping to return as much feeling as he could before Gavin struck back.

"I don't think he can control his powers as much as he wants us to believe," Rose stated.

"What do you mean?" Alicia asked.

"Look at his hand," Rose pointed.

"It's a hand," Alicia said. "A dumb hand."

Rose sighed. "Okay... so what about his other hand?"

Alicia took another look. "He's only wearing one glove?"

"He wasn't before," Evan said, finally beginning to regain some feeling in his hand. "When he attacked, not only did the wind come forward, but some went towards him as well. It's powerful, but it's damaging him as well. You can tell from the armor — not only the one glove missing, but his other pieces of armor have more cracks in them than they did when he first showed himself."

"Right," Rose spoke softly. "I bet if we attack from multiple angles, one of our attacks will be strong enough to break through that barrier."

"Rose and I will make the first attacks," Evan whispered. "Even if we only graze some of the alcohol with Alicia's fire that should be enough."

"It's no use!" Gavin screamed. "You can plot all you want! I can't lose!"

The ground beneath Gavin began to crack, while earth began to coil up his leg, tightening around him. He roared with anger as wind whipped around his feet, shattering his boots and carving away at the earth. Simultaneously, the wall to his left fell toward him. Wind gust out from his side, protecting him from the debris.

Evan made his way to Gavin's right side, as a burst of flame shot forward toward the wild-eyed leader of the outpost, threatening to engulf him.

"No use!" Gavin shouted, intensifying the wind all around his body. He then reached his arms out on either side of him, blowing away the debris that had fallen around him with a sudden burst of air.

In that instant, Gavin felt a sharp pain in his ribs. The wind around him began to subside. He looked down to see a frozen spire planted deep into him. He placed his hand around the ice, only to realize that several more were flying through the air towards him. Simultaneously, he felt the heat from the approaching flames in front him begin to consume his body.

As Alicia's flames wrapped around Gavin's body, the alcohol around him ignited all along the ground. A sudden explosion blew away the remaining wall around Gavin and sent a shockwave throughout the room.

As the initial impact of the explosion subsided, Evan, Alicia, and Rose regrouped. Where Gavin had been, all that remained was a smoldering pile of as ash and wood.

"Finally," Evan breathed. "Now we just – "

A sudden gust of wind erupted from the base of the previous explosion.

"Really?" Alicia sighed.

The dust settled, and Gavin stood among the rubble, a powerful barrier of wind swirling around his body. However, all of his armor had been completely shattered. He stood battered, bloody, and bruised. The skin on his chest had nearly completely charred, save a few spots of deep red.

"It's... not... over..." Gavin exhaled heavily.

A revamped blast of air flooded the area. Evan, Alicia, and Rose were forced into the crosswinds as the building around them began to crumble and collapse. The group swirled around, crashing into debris mid-air as they were pushed and pulled. When the winds finally died down, they all lay upon the ground.

Evan opened his eyes to see a blurry figured standing over him. He had hoped it would be Rose or Alicia coming to his aid. Slowly, the figure came into focus.

"I should really thank you," Gavin sneered. "A second time."

He brought the edge of his knife to Evan's neck, licking his lips with anticipation.

"You've given me so much," Gavin added.

"Thanks to me...?" Evan grumbled softly, his vision blurring.

"I guess you don't remember me after all." Gavin moved in closely to whisper into Evan's ear. "But I remembered you the moment you walked through the door of our bar."

Evan barely registered what Gavin had said. He had been hit so many times and lost quite a bit of blood. He couldn't even focus on Gavin; it seemed as though there were three men standing over him. At this point, there wasn't much he could do. *Is this as far as I go?* He thought to himself. *Sorry, Emma.*

"We had fun together once before." Gavin began to laugh maniacally, pulling away from Evan's ear. "That night on the road."

Suddenly, Evan's mother's voice echoed through his head, "Evan, run!"

His heart leapt, and he felt tears begin to cascade down his face. *Sorry Mom, I can barely move. Looks like I'll be seeing you, Dad, and Emma sooner than I thought, though.*

"Time to finish what I started," Gavin sneered.

He drew his knife back, before swinging it towards Evan.

Evan looked up at his parent's murderer, as the blade edged forward, he felt he could see more clearly than ever before. *Can't believe I have to die to this jerk*, he thought, looking Gavin once over when he noticed a dark mark on Gavin's neck.

Evan heard a cold voice hiss, "Pathetic."

Gavin's knife stopped in midair, and all at once, he was sent flying backwards into the debris of the bar. Evan stood up with ease. His body no longer felt heavy, and none of his wounds hurt. His vision had become much clearer than it was in the first place. He noticed he could spot even the tiniest details. A torrent of black energy suddenly swirled violently around his body.

"Is this all your talk of determination amounts to?" A voice not his own came out of his lips. "And all of your desires? You can't do anything without my intervention. You should be grateful."

Gavin stumbled, struggling to get to his feet. "What the hell just happened?"

Evan could feel the anger boiling off of Gavin's body, like an aura. It was almost like he was looking at another health bar designed specifically for emotions. Despite his intensity, the crazed man was barely standing. Evan slowly moved toward him.

"Stay back!" Gavin called out in desperation, struggling to raise his frantically shaking arm.

Evan ignored his cry, and once he was close enough, he could more clearly make out the figure on Gavin's neck: a black X.

"So," Evan's voice echoed, resonating through the bar. "It was you who killed my parents."

"So, you finally remember?" Gavin began to laugh uncontrollably, his body sinking as he did. "I'll kill you too!"

Gavin suddenly took a step, thrusting his arm forward with all his weight. A cone of air spiraled toward Evan, who raised his arm and opened his palm toward the oncoming gust. As though crashing into an invisible wall, the burst of wind halted against his hand. The air swirled violently, contained in the area just in front of Evan. He smirked, pouring his own energy into the air. As the air condensed, dark crystalline shards began to develop inside.

"You can't be serious!?" Gavin screamed, shocked at the boy's feat.

All at once, the air burst forward, rushing towards an unprepared Gavin. Before he could react, the air enveloped him, forcing him backwards into the ground. Evan stepped forward, and as though he had teleported, appeared within feet of the man's mangled body.

From the distance, Alicia opened her eyes, still on the ground. She looked over to see Rose lying next to her, eyes still closed. Alicia slowly got up and turned her attention to her sister, shaking her body. "Hey."

"Don't worry," Rose coughed. "I'm not dead."

Alicia helped her sister to her feet when suddenly, a shrill, ear-splitting wail echoed through the area. Evan had stabbed a spire of black ice deep into the man's left shoulder. The two, supporting one another, slowly made their way over to Evan.

"Does it hurt?" Evan smirked. "Don't worry, I won't let you die just yet. I still owe you for what you did to my parents."

Another spire of black ice formed in his hand. He stabbed this one into Gavin's other shoulder, prompting another wail of agony. The skin around where the spires pierced had begun to darken from its usual pale white. Slowly, that darkness began to spread from his shoulders. The skin on his neck and face began to grow darker and darker.

"What're… you… doing…?" Gavin barely managed to speak, a visible cloud coming out of his mouth with each breath.

"Feeling cold?" Evan sneered, taking great satisfaction in his superiority. "Your body is freezing from the inside out. Not just your skin, but your muscles, bones, blood, and organs."

Evan began to cackle, kneeling down next to Gavin. "Isn't this fun?"

"That's enough!" Rose bellowed.

Evan turned to see Rose and Alicia.

"Don't interfere," Evan warned, glaring at the two.

Rose immediately noticed his shimmering, golden eyes. "This isn't like you. Weren't we just trying to get the Holy Herb? Save those girls?"

Evan scowled, standing up. Gavin was already unnaturally still; his internal organs had likely already been coated in ice. He wouldn't last long as it was. Another spire of black ice formed in his hand, and with a single movement he pierced Gavin's chest, killing the man once and for all. Evan knelt down, placing his right hand in the pool of fresh blood that had formed under the body. Before long, the blood flowed into the mark on the back of his hand. With that, he stood back up, turning to the sisters.

They've seen too much already. They need to die.

"No!" Evan shouted suddenly. "I won't let you!"

Rose and Alicia took a step back, not sure what to expect.

Evan placed his hands on either side of his head, as if physically trying to suppress the voice.

"It's okay," Alicia said softly, reaching her hand toward Evan.
Rose immediately pulled her sister's arm back, clinging to her. "No, don't get too close."

You can't stop me, the voice in Evan's head resonated, louder than ever.

His body began to move on his own. His right arm extended out, and a spire of black ice formed. He took a step toward the sisters, drawing the spire back, poised to strike. Rose immediately erected a barrier of energy around herself and Alicia, bracing for impact.

"No!" Evan shouted, as his arm swung down toward the sisters.

Suddenly, he gritted his teeth. Blood began to flow from his mouth; the spire of ice had stabbed into his own stomach. The pain was more immense that he had anticipated. He could feel his stomach getting colder and colder.

Fool, the voice hissed. *You're lucky I can't allow you to die. But don't think you'll be able to resist me forever.*

Evan only smiled weakly before falling to the ground, unconscious.

VIII
Durian Forest

Evan awoke in an unfamiliar room. Soft light shone through a nearby window — the sun still hadn't fully risen. In the bed adjacent to his, Alicia and Rose were sprawled out, nude. The room was fairly small and quaint: there was a couch, along with a wooden table and chairs, and a bathroom with shower. Evan rubbed his eyes, exhausted. His body was covered in sweat and grime, and his memories from the previous night remained a haze. He pulled himself up, making his way to the bathroom.

He looked in the mirror. His hair was a mess — Matted on one side and sticking up on the other. Dark circles ran under his eyes. Since coming to this world — since teaming up with Alicia and Rose — he had been constantly on the move. Despite that, he had only just secured the first piece of the recipe. *Am I really doing enough?* He thought. He turned on the sink, cupping his hands and splashing some water onto his face before making his way to the toilet. Afterward, he turned to see a half-asleep Alicia standing in the doorway, "Good morning…?"

She swayed, yawning and rubbing her eyes as she made her way passed him and taking her place on the toilet, relieving herself. Evan hastily made his way out of the bathroom. To his surprise, Rose lay awake, sprawled out on the bed, looking up at the ceiling above, and lazily stroking her stiffening nipple.

"Err…I should go," Evan mumbled, taking a step back.

Alicia yawned as she walked past him. "It's fine. Or are you still unable to even look at us?"

Alicia took her place next to Rose, kissing her neck gently, their bodies beginning to weave together. Evan's heart raced; hearing Rose's moaning, his mind began to wander back to Emma. He remembered being in her room, arched over her, their lips interlocking as their pale bodies entangled in the sheets. The way she would kiss his neck as he climaxed and sinking into her and holding her afterwards. He heard her voice echo through his head, "Evan."

"Evan," Alicia's voice brought him back to reality.

He stood in a stupor, noticing the two had stopped and were staring at him.

"What a pervert." Rose scoffed.

"What...?" He glared at them. "Are you serious?"

"Do you want to join in?" Alicia smirked.

He sighed. "We've already been over th —"

He was cut off by a sharp pain in his forehead. He fell to his knees, placing his hand on his head. *Don't be afraid*, a familiar, ominous voice rang through his mind. With each passing second, his body seemed to heat up, his mind flooded with imagery of Emma.

"Is this your first time?" Her voice echoed.

"Yeah," he murmured, lying next to her in his room.

"Mine too…" she admitted, smiling weakly. "Don't be afraid. Let's just try and enjoy ourselves."

As the memory passed, he found himself still on his knees, staring at the ground. *What's happening?* He thought. He slowly brought himself to his feet, recognizing the small room he had been in. He turned around to see Alicia standing within inches of him.

"...Are you okay?" She asked tepidly.

"I don't know," Evan managed to breathe out, placing a hand on his stomach. "Lately it seems I'm losing track of what I've been doing. I mean, wasn't there a hole in my stomach?"

Alicia lowered her gaze, avoiding Evan's stare.

"You don't remember?" Rose interjected.

Evan shook his head, turning his attention to her.

After a pause, Rose finally spoke up.

"After you 'defeated' Gavin, you turned your attention to us. But it seemed like you were fighting yourself at the same time. You ended up stabbing yourself to avoiding stabbing us and passed out. We debated whether or not to continue to follow you after that."

After Evan had passed out, Rose shouted at Alicia, "He just tried to kill us!"

Alicia hesitated, glancing at Evan's fallen body before returning her attention to her sister.

"...But it seemed like there was something controlling him."

Rose shook her head, exasperated. "That's even worse. He's extremely volatile."

Alicia knelt down, combing strands of Evan's hair from his face.

"There's just something about him." She sighed. "We were given the quest to find and follow him for a reason. Are we just going to abandon that? Then what? Go back to being bored every day in that forest?"

Rose shifted uncomfortably, visibly frustrated with her sister.

"I know you're worried." Alicia turned toward her, smiling. "But, what do we really have to lose?"

"Our lives," Rose stated matter-of-factly.

Alicia smirked. "Since when did we start caring about those?"

"I suppose you're right," Rose chuckled. "But we still need to be careful about this boy. I'm going to be keeping him on a much shorter leash for the time being."

Alicia nodded, before focusing her attention on the spire of ice protruding from Evan's stomach. She reached her arms out, cupping her hands around the spire. She could feel the intense cold radiating off of it. Before she could touch it, she felt a sharp bite against her palms, forcing her to pull her hands away.

"Be careful!" Rose scolded.

Alicia glared at her sister indignantly, before cupping her hands around the spire once more. This time, her hands began radiating an intense heat, shimmering with a bright, red light. As she wrapped her hands around the spire, the cold had become no more than if she was holding a glass of ice water. The heat began to melt away at the spire, and slowly, Alicia pulled it from out of Evan's gut.

"You're up," she called out to Rose.

Rose nodded, kneeling on the other side of the boy.

However, before Rose could begin to treat the wound, the hole in Evan's stomach had begun to close on its own. The flesh seemed to swirl, making the hole smaller and smaller until there was nothing but a smooth patch of skin, as though the hole had never been there in the first place.

The sisters stared in awe for a moment before finally looking up to face one another.

Back in the small room, Evan stared at Rose for a moment, still processing the information.

"I'm not entirely sure how to react to that."

"You're telling us," Alicia exhaled. "Do you even have a high-speed regeneration skill?"

Evan shook his head, holding his tongue as he thought about his conversation with that voice and its eagerness to have him kill. *What exactly is that voice?* He thought. *And what does it want?*

Rose, noticing his hesitation, got up and made her way closer to him.

"Look." She paused. "Whether you want to believe it or not, you did try to kill us. Despite this, we've decided to keep helping you. I think we deserve some sort of explanation. If you have any idea about what was happening, you need to bring us into the fold."

Evan met Rose's eyes, looking into them for a moment before answering.

"I'm not really sure myself," he insisted. "In times of desperation, I start hearing a voice and suddenly I feel a surge of power. I can do things I normally wouldn't be able to do at my current level. My body sort of moves on its own." Rose turned to Alicia, who was already staring at her sister.

"For the time being —" Rose began.

"Then don't fight anymore," Alicia suddenly burst out. "Let me…let *us* protect you and help you find what you're looking for."

"Alicia…" Rose murmured.

"Why?" Evan finally replied, taken back. "Why are you insistent on going so far to be with me?"

Rose remained silent, turning to her sister, seemingly interested in hearing the answer as well.

Without another word, Alicia stepped as close as she could to Evan, placing her hand around the back of his neck and pulling him so that his lips met her own. She held him against her, resisting his own resistance. He slowly began to give in, feeling a deep yearning to let this happen. It was as though he had lost all sense of what he had been doing and he simply was drowning in the moment. Rose smirked, watching the scene unfold.

As the two continued to kiss, Evan grabbed her exposed breast before leaning down and kissing her neck. His body seeming to move of its own accord. *Take what it is you desire*, the voice rang through his head, driving him further and further toward Alicia.

Alicia pulled him along, backing closer to the bed until she spun him around and he was suddenly pushed down, plopping onto his back. Before he could react, Alicia loomed over his body on all fours, her hands placed flat on the bed on either side of him. Her breasts sank with her body, resting on his chest. He suddenly let out a soft cry as her crotch began to grind against his own.

"All you'd have to do is ask," she said slyly.

Rose had taken her place next to Evan, her breasts pressed into the side of his body. He turned to look at her, breathing heavily, his face flush. She smiled at him. "It'll be okay. You're only human."

He bit his lip, clenching his eyes tightly. Alicia turned to meet Rose's gaze, bringing her grinding to a halt. Rose gently kissed his forehead. "Sorry — perhaps this was too much."

"N…no," Evan stammered. "It's okay."

Alicia obeyed eagerly, and the next five minutes were a blur of touching, kissing, and pleasure.

"I'm assuming you hadn't touched yourself in a while," Rose remarked once they had finished. "Must still be pretty full — probably part of your problem."

He sighed as he sat up and closed his eyes. "I know it needed to happen. I feel better, and it felt amazing. But now I just feel guilty, like I've done something wrong."

"You've run yourself ragged," Alicia explained. "You had so much happen to you and you've let your feelings bottle up inside of you. It's therapeutic to let go, to vent."

"I'm sure your girlfriend wouldn't like what she saw if she were here, still alive." Rose stared at Evan. "Dark circles under your eyes. You've thinned. You hold so much in; even if it hurts, it's better to face it. You can't get better if you just ignore your feelings. You need to take a break and take care of yourself better."

"I'm pretty sure I'm good now." He sat up, beginning to stand.

Alicia stretched, slyly glancing at her sister and back at Evan. "Are you sure you don't want to watch?"

"Watch what?"

As though on cue, Alicia turned so that she was lying flat on her back while Rose loomed over her on all fours. Evan decidedly sat back down. The way the girls explored one another's bodies was very different from what Evan was used to. It was deliberate, soft, and tender. Despite a nagging of embarrassment in the back of his mind, Evan couldn't help but watch with intrigue.

Then Alicia's back arched, her grip tightened, and she gasped. After a few moments she exhaled, now breathing heavily. Rose pulled away from her sister. The sheets under Alicia's bottom were soaked, and Rose's mouth glistened. She crawled up her sister's body, kissing her. Alicia took her free hand and wrapped it around Rose's neck, bringing them closer together. Afterwards, they turned to see Evan, still watching, and he realized he had been holding hands with Alicia the entire time. Rose smiled. "Time for a shower, I think."

"I'll join you shortly," Alicia said, closing her eyes as she sprawled out.

Evan pulled his hand away, getting up and beginning to dress himself.

"You two really love each other," he said softly, making his way to the window.

Alicia opened her eyes, seeing him standing in front of the window. She stood up and walked over to him. "Remember, you're working on taking care of yourself. If you really believe you'll be reunited with your girlfriend, then make sure there is something for her to reunite with. No sense in reviving her, just to leave her alone."

She wrapped her arms around him from behind.

"I'm trying." He turned around, flashing a weak smile at her before suddenly being pushed up against the window and kissed.

"How do I taste?" She smirked.

He chuckled. "Sweet."

She nodded, heading toward the bathroom. Evan made his way to the beds and, looking at the wet spot, opted to lay on the dry one.

An hour later, Evan awoke in the middle of Rose and Alicia, who were still nude. He sat up and yawned before getting out of the bed and heading toward the table. He sat down and pressed a button in the middle, bringing up a window with pictures of various foods. He scrolled through the menu, looking for something to eat. Before long, Alicia came and sat next to him. "Hungry?"

"Yeah." He nodded.

"I've got something you can eat." She smirked.

He stopped, turning to her and smiling before resuming his search.

"Hey." She smiled. "It's the first time you've laughed rather than gotten frustrated."

"I suppose so," he said, finally picking a pork and egg sandwich. "Do you want anything?"

"Yeah…" she stared at him in silence for a few moments.

He turned to meet her gaze. After a few moments, "Um, what do you want?"

"Oh, um…" She began scrolling through the menu, picking a dense, square shaped cake littered with blueberries.

Within moments, the food appeared on the table, and the two began eating.

"So, um... tell —" Alicia began.

Suddenly Rose sat up, stretching her arms in the air. Her bright yellow hair draped over her shoulders.

"What's our next move?" She asked, taking her place at the table and skimming the visible menu.

Alicia sighed in frustration, turning her attention to her meal.

"Let me see…" Evan seemed not to notice Alicia as he withdrew the recipe he had received from Mike.

Holding it in one hand while taking a bite of his sandwich with the other, he began to read the contents aloud.

"After Holy Herb," he spoke in between bites. "The next thing is something called Pina Eyes…"

Alicia took notice of the item, her eyes glazed with excitement as they turned up from the bowl and focused on Rose.

"Yeah," Rose smiled to her sister. "That means we get to go to the Durian Forest."

"What's that?" Evan asked.

"Well —" Rose started.

Alicia had quickly swallowed her food to interject.

"The greatest place ever!" She exclaimed. "It's a forest filled with fruit-themed monsters. A culinary dream. I used to make Rose take me nearly every week."

Evan chuckled, continuing to eat.

"There is a boss at the heart of the forest," Rose said, regaining control of the conversation. "A giant electric spider, and it has the chance to drop those eyes. It's a fairly high-level boss, but we should be able to manage it."

With that, Rose picked her own breakfast, a bowl of assorted fruit. The group made quick work of their meals before preparing for their next adventure. The town of Riverton was small, only several buildings made of stone resting on either side of a riverbank. There were two bridges that connected the two banks, allowing passage from one side to the other. Not many people lingered, but there was a moderate amount of traffic through the town.

The group made their way south. As they stepped out of town, they could see a forest in the distance, just past a small field. Eventually, Evan took notice of a distinctive lack of enemy spawns. This appeared to be a surprisingly peaceful region.

Within the forest, he caught a faint, sweet aroma. Several berries grew from the surrounding brush, while larger fruits; melons, apples, and bananas grew from the trees.

" How rare is this monster?" Evan asked as they walked along the beaten path.

"It only spawns every three days, and the drops aren't guaranteed," Rose said. "Compared to other farmable enemies, this one is actually one of the worst to bother with. Therefore, we shouldn't have too much competition." Alicia smirked.

"And, even if there is, we are a much higher level than most players in this area. We shouldn't have too much trouble getting dibs on the creature."
The group passed a pool of thick, brown goop. A large worm made up of several purple balls erupted suddenly from it, screeching at the trio. The top ball, its face, had two white glowing eyes with several protruding fangs from its mouth. Its head snapped forward; fangs poised.

Rose reacted immediately, staring at the monster and flicking her wrist upward. "Pierce."

A jagged stone pillar erupted from the ground, piercing the worm's skull in mid-movement. It screeched in pain, and the balls making up its body began to burst one by one. A clear fluid flew in several directions, pooling onto the ground around them. The air was suddenly filled with a strong, sweet aroma.

"What's that scent?" Evan asked.

"Grape," Alicia said, kneeling in front of one of the puddles. "As I mentioned, this forest is full of fruit-based monsters that drop ingredients for food and medicines."

She brought up her inventory, adding some of the liquid to an empty vial.

"It's actually a pretty popular farming spot," Rose added.

They continued on, as they made their way deeper into the forest, a group of large stag beetles walked by. They were about two feet all, bright red, black spots scattered across their bodies, and a grassy green mane around their heads.

They stomped by without attacking the group.

"Ohmygod!" Alicia shouted, turning her attention to them. "I need some strawberry essence!"

"We don't really have time for this…" Rose shifted her eyes.

"Strawberry Beetles are super rare," Alicia glared at Rose. "As many times as we've come here, I've never seen one."

Evan sighed, "It's fine — how long can it take to kill a couple of bugs?"

Alicia nodded, turning to see the beetles walking away. She raised her right arm and, using her fingers as a sight, lined up the bug so that it was between her middle and ring finger. "Ignite!"

Wings of flame erupted from her back, and small embers flickered from the top and side of her eyes. Rings of fire formed around both her wrists and ankles. Then, in an instant, she vanished, reappearing within the center of the beetles. A sudden crash echoed throughout the area and a ring of fire shot out from her body, igniting the beetles in flames. She stood in the center of the burning carcasses, her body reverberating from the transportation.

Rose rolled her eyes. "Show-off."

Evan and Rose made their way over to Alicia. She had already begun filling empty vials with the liquid that had spilled from the beetle's bodies.

"What the hell was that?" Evan asked.

"It's just the base of my skills," she shrugged. "If I was serious, I'd have cloaked my entire body in fire."

"The eyes seemed unnecessary," Rose said.

Alicia glared at her sister.

"What is it for?" Evan asked excitedly. "It's like having flaming eyeliner. Does it let you see further or something?"

"Nah, I just think it looks cool," Alicia stated. "Ready? We have a boss to kill."

Rose shook her head, and Evan chuckled as the group resumed their search. As they walked, Evan could hear the murmurs and shouts of other players from behind passing brush and trees. Above them, a group of colorful dragonflies — significantly larger than Evan was used to seeing — flew overhead. As they passed, he noticed that their tails were made up of clusters of dark blue orbs.

"Can you transform your body too, Rose?" Evan asked suddenly as they continued forward.

"No," Rose replied. "I manipulate Earth. It seems like it'd be unbecoming to become a rock. Although, I would be the most beautiful rock in all the land."

"I'm not sure if that's something to be proud of," Alicia pointed out.

"Shut up," Rose scoffed. "It's more important to have skills that are useful, and not just there for aesthetic value."

"Luckily my skills are both useful and aesthetically pleasing," Alicia stated proudly.

Rose sighed.

"Heh, so what are we looking for anyway?" Evan asked as they came around another bend in the forest.

Rose pointed. "That."

Before them was a vast depression. Rising up from the bottom were numerous pillars and spires of all shapes and sizes. Many of them held up plateau's that served as steppingstones across the gap. Scattered throughout the bottom of the pit were various pieces of armor, weapons, as well as remains of monsters and humans.

Rose brought up her menu, checking the time. "We're still a little early. Usually spawns around 2:00pm. It's only 1:45pm. Might as well take stock of what we have, perhaps go over a plan."

In the distance, dark clouds had begun rolling in, blocking out the sun and darkening the forest. Rose brought up a screen in mid-air, tapping the bottom corner it spun around facing Alicia and Evan. "This is our target, Electric Spinner, as you'd expect from the forest, it's a fruit-based monster."

The creature had a gelatinous thorax with spikes extending out all over, as well as eight long spikes protruding from the sides. They arched and touched the ground underneath the creature's body, acting as legs. Its head was a ball of messy, yellow fur with several red eyes scattered and two pincers extending out of its mouth.

"It's essentially an electric, pineapple spider," Rose stated.

Alicia's eyes lit up, like a beacon cutting through the darkness of the now dimly lit forest. "What all does it drop?"

Evan smirked.

"Aside from the legendary material, Pina Eyes, which is what we came for, it can also drop Pineapple Essence and Toxic Needles," Rose stated.

"Pineapple Essence," Alicia whispered, fidgeting in her excitement.

A drop of rain fell from the dark clouds hovering overhead. Soon a steady, yet light pace of rain began to fall. The group took cover under a nearby tree.

"Any strategies listed, or attack patterns?" Evan inquired.

Rose nodded. "As you might assume from its name, Electric Spinner, it can use lightning-based attacks. However, it also can spew a deadly acid, and the various needles extending from its thorax are poisonous to the touch. The most common attack seems to be electric webbing combined with biting and stabbing."

"Its stats aren't too high," Alicia observed. "I guess it helps that we're in a fairly mid-level area. And aside from being used for our purposes, fruit-based drops are generally only used for foods."

"I think a basic strategy can be Alicia will take the sky with her flame cloak." Rose pointed to the sky. "I will stay outside of range and provide buffs and healing and any residual damage I can, and then Evan will stick to mid-to-close range combat."

Rose spoke directly to Evan now. "Don't. Push. Yourself. I'll be keeping an eye on you, but let Alicia handle the majority of the attacking."

A sudden crack, and then a boom echoed through the forest.

"Thunder?" Evan asked confusedly.

"It must be here," Alicia said, turning to see a swirl of clouds converging over the hole.

A bolt of lightning dropped, striking the centermost pillar, where the Electric Spinner stood balanced on its tip. Without any hesitation, it quickly leapt to the closest pillar, and then began spinning a web from that point. It moved from pillar to pillar, creating lines of webbing between them all until the entire hole was covered by a completed web.

"Come on," Alicia urged, pulling the other two with her. She quickly jumped onto the nearest pillar.

The Electric Spinner had taken its place back at the center of the hole. It let out a screech, and suddenly electricity poured from its body, flowing down into the web. The web conducted it in all directions until the entire webbing was electrified, Alicia grimaced.

"Don't worry," Rose affirmed. "As long as you stay planted on a stone plateau the electricity will disperse against it and you'll avoid any residual damage. Do try not to fall directly into the webbing though."

Suddenly, the monster's eyes shined deep amber. The electricity swimming within the web traveled in all directions to the edges of the circle. The electric energy shot up into the air, arcing until it converged into a single point above the spider. The entire hole was now encased in an electric dome.

"Um…?" Alicia turned to Rose.

"This wasn't in the data…" Rose took a step forward, away from the edge of the dome and looking up and all around her.

From outside of the dome, Alexa's three assassins stood in watch.

"Unlucky for them," the blue-haired one stated.

"What are the odds of that?" The redhead asked. "That boss only enters berserk mode, maybe, once every thousand spawns."

"Well, either they die to it, or they get killed right after the battle by us," the blonde smirked.

They kept hidden, waiting to see the result of the battle.

"The plan hasn't changed," Rose shouted. "Alicia, use your fire cloak and just be careful about how high you go. Evan, keep an eye on the boss and do your best to avoid the webbing."

Alicia crouched down, and pushing herself up with her legs, leapt to the closest plateau. Once stable she closed her eyes and balled her right hand into a fist, placing it against her chest. "Ignite!"

"Brace yourself," Rose warned Evan.

Alicia's body let out a pulse, the wave of energy swept over Rose and Evan. Wings of flames erupted from her shoulder blades, and flames began to spread from her back, up her arms and legs, stopping at her ankles, wrist, and neck. Her body was submerged in a layer of fire, like a suit of armor. In her right hand she held a long pole and attached to the end was a sharp block of metal — a glaive. Her wings flapped, bringing her up off the ground slightly. Then, all at once, she shot forward toward the monster.

Evan opened his hands; the tattoo on his right hand began to glow. Jagged shards of ice began to form around his body, gathering residual moisture from the air and growing into swords of pure ice that hovered around him. He leapt from plateau to plateau, making his way toward the monster. As he moved, he noticed a thin veil of purple draped over Alicia's body before fading away. Evan caught a glimpse of the same veil over him before it faded away once more. He turned to see Rose chanting, her arms extended outward, firmly gripping a staff. Below her was a white, shimmering circle of energy.

The monster screeched. Evan turned to see Alicia pulling away her glaive, fresh yellow blood dripping from the metal. She shot herself back, closer to Evan, avoiding a spray of acid from the monster's mouth. The acid flew through the air before falling onto a nearby stone plateau, melting away at the surface. An orange veil now fell over Evan and Alicia.

"Focus!" Alicia commanded.

"Wh —" Evan began, before a sudden screech filled the area.

The two looked over to see another wave of electricity pouring from the monster's body. It flowed down into the web, spreading throughout the area.

"Heh, stupid thing." Alicia pulled the skin under her eye down with her free hand and stuck her tongue out at the creature.

Evan felt the creature probably didn't comprehend the gesture.

The electricity continued to spread along the inside of the dome, heading up to the topmost point. It converged, gathering into a shining orb.

"Above you!" Rose pointed her staff.

A bolt of lightning fell toward Alicia, it halted inches from her head, as if pushing against an invisible wall, the space above her cracked. The lightning began flowing around her body before fizzling out. Alicia's invisible shield shattered. She turned her attention to the monster, flexing her wings and shooting herself toward it. The monster spewed acid toward the incoming Alicia, who spun through the air, gracefully avoiding the gunk and forcing her glaive into the monster's mouth. Its wail was muffled by the mouthful of metal.

"Hm," Alicia murmured, noticing a shift in her weight.

She withdrew her glaive to find the head had been corroded off by the monster's saliva. She dropped the now useless weapon as the monster quickly spit another vat of poison at her. At such a distance, she instinctively crossed her arms over her body, her wings following suit, folding around the front of her body. It was too late. Her scream echoed through the area. Evan's eyes widened as he made his way closer to her. She suddenly kicked, her wings extending back out as she drifted back towards Rose. Evan stopped in place, watching her for a moment before turning to face the monster, his blades at the ready.

The monster let out a powerful screech, blood still dripping from its mouth. Evan leapt forward onto the next plateau. A shot of acid had already started rushing towards him. He immediately crouched, and with a powerful push, leapt forward to the next space. The acid struck the plateau he had just been on only an instant after he had moved.

He landed, much closer, but still a good twenty feet from the creature. The monster's wails echoing through the dome, electricity began pouring out from its body, refreshing the webs with another surge of electricity.

"This sucks," Evan mumbled.

Alicia had safely landed next to Rose, although her breathing was heavy. The cloak of flame that had wrapped around her body had begun receding towards her shoulder blades. Smoke rose from her bloodied forearms; the skin had nearly melted away completely. Rose immediately took her sister's arms, looking at the damage, and sighed. "Idiot. It's like you're not taking this seriously."

Alicia smiled weakly. "Something's wrong, though. It's stronger than your data said."

"Yeah, must be a super rare spawn," Rose said. "Lucky us. Hold your arms up." Alicia obeyed.

Rose hovered one hand over each forearm, a bubble of energy forming around each. Excess poison began to flow out from the wound, hovering within the bubbles before dissipating, simultaneously the skin began to scab and heal.

"Evan!" Rose shouted. "You're on your own for a while!"

"Can't you heal any faster?" Alicia gritted her teeth. "Leaving him alone with such a strong monster is the kind of situation we wanted to avoid."

Rose remained focused on her sister's wounds. "I'm aware."

The electricity had converged at the top of the dome once more.

Evan quickly swung his left arm forward, freeing one of the levitating blades around him and tossing it at a distant plateau. It spiraled through the air, planting into the distant surface. Upon impact, the plateau froze over. Evan reached his arm out, lining up his free hand with the frozen structure. The plateau began to glow, and the ice began to build upon itself until it became its own pillar. The orb in the sky pulsated, then lightning fell striking the highest target, the tip of the ice pillar. The force shattered the ice, which then quickly melted and evaporated.

Evan had already turned toward the monster, throwing another sword. It spun through the air, sinking into the monster's face. A sheet of ice spread out, covering the monster's entire head. Evan kept moving, leaping to a closer plateau, and throwing another sword at the pillar the monster clung to. The pillar froze over; and the monster began to slip. Unable to gain traction, it crashed into an adjacent plateau. Evan now stood on the plateau directly next to the monster.

As he moved the remaining shards of ice around him, poised to attack, he heard the familiar voice of one of his teammates.

"It's mine!" Alicia roared, her voiced echoing through the dome.

She dropped down from the sky, and her fist, wrapped in flames, extended out. As she came down, she pierced through the monster's thorax. Juices began to flow out from its body as its legs gave out, and it collapsed. Alicia withdrew her fist as more juice began to spurt out. She dropped down, standing next to the monster's corpse. Evan jumped over to join her.

"That was rather anti-climactic," he noted, dispersing his remaining ice swords.

"That's just because I'm so awesome," Alicia stated matter-of-factly as she scrolled through a pop-up menu of their spoils.

"What did we get?" Evan asked.

"Aw YEAH!" Alicia shouted enthusiastically. "Pineapple Essence!" Evan watched her in anticipation.

"Also, your thing is here too." She shrugged. "That's cool, I guess."

Evan suddenly noticed a small window in front of him. It read "Accept Trade Request?" He pressed the green button and was prompted with a second window reading "Acquired Pina Eyes."

"Two down…" Evan murmured to himself, closing the excess windows.

Alicia glanced at him, her gaze falling to the ground immediately after. She sighed.

"Well, let's go!" Evan said, oblivious.

Alicia raised her head, nodding. The two turned to see that Rose had connected all the plateaus together, making an easy path for them to return.

"Why didn't you do that in the first place?" Evan asked as they united at the edge of the hole.

"I didn't have time. If you hadn't noticed, we did kind of get screwed over there. I hope it was worth it." She stared at Evan.

"Yeah, we got them." He smiled.

"And you!" Rose began, turning her frustration toward Alicia.

Alicia's eyes had remained glued to the ground.

"…just… be more careful," Rose's voice trailed off.

Evan looked to see Alicia. "Did something happen? I know you took a hit, but you delivered the finishing blow."

"Nothing, it's fine," Alicia said, raising her head and walking back toward the entrance of the forest. Evan watched her, and then turned to Rose who had already started walking after her. He trailed behind them.

"What's going on?" Rose whispered, staring at Alicia.

"I guess I let myself forget what we're doing…" Alicia rubbed her left eye.

Rose glanced behind them. Evan was keeping his distance. "Well, what do you want to do?"

"I don't want to stop," Alicia said.

"You know this won't end well if you keep on this path," Rose sighed.

"I'll still have you, even if it ends the way he wants." Alicia glanced over at her sister.

"Yeah, you'll always have me," Rose said, wrapping her arm around Alicia's shoulder.

As the group emerged from the forest, Evan was met with three women, standing in a row and blocking the group's way.

"It's time," the blonde assassin stated.

IX
Assassins

On the plains between the forest and town, Evan, Rose, and Alicia stood in front of the three assassins. Directly across from Rose stood the tallest of the group. Her long, blonde hair was braided down the length of her back. She wore a leather tunic with a short, leather skirt reaching down to her knees, and her hands and feet were wrapped in bandages. Her deep blue eyes focused intently on Rose.

To her right, across from Evan, was a slightly shorter woman with shoulder-length blue hair and matching eyes. The most petite of the three, she wore a white robe with sandals. Around her wrists and ankles were golden bracelets and draped from her neck was a silver necklace embedded with a deep purple gem.

The final assassin, across from Alicia, was the most muscular of the three. She had a single plate of metallic armor covering her torso and chest, with matching gauntlets and gloves. The left half of her head had a patch of short, spiky red hair, while the right half was completely shaven.

The woman in the center spoke first. "My name is Tulli." Her voice glided through the air as she withdrew a curved dagger.

"I'm Viviana," the blue-haired woman chimed in, reaching into her robe to pull out a straight wand with a purple gem protruding from its tip.

"Flaire," the red head grunted, a large axe appeared within her hands.

"We've got orders to kill Evan." Tulli glanced at him. "We are willing to let you other two leave unharmed. Just stay out of our way."

"Don't be stupid." Alicia smirked. "It's more like —"

"We're willing to let you leave," Rose interrupted, "but if you insist on fighting, you will die."

"Don't push your luck!" Flaire charged toward Alicia.

Suddenly, the blade of Flaire's axe erupted in flames. She swung it through the air toward Alicia, who leapt backwards to avoid the crushing blow. The axe stuck into the ground, the grass burning away beneath it.

Alicia grinned. "I don't even need my weapon to beat you."

Flaire gritted her teeth before freeing her axe from the ground. By the time she'd retrieved her weapon, Alicia had disappeared.

"Fool," came Alicia's voice from behind.

Flaire spun on her feet, her face turning right into Alicia's flame-coated fist. The blow knocked Flaire back; she hit the ground hard and slid back several feet. Her axe had fallen from her grip, sticking into the ground where she had just stood. Alicia stepped forward, blocking the path between Flaire and her weapon.

Tulli sighed, glimpsing Flaire's fall from the corner of her eye. She extended her arm out, pointing the tip of her dagger at Rose, and, without warning, shooting a bullet of condensed air. Rose immediately crouched down, slamming her palm onto the ground. A wall of thick earth erected before her, the air dispersing against it. Rose then stood up, placing her free hand on the stone. The wall shattered into a collection of shards that shot forward toward Tulli. She smirked as the air around her began to swirl violently, the shards of earth grinding into dust as they approached. Rose took the opportunity to withdraw her staff, holding it defensively in front of her body, meeting Tulli's gaze with her own.

For a moment, Evan and Viviana stood in silence, until a sword of ice formed within Evan's right hand. He stepped forward, thrusting the blade toward Viviana. With a flick of her wrist, her wand swished through the air and the ice melted to water in Evan's hand. The water immediately gathered to the tip of Viviana's wand. Then, swinging her arm forward she tossed the concentrated ball of water at Evan. It struck his chest with force, knocking him backwards onto the ground.

Flaire placed her hand on the grass, pushing herself up to her feet. She could smell the burning flesh from her face. She raised her hand up to her singed cheek, glaring at Alicia. "Must think you're really something." She scowled. "Well, I can manipulate fire too!"

She opened her hand, thrusting her arm forward. Then, she made a fist, and the small embers burning around the axe erupted, flames exploding up and around it. Alicia immediately leapt away, while Flaire simultaneously dashed forward. The flames died down, wrapping only around the head of the axe as Flaire grabbed the handle. She pulled it from the ground and charged forward, swinging her burning axe toward Alicia, who was still in mid-landing. Alicia planted her foot on the ground, using the momentum from the jump to turn, and thrust her arms upward. She slammed her palms on either side of the axe's blade, gritting her teeth to endure the flames, but still managing to halt the blade inches from her body. Her arms shook as she pushed up against the blade, struggling against Flaire's strength.

"How's that!?" Flaire exclaimed. "You think you're so fast and strong!" Evan had pushed himself to his feet, Viviana chuckling, "Silly boy."

With a step forward, he pushed off from the ground, dashing toward her. She smirked, swinging her wand through the air. The ground beneath Evan's feet cracked. Feeling it give way, he instinctively rolled to his left. As he got back to his feet, a pillar of water erupted from the ground. He stepped forward, when suddenly the ground began to collapse once again. He leapt back, avoiding another explosion of water. Spots all around him had begun to crack, water emerging from each of them until he was surrounded on all sides by several constant geysers.

Suddenly, the water began to converge toward his body. The pillars had receded back into the ground as he became trapped in a large, floating orb of swirling water. He struggled to hold his breath as his body was pushed and pulled with the current. Finally, he and the water came to abrupt stop. He felt a great weight bearing down on him as his lungs gave way. He coughed, inhaling water when suddenly, like an explosion, a burst of air erupted from the center of the ball, forcing Evan onto the ground. The water shot out in all directions. Evan continued to cough violently.

Flaire smirked. "Sounds like your little boy toy is about to die."

Alicia strengthened her grip. "You'd better hope not."

"What're you —" Flaire began.

A loud *crack* echoed through the air as the head of Flaire's axe split into two. Once Alicia released her grip on the blade, she swung her fist up into Flare's chin, snapping her jaw shut and causing her to bite down on her tongue. Blood began to flow from between her lips. Alicia's free hand became wrapped in flames; she threw a punch into Flaire's stomach. Her plate-mail cracked as she fell backwards. Alicia immediately mounted Flaire as she was hitting the ground, thrusting her left forearm down and clamping onto Flaire's throat. She raised her right arm, clenching her hand into a fist. Flames violently erupted around it as she muttered, "Die."

Having remained in a standstill, Tulli and Rose kept an eye on the adjacent battles. Noticing her team lose the upper hand, Tulli's voice echoed, "Stop!"

Alicia hesitated, her fist a mere few inches from Flaire's face. The flames still swirling violently, they kissed Flaire's skin, just beginning to sear it. Alicia turned to see Tulli looking at her, and Rose staring at Evan and Viviana. Evan lay on the ground atop of a frozen puddle with Viviana's wand pointed at his face, and a spire of ice stretched up to the tip of her throat.

"We'll fall back…" Tulli said tepidly.

Rose glared at her.

"Like hell!" Alicia screamed. "I'll kill this girl, Evan kills that one, and then all three of us team up and kill you."

She refocused on Flaire, raising her arm back up in the arm, the flames around her fist swirling even more violently.

"No! Wait!" Tulli cried, reaching her arm out. "If you let us go, I'll tell you where you can find something you're looking for!"

Rose turned her head slightly, looking at Alicia, who sighed. The flames around her fist began to fade away, but she remained mounted on Flaire.

Tulli exhaled in relief. "The verbal incantation for the revival spell can only be learned from a book kept in Queen Alexa's private library. If you let us leave, I will transfer map data to you that will show you a way that you can sneak into the castle."

"No!" Flaire exclaimed. "You'd betray our Queen!?"

Tulli turned toward Flaire, shaking her head. "You'd rather die?" Flaire scowled, looking away.

"Seems like Queen Alexa would be the type to have no problem murdering over betrayal." Rose raised her brow.

"We'll just run away. I care more for my subordinates — no, for my sisters — than I do for Queen Alexa's ambitions." Tulli glanced from Rose to Alicia. "I'm sure you two agree."

Alicia glared at Tulli.

"Well?" Tulli turned to Rose.

Rose turned to Evan, who mouthed the word, "no." She nodded, turning to Tulli and sighing. "This is clearly a trap, but at the same time, there is likely no way around it. I am certain that Queen Alexa would have the only copy of that book. At least this way, we don't have to charge through the center of the city." Evan turned away from Rose. Alicia clenched her fist.

"Give me the data," Rose instructed, "then teleport away from here as fast you can."

Tulli nodded, bringing up her map. She pressed a button, and a window with the map popped up in front of Rose. The data was immediately uploaded to her account. Tulli then stepped back; her body began to glow, Flaire and Viviana's bodies glowing in conjunction. In an instant, they became orbs of light and shot upward into the sky.

Alicia walked over to Rose, staring huffily at her. "Why?"

"You know why," Rose said, turning to see Evan get to his feet. He made his way over to the two.

"We could have just killed the other two and forced her to give us the data," Alicia complained.

"If she had nothing to live for after we took away her sisters, then she likely would have just tried to kill us without a word," Rose argued. "It may be a trap, but this way we have an opportunity to get what we need."

"What if they just lied about the book?" Evan asked.

"Unlikely," Rose retorted. "That book is one of a kind. Many people have already confirmed that it's no longer in its original resting place. I don't see why she wouldn't have it, all things considered."

Alicia sighed. "Still, there's a good chance they lied about fleeing. To be honest, it wouldn't surprise me if Alexa had them leak that information on purpose."

"True enough," Rose exhaled. "If she has that book, she may have her own use for it. She's been keeping tabs on us with those three; if she's only missing what we're carrying, we'd essentially be delivering the materials she needs right to her."

Evan turned his eyes to the ground. "Sorry, this is pretty much my fault."

Rose and Alicia nodded before speaking in unison. "Yeah."

"I've dragged you two through a lot," Evan continued. "I can't expect you to put yourselves into such a dangerous situation for me. It's okay if you want me to go it alone." He sighed.

Suddenly, Alicia smacked Evan across the face. "Don't be selfish."

He raised his hand up to his cheek, glaring at her.

"Besides," she went on, returning his glare. "We attacked those assassins on our own. You think we won't be marked now?"

"We've probably been marked since we decided to leave with you from Alchemilla," Rose pointed out. "After all, we were the ones who originally stopped them when they snuck into your room."

"We're in this together," Alicia stated. "It's too late to turn back now."

Evan nodded. "Sorry, you're right. Thank you."

He reached out and, without thinking, found himself hugging the two. They had continuously been there for him and refused to leave his side. At this point, he couldn't just turn them away. He owed them, in more ways than one.

Rose and Alicia smiled, returning the embrace before they all headed back to the inn.

Evan stood in the bathroom, alone. He ran a towel along his naked body, wiping off all of the excess water from his encounter with Viviana. He sighed, looking at his reflection in the mirror. "Am I doing the right thing?"

He placed his hands on the sink, his eyes gazing into it. The tattoo on the back of his hand began to glow. He gritted his teeth, his eyes flinching shut as a stinging pain ran through his body. When the pain subsided, he opened his eyes. Instead of his reflection, a girl with golden brown hair stared dark eyes at him in the mirror. It was Emma. He took a step back, his mouth gaped open. "W…what the?"

She smiled, her voice echoing through his head. "You don't look well, Evan."

"How're you here?" He reached out, touching the mirror. "Didn't you… die?"

"Of course," she whispered, "but that night when you awoke to your gift, and… murdered that boy… your strong desire to save me coupled with your new powers gave birth to a miracle."

Evan blinked, curious not only to the situation, but what Emma had meant.

"I don't understand," he exhaled.

Emma smiled gently, her reflection placing her own hand against his.

"With your goal made clear and the necessary sacrifice made, your powers acted as a magnet for my soul," Emma explained. "My lingering spirit from my fresh corpse was pulled and latched onto your own, further boosting your strength."

Evan's eyes widened as he began to piece together his own hypothesis.

"Are you saying?" He hesitated, his eyes shifting frantically as the wheels in his head turned. "The times I've lost control of my body… housing two souls— "

"I've been watching over you all this time." Emma smiled. "It wouldn't be a stretch to say I am like your guardian angel, protecting you. Not only a hidden power, but a *hidden* hidden power that was gifted to you and you alone. All this time, I've seen everything you've seen, and everything you've done."

He turned his gaze down, staring pathetically into the sink.

"Don't worry," Emma added. "I don't hold anything against you. I love you, and I only want what's best for you. But why is now that you're wavering?" Her voice filled with despair, her eyes welling with tears. "After you've come so far…don't you miss me?"

His head shot up, a fresh tear running down his cheek. "More than anything!"

You're so close," she insisted. "I'm eager to see you, to be able to feel your warmth once more. Don't leave me waiting too much longer."

With that, her image slowly faded away, becoming his once more. *What does this all mean?* He thought, still trying to wrap his head around everything Emma had told him. *This whole time I thought I was chasing a pipe dream, but all along my goal has been this close?* He wiped his eyes, staring at his reflection in the mirror for another few moments, hoping he might catch Emma's reflection one more time.

Outside the bathroom, Alicia and Rose sat at a table, talking over slabs of fish. Rose cut off a small square of hers, stabbing it with a fork and bringing it up to her mouth. She chewed, watching Alicia poke at her food begrudgingly.

"Why don't you just be blunt?" Rose asked as she sliced into another piece of fish. "That's your specialty, after all."

Alicia sighed. "He doesn't seem the least be interested, despite everything that's happened. He only has eyes for her. At this point, bringing up a triangle would only hinder us for what's to come."

"He can't choose if he doesn't know there is a choice." Rose bit off a piece of fish from her fork. "You know very well that going to Alexa's castle could mean we'll all end up dead. Wouldn't you rather he knows how you feel before that?"

"Yeah," Alicia murmured, "but even so…what about you?" She looked up at Rose pitifully.

Rose gave a small smile. "I just want you to be happy."

Alicia blinked. "I thought you wanted him, too?"

"Oh, don't worry," Rose assured her, smirking. "If you don't want to make a move, I certainly will."

"H… hey!" Alicia stammered, flustered. "That's not what I asked!"

"He's fun, but only for so long." Rose shrugged. "He's too much of a project for me. You've always been the one enamored by him. It's better to be in a relationship on equal grounds. I'm quite a bit higher up than him, after all."

Alicia stared at her for a moment. "Wait… if you're saying he and I are on the same level that means you're above us both…?"

Alicia glared at her sister. Rose smirked again, taking another bite of fish. Suddenly, the bathroom door opened. Evan stepped out wearing plain black pants, and a matching black shirt. His eyes focused on the ground as he made his way to the table and slumped into a seat. Rose winked at her sister, and Alicia scowled back.

"Are you hungry?" Rose asked innocently.

"Mm…I don't know," Evan muttered.

"You should eat," Alicia scolded. "You can't take on Queen Alexa on an empty stomach!"

"*Your* plate is still untouched," Rose pointed out.

Alicia glared at her. "Whatever! I'm getting to it!"

Rose grinned, pressing a button which warped away her empty plate. She got up, glancing nonchalantly down at Alicia. "I'm going to shower."

Alicia turned toward her plate, blushing. Evan hadn't noticed a thing; his eyes only stared blankly at the table.

"Evan!" Alicia shouted.

"Huh?" Evan's head shot up.

"I asked if you wanted some of my fish?" she repeated.

"Oh…um, sure, I guess," he said, looking at her plate.

She pushed her plate over so that it sat between them both. She handed him the fork, using her fingers to pick pieces off for herself.

After a few seconds of silence, Alicia asked, "What's wrong? Did the assassins shake you up that badly?" She pulled a sliver of fish off of the slab and placed it in her mouth.

"Oh, um…I guess?" Evan answered absently. "No, I suppose not really…I, I just can't believe how close I am…" He began cutting into the fish with the fork.

"Oh…yeah, of course…" Alicia said, her hand hovering over the fish. "You must miss her…"

"Of course I do!" Evan shouted, defending an accusation no one had made. "She means everything to me!"

Alicia flinched, glancing away from him.

Evan's head throbbed; he raised his arm up to his forehead.

Alicia turned back, noticing a faint tint of blackness swirling around his body. “Are you okay…?”

Evan rubbed his head, lowering his hand, “Yeah… sorry.”

Alicia averted her eyes back to the fish. “…So, what’s her name anyway?”

“…Who?” Evan asked.

“Your girlfriend?” Alicia responded, growing increasingly concerned.

“Oh…” Evan murmured. “Emma Hayes.”

“That’s a pretty name,” Alicia said softly. She suddenly perked up, staring directly at him, “H…hey! So, I never told you our last name!”

“No, I suppose not…” Evan muttered, lazily stabbing at the fish with his fork.

Alicia paused for a moment before breaking the silence.

“Do you want to know what it is?”

“Huh, oh… yeah.” Evan said, as if he had suddenly realized who he was talking to.

“Sherwood,” Alicia said, smiling weakly.

He raised his hand back up to his head, rubbing it once more.

“Um, let me go check on Rose,” Alicia stated.

She hastily made her way to the bathroom, opening the door and stepping inside. Hot water was running over Rose’s body as she rubbed soap along herself. As she turned, she noticed the curtain open with Alicia standing, eagerly staring at her.

“What’s wrong?” Rose asked, pausing to stare at Alicia.

“Something isn’t right,” Alicia complained.

“What do you mean?” Rose responded, confused.

“There’s something off about Evan,” Alicia explained. “I noticed a strange aura.”

“Okay,” Rose sighed. “Let me dry off and I’ll go talk to him.” Alicia nodded frantically.

Evan hadn’t moved from his spot in the chair, holding his head. The sound of running water stopped, and after a few moments, the door opened. Rose stepped out; Alicia close behind. Rose raised her brow as she made her way toward Evan. “Are you okay?”

“Yeah,” Evan said weakly, exhaling.

She noticed the black mist outlining his body. She knelt down, replacing his hand with her own. “Are you sure?”

There was no fever.

“Probably,” Evan replied softly. “Just stress or worry…”

“No sense in pushing yourself,” Rose told him. “This won’t be an easy battle. We should rest as much as possible before we depart.”

Alicia nodded in agreement.

“It’s okay — we’re almost done,” Evan insisted, standing up. “I’ll eat some more and be okay.”

Rose watched him move to the table. “Okay.”

Alicia and Rose joined Evan at the table, both keeping their eyes on him. Evan ordered a fresh piece of fish, while Alicia ordered a bowl of assorted fruit.

Rose brought up the map data they had just received. “So, we should be able to warp to the outskirts of the city. Then, we can enter the castle from a cave that goes underneath."

"It's safe to assume the assassins, among others, will be waiting for us," Alicia said.

"Of no concern…" Evan whispered to himself.

Rose lowered her brow, staring intently at Evan.

"Should we keep the same combat configuration?" Alicia interjected. "Evan versus Viviana, Rose versus Tulli, and myself versus Flaire?"

Evan blinked, and suddenly the black tint faded. He appeared to regain his normal demeanor. "Um, I don't know. When it comes to spell casters, I'm not as strong as both of you. I seemed to barely hold my own this last time."

Rose and Alicia exchanged glances, then Alicia grinned. "We can switch, then. Flaire was a lightweight."

"Will you be okay, Rose?" Evan asked.

"I'd be most worried about Alexa herself showing up," Rose explained, sighing. "Or her second in command, Mike."

"We'll need to get in and get out," Alicia exclaimed.

"Right — don't be a hero." Evan smiled. "I want my girlfriend to be able to meet you: the two who've helped me the most. It's thanks to you I could get this far. I probably would have just looked for a place to die without you two by my side."

Alicia smiled weakly, looking down at her food. She began to pick at the fruit, biting small pieces and putting them back. Rose sighed, looking over at her.

"Evan," Rose stated plainly. "Don't thank us yet. We've got quite the hurdle to get over. Besides…"

Evan looked at her expectantly.

"I never mentioned this was free work." Rose smirked at him. "After we finish this job, you'll owe us."

Alicia glanced at her sister, confused, while Evan stared at her blankly.

"Uh...but..."

"Just keep that in mind." With that, Rose got up and headed back to the bathroom.

Alicia closed her eyes, exhaling.

"Evan, don't get reckless," she warned him. "If you're afraid, come find one of us." She popped a final piece of fruit into her mouth before following Rose to the bathroom.

Evan sighed, lying his head on the table.

"Well?" Alicia asked as Rose turned the shower on once again.

"He seemed a little out of it," Rose admitted, removing her clothes. "I noticed the tint you mentioned. But it's gone now. Likely just nerves. Emotions play a large role in how your abilities work in this world, after all. He certainly wouldn't be the first player to have developed a strange power during an emotional crisis."

"I suppose," Alicia said slowly, undressing as well.

Rose stepped into the running water.

"What is he going to owe us?" Alicia asked, stepping into the shower alongside Rose.

Rose rested her hand on her sister's waist. "You'll see."

X
The Ritual

Evan stood on the outskirts of Riverton, staring up at the starry night sky. His hair swaying from the slight breeze, he thought about everything he'd been through up to this point. He sighed as he closed his eyes. He had thrown himself into dangerous situations since getting to this world. Despite the risks, looking back on it all, he hadn't enjoyed himself this much in such a long time. Since before his parents died.

What's going to happen to me? He thought to himself. *What will happen when — if — I get Emma back? Can we simply return to Earth? After everything that's happened, will I be able to adjust back to normal society? I was already struggling to cope. How can I hope to return to a normal life?*

"Do I even want to?" he exhaled.

"Want to what?" Alicia's voice rang through the air.

He opened his eyes, turning to see her walking toward him.

"Nothing…" he said.

"Oh…" Her voice faded. "You're early…"

"I just had nothing else to do," he stated. "Everything is in order, and I'm good on gear and items."

She stared at him for a moment, before turning her head up toward the sky. "Even here, there are so many stars. I wonder exactly where we are…which one of those might be Earth?"

Evan looked back up at the sky. "I don't —" he began before he was suddenly embraced by Alicia.

"I have something to tell you," she whispered in his ear. "I lov —"

"Already here, I see," Rose's voice flooded into his ears.

Evan's eyes lingered on Alicia for a moment, before he turned his attention to Rose. Despite the interruption, he had actually managed to hear Alicia perfectly.

Meanwhile, Alicia smirked at her sister as if nothing had happened.

"Anyway, are we all ready?" Rose asked.

Alicia and Evan nodded.

"Good," Rose said, withdrawing a cubic purple crystal from her inventory. "When we activate this, we'll be sent to the outskirts of Alexgrad."

"I have the one that will bring us back," Alicia chimed in.

"We simply need to get the book, and warp out," Rose stated.

Evan nodded. "No heroics."

"Here we go," Rose said, holding the crystal out in front of her. She tapped the top of the block and a thin, purple dome began to expand outward, enveloping all three of them. The next thing they knew, they were standing adjacent to a large wall.

"We're here," Evan whispered.

Rose nodded, pointing to their right side. They all moved along the edge of the wall, following it around until they reached a stream of water. It flowed into a small opening at the wall's base. Across the stream was a hill, with various boulders and rubble scattered and piled up at the bottom.

"The top of the hill has to be a hundred feet up, with a straight vertical edge," Alicia sighed.

"Let's hope we don't have to climb it," Rose whispered, pulling up her map data.

The group waded their way through the shallow waters, Rose and Evan reaching the other side first.

"According to the map, it should be behind some of this rubble," Rose said, turning to see Alicia still standing in the river.

"Must be their drinking water," she whispered.

"Yeah, so?" Rose whispered, exasperated. "Why're you —"

Alicia stood with her feet spread apart, her fingers pulling her panties to the side and a stream of fluid spraying down into the water. She exhaled in relief as it rushed out of her.

"Really though…" Rose sighed, lowering her head.

Evan chuckled as Alicia finished up, her fluids flowing into the city with the stream.

"I forgot to go earlier — I couldn't hold it in much longer anyway." Alicia shrugged, walking toward Rose and Evan.

"Get in, get the book, get out," Rose sighed, turning toward the rubble.

Alicia winked at Evan, before turning her attention to the rubble as well.

"Somewhere around here," Rose whispered.

The group spread out slightly, pushing and lifting pieces of rubble.

"Here," Rose whispered, pointing toward an opening.

They removed several more rocks revealing the entire entrance, a mid-sized crawl space. Alicia knelt down, creating a small flame within her palm and holding it up like a lantern. "I'll lead."

Rose and Evan followed after her. The space opened up little by little as the group crawled through. Other than the light of Alicia's spell, the cave was dark and dank. Evan was sure this passage must have housed more than a few creatures he'd rather not come face-to-face with. After a few minutes, the space opened up into a much wider room. As they filed out of the crawl space, they took to their feet. In the center of the room was a glowing, circular pad. They looked at one another.

"This is likely it," Rose announced.

Evan stepped forward onto the pad. Instantaneously he was transported, appearing in a large room. Alicia and Rose appeared next to him soon after. The room was vast, filled with numerous wooden tables and chairs. Shelves, filled with books, lined the walls while several isolated rows of shelves were spaced out throughout the room.

"It seems a little too convenient that we would appear in a library..." Rose whispered, looking around.

"Let's start looking," Evan said sternly.

Rose and Alicia turned to see his backside as he walked toward a far wall.

"Did you tell him the name of the book?" Alicia whispered.

"…No," she whispered back, their eyes locked onto him.

A familiar voice rang through the air, drawing away their attention from Evan.

"You don't waste any time," Flaire exclaimed loudly.

Rose and Alicia turned to see Tulli, Flaire, and Viviana only several feet away.

"Where's the boy?" Viviana asked. "Leave him behind?"

"What? No, he's —" Alicia turned to see that Evan was gone.

In the direction he had been going, there was now a doorway that hadn't been there before.

"How did he know where that was?" Tulli asked, perplexed. "No matter. The book is protected by a powerful spell. Viviana, go catch up with him just to be safe."

Viviana nodded, leaping from table to table and covering the distance to the secret passage in no time at all.

"Not going to go help your pathetic friend?" Flaire goaded Alicia. Alicia glared at Flaire.

"Ooooh, *soooo* scaryyy," Flaire teased. "Unfortunately — for you, that is — Queen Alexa has given us much better gear. This fight won't be the same as before!"

"We'll see," Alicia said calmly as her hand balled into a fist.

She leapt toward Flaire, bending her arm and thrusting her elbow toward her. Flaire leapt backwards, avoiding the blow with ease. Alicia followed up immediately, pushing forward with a flurry of punches. Flaire, moving backwards, avoided the blows until, after several feet, she reached out, catching Alicia's fist. "Pathetic. I'm bored."

Alicia smirked. "Idiot."

Wings of flame erupted from her back, the flames beginning to spread and coating her entire body. Flaire took a step back, quickly releasing Alicia's burning fist. Alicia's skin became pure red, with wisps of yellow and orange swaying around her. She glared at Flaire, who had continued to slowly step backward.

"This time, there's nothing to stop me." Alicia glared at the woman. "I'll kill you, then Tulli, and then go make sure Evan killed Viviana."

"Your sister is scary," Tulli teased Rose as she withdrew her knife, a gust of wind forming around the blade.

Rose withdrew her staff, gripping it with both hands. She stepped forward, pushing the staff horizontally toward Tulli, who immediately swung her knife down, striking the staff. The two stood locked in place, pushing against one another.

"Keep your eyes on the monster in front of you," Rose murmured, glaring at Tulli.

In the passage, Evan stood in a small room before a white, marble pedestal. Atop of it sat a thick book with black binding and bright purple lettering embroidered on the cover, encased in a golden veil. On either side of the pedestal were two glowing, floating orbs, emitting enough light to fill the whole room.

"Finally," Evan breathed out.

"Jeez!" Viviana complained as she finally reached Evan. "I said 'stop,' like, a thousand times!"

Evan turned, his eyes now gleaming gold. He stared blankly at the girl. "...Who're you?"

Viviana stared back, her expression quickly turning from confusion to rage. "At least have the common courtesy to remember people who almost kill you." She took a deep breath. "I'm not going to let you lull me into —" she stopped suddenly; a black beam had extended from the palm of Evan's hand, piercing her throat. Viviana gasped for air as she fell, raising her hand up to her neck, but only silence escaped her throat as she struggled to speak. Blood poured from the wound as the beam shattered into shards, floating into the air before fading away. He stepped over to the girl, extending his right arm over her body. The tattoo on the back of his hand, normally blue, had become pitch black.

The blood pooling around her neck began to flow upward, gathering at the tattoo and sinking into his skin. Evan's body became outlined by a faint red glow as the blood continued to gather from Viviana's body. Soon the remaining blood in her body flowed out from her pores, eyes, nose, ears, and every orifice it could escape from. Her body shriveled up as it lost more and more blood. Finally, when all the liquid had been absorbed, she lay as a mass of skin and bone. The glow around Evan's body faded, and he turned away, walking over to the book.

He extended his arm out, his palm facing the book. The veil around the book and the orbs of light floating next to it all shattered at once. He reached out, grabbing the book and placing it into his inventory. Then, turning around, he walked past the corpse without so much as a flinch, making his way back to the main library.

The flames extending from her back raged violently as Alicia's fist crashed into Flaire's face, searing her skin. Flaire flew backwards, crashing onto the ground, the smell of charred flesh ripe in the air. Alicia effortlessly closed the distance, her wings flexing and propelling her forward. She stood over Flaire's body.

"Give up?" Alicia suggested.

Flaire struggled to lift her body up, her face soiled with blood and tears. Patches of her skin had been burnt away completely, revealing muscle and bone.

"Finish her," a voice whispered in Alicia's ear. The words echoed through her head along with a stinging pain.

She raised her hand to her forehead. The flames coating her body began to fade away.

"What're you doing? Finish her," Evan whispered, now standing directly next to Alicia.

Alicia opened her eyes; the pain had subsided. She turned to see Evan, immediately noticing his golden irises.

"Wha…wait, Evan?" She stammered, confused.

"Hurry!" Evan shouted; his eyes focused intently on her.

Alicia took a step backwards, taken back by his unnatural demeanor. The flames around her body began to disperse, slowly dying down until she had returned to her normal state.

"Very well," he stated flatly, turning his attention to Flaire.

He brought his leg up, striking Flaire in the chin with his foot. She collapsed onto her backside. He was already mounted atop her, a beam of black energy held firmly in his right hand. He stabbed it down, piercing her heart. Fresh blood flowed out from her body and into his tattoo upon her death. Once drained, he stood up, the black beam shattering into shards. He turned to Alicia, sneering.

"Who…are…you?" She asked softly, stepping backwards.

Meanwhile, Rose and Tulli remained clashed in a deadlock, Rose's staff pressing against Tulli's knife. A small crack had appeared where the blade dug into the wood.

Tulli smirked. "See that crack? Eventually the whole staff will split apart and you'll follow suit."

Rose pushed her staff further against the knife, the crack widening slightly.

"Fool!" Tulli screamed. "There's no earth here for you to manipulate! You'll soon fall, just as your friends likely already have!" She turned, expecting to see Flaire fighting, only to see Evan facing Alicia.

"What!?" Tulli cried furiously. Her knees suddenly buckled, and she fell to the ground.

"You're the fool," Rose stated, looking down at her.

"What… happened?" Tulli gasped, her breathing becoming more rapid. "I feel, so weak…"

"So excited about a little crack, and so sure you were aware of the extent of my power," Rose scolded.

Tulli struggled, attempting to climb to her feet, only to collapse back onto the ground.

"Manipulating earth is only the first step in the skill tree I chose," Rose stated.

Tulli craned her neck, staring up at Rose. Her eyes widened with shock.

"N…no…" Tulli breathed out.

"The whole time, I simply drained your life energy," Rose told Tulli, kneeling down to look her in the eyes.

"Finish her," Evan breathed out, as he and Alicia approached Rose.

Rose turned to Evan, glaring at him. "Who're you?"

Evan smirked.

"Alicia, get next to me," Rose said, taking a step away from Tulli and toward Evan.

Evan took a step forward, his body disappearing from sight. Rose ran over to Alicia, and the two looked around frantically. Evan appeared kneeling next to Tulli, a beam of black energy held firmly in his hand. He stabbed her effortlessly, killing her in an instant. The beam shattered into shards, and he stood up to face Rose and Alicia.

"I've got the book, and this girl will do for a corpse," Evan stated, pointing to Tulli's body. "We just need a little blood from one of you two, and then we'll be good. Let's escape while we can."

"No," Rose said, staring at Evan in disbelief. "We can't help you as you are."

Evan glared at her. "Is that so?"

The two sisters hesitantly took a step back, getting closer to one another. Rose could feel the malice pouring out from the once timid boy.

"I should've noticed sooner…" Rose exhaled.

Alicia closed her eyes, clenching her fist.

"It's fine," she said after a moment. "I'll use some of my blood. Just promise to leave us alone after that…"

Rose turned to her sister, sighing and shaking her head.

"No problem," Evan sneered. He turned to Tulli's corpse.

"Not so fast," a voice boomed.

Alexa stood in the center of the room, her body covered in a thin chain mail with a thicker plate of steel encasing her torso and breasts, and a flail in hand. Next to her was her right-hand man. Mike wore a heavy plate mail, complete with greaves, gauntlets, a tower shield, and a broadsword.

"You pathetic elves," Alexa scoffed. "You'd do good to get away from that demon."

"Alex," Mike whispered, "This aura is so dense. Even from here it feels like something is pushing against me. I can't believe he developed this much."

Alexa nodded; her eyes focused intently on the boy in front of them.

"You…" Evan began walking toward Alexa. "Are you having fun playing Queen?"

"Shut up!" Alexa shouted. "I've got you all figured out at this point. It's over."

"At this point, it's too late." Evan shrugged, then reached out his arm as a black beam extended out about three feet. He gripped the beam of energy tightly, slashing it through the air before pointing it at Alexa.

"Use the crystal," Rose murmured to Alicia.

"I've been trying," Alicia hissed back. "It won't work here. Must be blocked by one of Alexa's spells."

"I guess you were right…something was off." Rose sighed. "At this point, Alexa is our best hope. First chance we get, we'll provide support. Four-on-one is the best bet."

Alicia nodded, her eyes averting to the floor.

Mike raised his left arm, holding his sword pointed up toward the ceiling. Suddenly, flames spun around the length of the blade, like a handheld, flaming tornado. He pointed the blade at Evan, and moved his shield so that it covered the front of his body before charging toward Evan.

As he moved closer, he thrust his flaming blade toward Evan. As the blade came toward him, Evan sprung off his feet, flipping backwards onto the table behind him. Mike had already followed up, leaping forward and swinging his sword downward toward Evan. The flames danced around the blade, erupting and raging violently. Evan leapt up into the air, Mike's sword crashing through the table. Pieces of wood lay scattered and burnt on the charred rug. The flames receded from his blade and he looked up to see Evan firing a beam of black energy toward him. A prismatic barrier surrounded Mike, the beam dissolving against it.

Evan scowled, hovering in mid-air.

Suddenly he was enveloped in a mass of light, being forced toward the ground. He crashed, lying face down in a small crater. Alexa took her place next to Mike, and the two made their way to the crater just a few feet away. They looked down to see Evan struggling to get up.

"We're well aware of what type of magic you use," Mike said smugly.

"Your time is over," Alexa declared. "This truly is the end."

Mike stepped into the crater, gripping his blade tightly. Evan had barely gotten to his feet. His body numb, he struggled to keep his balance as his legs trembled. He glared at Mike, furious. Mike remained silent, swinging his sword horizontally through the air with grace. Evan's head rolled off his shoulders, and his body fell to the floor, limp. Mike stared at the body for a moment before turning his back and making his way out of the crater.

Alicia's screams filled the air, as she was suddenly enveloped by her sister.

Alexa closed her eyes, turning away. As he stepped out of the crater, Mike turned to see three black tentacles stretch out from the base of Evan's neck to his detached head. The tentacles slipped up through the bottom of his neck and pulled it back towards the body, reattaching the two back together.

Evan opened his eyes and stood up, cracking his neck nonchalantly. "Kind of stings." He smirked.

Flames erupted around Mike's sword once more and he charged into the crater, toward Evan. Alexa took a step forward, extending her arm in protest. "Stop! Don't be reckless!"

As Mike approached, a beam of black energy formed in Evan's right hand. Mike roared, swinging his blade of flames downward toward Evan with a speed even greater than before. Evan swung his right arm up, crashing his beam of energy into the blade. The energy cut through the sword, the top half spiraling through the air and stabbing into the side of the crater. Mike stared in disbelief as the flames faded from his broken sword.

"Just because you know what my power is doesn't mean you have the strength to stop it," Evan sneered.

Mike hastily thrust his shield forward to bash Evan, who simply stabbed with his energy beam, piercing through the center of the shield. As Mike reeled backwards, his shield began to crack and eventually crumble at his feet. He raised his right arm, forming a fireball in his hand. As he moved to throw it, Evan stepped forward swinging his beam upward, diagonally from Mike's right hip to left shoulder. Mike's armor shattered instantly; the fireball in his hand faded and he fell to his knees. Evan quickly stabbed Mike's chest with the beam of energy. Blood spurting from his mouth and from the hole in his chest as Evan pulled the beam away.

Alexa's eyes widened as she watched Mike fall forward, face down.

"Shall I, absorb this one too?" Evan smirked, holding his arm over Mike's body.

Before he had the chance, Alexa extended her arm out, shooting a bolt of lightning toward Evan. He flipped backwards out of the crater, landing back on level ground opposite to Alexa, the crater between them.

"Guess you want to go together?" Evan shrugged, pointing the beam of energy at Alexa.

She brought her arm up, shooting another bolt of electricity toward him. He moved the beam slightly, catching the electricity with the tip of it. The energy dissolved against it. Alexa glared at him, leaping forward and swinging her flail through the air as she did. Evan stepped back, allowing her to land where he had been, the flail moving through empty space. She shot forward, swinging her flail around once more. Evan formed a second beam of energy in his free hand. He stepped to the side, parrying the flail and shattering it. He then thrust his free arm forward, piercing Alexa's side with the second beam of energy. Her armor began to crack, and she was sent flying into a nearby bookcase, Alicia and Rose remained hesitant. They stared at her, reluctant to join the fray.

Alexa groaned, standing up slowly. She looked over to see Alicia and Rose, stationary. Alexa coughed, blood spilling from her mouth. She turned to Rose. "Thought *you* were a monster?"

Rose glared at her, taken back by the woman's contempt.

"Guess you're just a coward. This is a real monster," Alexa pointed at Evan. "He's the one who trapped us here, he's the one who stole your humanity, and he's the one who took your friend. Are you just going to cry about it?"

Evan began walking toward the group. He held a beam of black, dense energy in each hand, the skin around his golden eyes now stained with black that slowly continued to spread.

"I'll help you," Rose sighed, gripping her staff.

"Rose," Alicia murmured.

"Stay back, Alicia," Rose stated firmly.

Alexa clapped her hands together, and light and sparks began surging around them. When she pulled them apart, each hand was surging with electricity. She shot forward, within ten feet of Evan she knelt, slamming her left palm on the ground. Sparks spread out along the ground like a fan, moving in Evan's direction. He stabbed one of his beams of energy into the ground, the sparks all feeding into the black beam like a lightning rod. Once they all dissipated, the rod shattered. Alexa glared at Evan before extending her other arm forward, shooting a bolt of lightning directly at him. He leapt into the air. Rose, already airborne, looked down at him. Her right arm extended, she shot a wave of white energy toward Evan. He thrust his black beam forward, extending it to meet her attack. The waves enveloped the rod, shattering it and moving forward to envelope Evan. His body reverberated within the energy as he crashed into the ground.

Rose landed gracefully next to Alexa.

"Look, I'm leaning on you because your ability is the direct opposite of him," Alexa exhaled, exasperated. "You have the best chance to kill him."

Rose glanced at her.

"But you need to stop holding back." Alexa scowled. "Your friend is already gone."

Evan stood up, moving toward the two once again. "A bit stronger than I expected," he sneered.

"Now what?" Rose asked.

"I should be able to at least hinder his movement," Alexa explained. "However, he'll likely dodge the attacks as he has been if we go for a frontal assault."

"I'll help create the diversion," Alicia interjected, stepping forward to stand next to Rose.

"Alicia, no," Rose stated in protest.

"We don't have time to argue," Alexa shouted. "You two distract him; I'll hit him from behind. Then, Rose should deliver a finishing blow."

Alicia nodded.

"Very well..." Rose sighed.

Alicia took the lead, running toward Evan. Wings of flame erupted from her back as she closed the distance.

"Feh," Evan murmured. "This is getting out of hand."

Alicia swung her arm forward, fist wrapped in flames. As she came within reach of Evan, he took a step back, avoiding the blow completely. Then, he snapped his right leg upward, into her throat. She gasped, reeling backwards as a beam of energy formed in his right hand. He stabbed it into her right shoulder blade, forcing her onto the ground.

"Since you had stayed out of it before," Evan began, pushing the beam further into her shoulder, pinning her to the ground, "I was planning to leave you alone. However…"

Suddenly, he felt a force weighing him down. He turned to see Rose firing off another wave of white energy.

Evan smirked. "You'll need to hit harder than that."

The black beam pinning Alicia to the ground shattered. Her left hand formed a fist, flames surging around it. She let out a yell, lifting her upper body and thrusting her fist toward Evan. He turned to see her fist connect, striking him square in the face. He groaned, sliding backwards onto the ground. As though on cue, a bolt of lightning fell toward Evan's body, enveloping him in light.

Alicia, breathing heavily, slowly made it to her feet. "Now… Rose…"

Rose nodded, extending her staff in front of her body.

Then, Evan stood up, staring at Alicia. His body showed no evident wounds. Surprised, she took a step backward. A beam of black energy extended from his right hand, he started walking toward her. Alicia stood in place, staring in disbelief at Evan as he got closer.

"Why did it have to end this way?" Alicia whimpered. "Rose and I worked so hard to protect you, to help you. We did it all for you. I did it all for you…"

Evan sneered, raising his arm up to slash her.

Alicia suddenly smiled. "I love you."

Evan swung his blade down, slashing from her left shoulder down through her right hip. Despite the gaping wound, no blood flowed from her body. In fact, the wound began to regenerate rapidly. Alicia stood, more or less unharmed. Surprised, Evan took a step back. "What's going on?" he asked, before noticing a thin green string of energy attached to Alicia's chest.

"…No…" Alicia stumbled backwards. "Rose!"

Evan turned to see the string connected to Rose's heart. Across Rose's chest was a large, gaping wound with blood flowing freely. She collapsed to the ground, the string connecting the two sisters shattering.

"Shit," Alexa scoffed, keeping her distance.

"You can live… for now." Evan smirked. "But I'll be back soon to reclaim what's mine."

His body faded, reappearing next to Rose's. A black ring of energy surrounded the two.

"NO!" Alicia screamed, her left fist erupting with flames, the skin on her hand beginning to peel away. She pushed herself forward, thrusting her left arm at Evan. In an instant, all three were consumed by the black light. When it had faded, they were gone. Alexa rushed over to Mike. Kneeling next to him, she noticed he was still breathing.

Meanwhile, Evan, Alicia, and Rose appeared within a large cave. Rose's body lay on the ground, with Evan standing next to it, and Alicia's fist planted firmly on his face. He smirked, raising his arm and placing it on her chest. Black energy flowed out, silky and wavy like a ribbon. It wrapped itself tightly around her body and then her mouth. Unable to move, Evan easily pushed her onto the ground.

In the cave was a large, wooden table with assorted beakers, flasks, and instruments, as well as a large pot adjacent to the table. Evan stepped toward the table, bringing up his menu. He pressed a couple of buttons; the Holy Herb and Pina Eyes fell onto the table.

He placed a large bowl in front of him, and picked up the herb and eyes, tossing them in. He then reached over, grabbing a small metallic cylinder. He used the butt of it to smash and grind the two ingredients together. Once adequately mushed into a paste, he scooped it into a nearby flask.

He turned, looking down at Alicia, her eyes flooded with tears and terror. He smiled as he knelt down, and with a flick of his wrist, using a small knife, he slit her wrist. He held the knife over the flask, tilting and flicking the blade to trap as much of her blood into it as he could. He then stood up, turning his back to her and moving to the table, where he began stirring the mixture with a long, thin glass rod. He stirred rhythmically until the ingredients began to blend into one another, becoming a brownish goo.

He poured the completed mixture into a smaller bowl, discarding the flask, and turned his attention to Rose, pulling her body into an empty area of the cave. Alicia's screams were murmured by the ribbon as Evan retrieved the bowl, dipping his index and middle finger into the gunk. He knelt down, placing his fingers on the ground and drawing a circle around Rose with the mixture. Once complete, he dipped his fingers into the goop once more. He placed his fingers at the northernmost part of the circle, drawing a straight line down just to Rose's head. He repeated this with the east, south, and west parts of the circle, drawing lines up to her body, creating a cross section with her body at the center.

He stood up, walking over to the table. As he placed the bowl down, he brought up his menu. With the press of a button, the black book appeared in his hand. He made his way back over to Rose, holding the book open in his left hand he reached his right hand out over her body. His black tattoo began to glow as he chanted a spell from the book. A black mist began to pour from the tattoo, flowing into the mixture around Rose. The concoction began to shine a bright purple, and Rose's body began to hover slightly off the ground in conjunction. Alicia continued with her muffled screaming as tears rolled down her cheeks.

As Evan finished chanting, the tattoo on the back of his hand returned to its usual blue. His eyes fluttered shut, and he fell backwards. The book in his hand shattered into black orbs, which flew into Rose's body. The purple energy radiating from the mixture began to flow into Rose and her body began to glow in turn, becoming enshrouded in a cocoon of violet light. When the energy around her had finally been absorbed and faded away, she stood up.

Her body had been transformed. What stood before Alicia now was more of a demon than an elf. Its torso and body were wrapped in a black ribbon, with its limbs and head bare. It stood slightly taller than Rose had, with long silver hair, pale purple skin, black lips, and golden eyes. Long nails stretched out from its fingers and toes. From its shoulders grew two large black wings, and from its lower back extended a thin black tail with a pointed tip.

It looked down at Evan and Alicia. "Elf bodies are great."

Alicia watched in horror, a fresh wave of tears pouring from her eyes at the realization of what was unfolding.

The demon raised its right arm, and with a flick of its wrist, the ribbon around Alicia split apart, freeing her. "I suppose I owe you that much. You did help me get this body, after all,"

Alicia glared at the demon, her eyes stinging as tears continued to flow. She clenched her left fist tightly, intense flames beginning to dance violently around her fist. The fire burned far hotter than it had ever before; her own skin began to peel and char.

"I will kill you!" Alicia shouted, leaping toward the demon.

Not a moment after she had left the ground had she stopped herself. Evan's body was now dangling between the demon and herself.

"Now, now." The demon wagged its finger as if scolding a child. "You do want to salvage something out of this situation, don't you?"

Rose wouldn't let herself be controlled by this thing, Alicia thought as she gritted her teeth. She took a deep breath, as the flames around her fist died down. "So what? You just used Evan to get what you wanted this whole time? Did he even have a girlfriend? How much did you lie to him?"

"Ho, now you're asking the right questions." The demon applauded. "However, I'm not ready to reveal my plans. I'll ease your conscience though. Evan had no idea what he was doing the whole time you were in the castle. I took over his body to ensure you all wouldn't fail. I think thanks are in order."

"I see," Alicia said softly, struggling to contain her rage. "You used the pain in his heart to drive him to get what you needed in order to come back. He may be the worst victim of this whole situation."

The demon sneered delightedly, watching Alicia squirm.

"So… now what?" Alicia exhaled, trying to calm herself down.

"Now, I go finish what I started. That girl in the castle has the other half. Until then, you are of little consequence," The demon smiled. "In fact, I like you and him. Not only did you serve me well, but you are both extremely powerful. I could use you for the next stage. So, I'll let you go free, and I'll expect to see you on my side in the future as thanks."

"Yeah — just — give me Evan and get us out of here then," Alicia blurted out.

The demon sneered, nodding. It lifted its arm, and a black circle surrounded Evan and Alicia. With a flash, they were warped away.

XI
Expansion

The next morning, Evan laid in bed, looking up at the ceiling with Alicia in the adjacent bed. The events of yesterday were a blur; visions flashed through his head, images of the battle with Alexa and Mike, and finally of Rose's death.

"Everything, was a lie?" Evan sighed.

Alicia closed her eyes.

"This whole time, that old man from *that* day was just using me as a vessel for some… demon." Evan's eyes clenched shut as he let out a sigh of frustration.

Alicia sighed, lifting herself up. It was hard not to share Evan's sentiment; so much had changed in the past day. Rose's voice echoed through her head: *You'll always have me. I just want you to be happy.* Her sister was gone. She was truly alone. She could feel the tears building up behind her eyes. "What am I supposed to do?!"

Evan glanced over at her.

"She knew," Alicia whispered, turning to face Evan. "She was more aware than she let on. She probably recognized you the moment we met you. Saw the darkness that rested within you."

Alicia continued to remember her sister's words. *People in a relationship should be on equal ground.*

"What does that mean for me...?" Alicia whispered.

Evan buried his head into a pillow. *It's entirely my fault*, he thought. *All I managed to accomplish this whole time was hurting more and more people.*

Alicia stood up, moving next to Evan's bed. Watching him, she heard Rose's voice once again. *He's too much of a project for me.* She smiled weakly, looking down at him. "Evan."

He slowly lifted himself off his pillow, eyes glazed with tears as he looked up at her.

"You made this mess, but you were used," Alicia explained. "Plus, I helped, and so did Rose. We were all in this together, and, at least, you and I still are. Do you remember what she said last night?"

Evan shook his head, his puffy eyes stinging from tears.

"We aren't doing charity work." Alicia told him. "Whether the outcome is what you wanted or not, we helped you meet your goal. You owe us."

"I understand… I'll pay…" Evan lowered his eyes. "I took away your sister's life. If you feel you need to take mine away, I won't resist."

"Idiot!" Alicia screamed, her wall finally breaking down, tears streaming down her face. "You want to make up for what you've done? Then take her place. Give your life to protect what she did: me."

"What?" Evan asked, confused.

"You heard me," Alicia shouted. "Time to pay up! You'll become my new family!"

Evan closed his eyes, his mind raced with thoughts of Emma. He had spent all this time searching to bring her back. He hadn't really had time to recover from losing her, let alone losing the possibility of reviving her. He hadn't even really had the chance to mourn her. He had never believed that she was gone for good. Alicia's suggestion was rather sudden — it hadn't even been a day. *Is it okay to just move on?*

Yes, a familiar voice filled his head.

His eyes snapped open. For just a moment, the image of a pale skinned girl with shoulder-length brown hair appeared before him.

"Emma," he murmured softly.

The image disappeared just as soon as it had appeared, revealing the pink-haired Alicia, who stood face-to-face with him.

"Your girlfriend is gone." Alicia stated. "She can't come back. You were tricked. As a result, you let my only family die... Despite this, I love you."

Evan watched her tepidly, unsure of what to expect.

"You've suffered enough, and you've lost enough," Alicia continued. "I know it wasn't your fault my sister died. There is no reason to beat yourself up. Give yourself a chance. You promised me you'd work on giving yourself a break. We can be happy together. I promise."

Evan exhaled. Despite her numerous advances, he never thought she had been seriously pursuing him.

"I thought I was just a form of amusement for you," Evan pressed her. "The butt of a joke. You always teased me."

Alicia flashed a genuine smile, placing her hand against his cheek. "I'm not exactly a perfect person."

Evan reached his arm up, placing his hand atop her own. The warmth of her touch seemed to ease his troubled thoughts.

"I reached out to you the only way I know how," Alicia insisted.

Evan smiled weakly. It had been a long road. Only now did he realize how reckless he had been. If he had only slowed down, would things have turned out differently? He had believed everything he had done up until this point had been justified. In the end, everything he worked toward had been meaningless. His selfish journey had only spread more pain, more death. A tear formed in the pit of his eye.

Without missing a beat, Alicia flicked it away, leaning down and pressing her lips to his own. He didn't resist, allowing himself to indulge in her kiss. He had to accept the fact: more than anything, when he was with her, he felt happy. As they pulled away, their eyes lingered on one another's.

If he was going to salvage the situation, there was only one thing he could do.

Slowly, he rose to his feet, embracing Alicia. "I understand. I will be with you as long as I live."

Alicia smiled, returning his embrace as tears began to flow down her face. After a moment, she pulled away, wiping her eyes. "First things first. Evan, what's your last name?"

"Farrant."

"No, not anymore. Today you're mine, forever… Evan Sherwood."

He began to nod before being cut off by Alicia's kiss.

As they kissed, Alicia thought back once more to what her sister had said.

"What is he going to owe us?" Alicia asked.

Rose smiled. "Your happiness."

Alicia pushed Evan onto the bed, removing various articles of clothing as she fell atop of him, her legs weaving within his own as her lips ran across his neck. She tugged at his clothes as her lips continued to move down his body. She quickly undid his pants, revealing his throbbing erection. Smirking, she mounted him, allowing it to slide inside of her.

"This time, you're all mine," Alicia leaned down, panting into his ear.

Meanwhile, Alexa had moved Mike from the hall to a private room. She began tending to his wounds as he lay unconscious. Despite their best efforts, the battle had been less fruitful than she had anticipated.

"Those girls were basically useless," Alexa sighed. "It won't be long before that *thing* comes back here."

She had spent much of her time researching the properties of this world. It wasn't hard to figure out that the old man who "blessed" her with this tattoo was more than he seemed.

She finished wrapping Mike's bruised arms. He, however, had been more helpful than she could have ever hoped. Even before coming to this world, Mike had always been a shoulder to lean on. At least, more so than Gerard. He certainly stepped up to the plate once he had joined her in this place. She wouldn't let him die so easily. She needed him.

Wait for me, a deep, foreboding voice rang through her head.

Alexa gritted her teeth as a deep pain pulsed in her head. "Again?!"

Whenever this voice rang, it left her with a pounding headache.

"I guess I'll have to finish this up later." She smiled weakly, placing her hand on Mike's forehead before turning and exiting from the room.

She slowly made her way back to the large hall. She had spent all of this time working out how to combat this threat, but still had not found any guarantee of victory. At this point, all she could do is give it her all. As she entered the hall, a loud crash echoed from overhead. The roof collapsed, bits of stone and wood scattering about the ground along with a dark figure.

Standing before Alexa was a grotesque, black creature so thin it resembled a tower of bones. Each of its limbs, fingers, and toes were unusually long, as was its slender body. Protruding from its spine were large wings that stretched out, before slowly folding neatly onto its back. Its thin face was essentially a skull with protruding horns.

"Long time, no see," it sneered, stepping toward Alexa.

Alexa's head throbbed and ached as she walked toward the demon. She felt heavier, as if she was weighed down by a great pressure that had filled the room. As they approached one another, a black mist exuded from the demon's body.

"What do you want?" Alexa bellowed.

"What I left with you," the demon replied. "You have at least half of what I am."

Alexa withdrew her flail, taking a battle stance. "As if I'll let you just take it."

The demon smirked, raising its arm and opening its hand to face Alexa. "So be it." As it spoke, a purple aura flowed around its hand.

Alexa dashed forward, closing the distance almost instantly. She swung her flail through the air, crashing it into demon's side. It grunted on impact before collapsing to the ground. *It's still weak*, Alexa thought as lightning began to spark around her free hand.

The demon struggled to stand as Alexa swung her free hand down through the air. A bolt of bright light came crashing down, piercing the demon's body. She watched as the corpse lay limp, a gaping hole where its chest had been.

However, it wasn't long before the demon made its way to its feet. It smiled as the hole slowly filled with fresh bone, blood, and flesh.

Alexa scowled. "Regeneration."

"Leave it to you to call lightning down," the demon complimented. "You should really thank me for the blessing that was bestowed upon you. If not for my gift, you never could have accomplished so much."

Alexa shook her head. "So, you are the old man."

"Of course," The demon sneered.

I'll have to take him by surprise, Alexa thought to herself.

"What's the point of all this?!" She asked. "I thought you were giving us a paradise! What are you doing here? Why are you trying to kill me?"

"Paradise?" The demon spoke slowly. "I am fairly certain I have made good on that promise."

"You said I would bring about peace!" Alexa shouted.

"You will," the demon stated. "Or, at the very least, your body will. We will need to become one before we can move on to the next phase."

"That's not an option!" Alexa roared. "If you want to give me more power, then fine. But I won't give myself over to be used as a puppet!"

Alexa began swinging her flail through the air. As it sped up, sparks of electricity wrapped around the swinging metal. The flail continued building speed until a small vortex spiraled around the head of the flail. As she swung it forward, the mini tornado flew onto the ground, expanding into a massive twister. The wind bellowed through the hall as the tornado moved toward the demon, coursing with sparks.

The demon watched as the twister advanced towards it. It's back flexed and its wings swung toward the tornado. A massive gust of air rushed forward, pushing the tornado backwards at twice the speed.

"Shit," Alexa watched wide-eyed, unable to react in time as the wind and lightning enveloped her.

She was caught in the current, spiraling through the air as her armor cracked and gashes opened up all along her body. She felt herself being pulled in every direction at once, as more wounds open up along her body. Before long, her armor had completely shattered, pain shooting through her as she swirled through the air. As the twister finally dissipated, she fell hard to the ground. Her eyes opened slowly to see the demon looming over her.

"Well," the demon said softly. "Guess this is the end."

Dammit, Alexa thought. *Sorry, Mike, this is as far as I go.*

The demon kneeled down, grasping one of Alexa's exposed breasts. A sharp pain shot through her chest as the demon melted into a black liquid, seeping slowly into her skin. She writhed in pain as her insides burned. Her body wriggled as tears began to flow down her face. It was the worst pain she had ever felt. Once the liquid was completely inside her, she let out a horrible wail of agony. Black blotches began to spread across her normally pale skin until her entire body had become black. Her eyes gleamed gold, and her hair faded, becoming a shimmering silver.

"Good," the demon proclaimed as it stood up. "This body will do just fine. I will make sure *you* free everyone from their pain."

The demon, now in Alexa's body, made its way out of the hall. Drawn by instinct, it didn't take it long to make its way to where Mike was resting, feeling his energy and following the trail to the small medical room. Once inside, it stood over the sleeping boy. The demon reached its arm out, holding its open palm over the boy's body as it glowed with a red energy. Before long, his body writhed and sweat began to flow from it. From the boy's tattoo, a ball of light blue energy emerged, his tattoo fading away shortly after. The ball gravitated toward the demon's hand. The demon grasped it gently and brought it up to its own mouth, swallowing it in one gulp.

"One down, thousands to go," the demon sneered, standing over the lifeless corpse.

Back at Riverton, Alicia nuzzled up against Evan, gently kissing his neck.

"I don't know if I can handle anymore," Evan exhaled.

"We can take a break." Alicia smiled. "But we do need a clear head to plan our next move."

"Do we even know where to start?" Evan asked.

"*It* told me it spared us so we could be used," Alicia said somberly. "It must have something in store for everyone involved in this *game*."

Evan sighed. "I barely remember anything. It's all so hazy."

"That's okay." Alicia sat up, smiling as she gazed down at him. "I'm just glad you're alive."

"About that." Evan returned her stare. "What's so special about me? All this time, why do you care so deeply about me? Why did you help me?"

Alicia chuckled, her smile widening. "For a long time, it was just me and my sister," she explained. "When we were on Earth, even then, we only really had each other. Our father died, our mother became abusive, and life at school sucked."

Evan watched her with resignation. He knew what it was like to be alienated, to have no one to turn to. His aunt wasn't much of a support system. If it hadn't been for Emma, who knows how much worse off he would have been?

"We basically only had each other," Alicia continued. "That's how our relationship started to get unconventional. Of course, we kept it a secret, or tried to…"

In a classroom stood a tall, dark-haired man, jotting equations onto the board in the front of the room. Numerous students diligently copied the content into their notebooks. In the very back row sat a slim, blonde girl dressed in a pair of jeans and a black hoodie, her head resting on her desk. Her emerald green eyes were focused on the clouds outside of the nearby window. She felt as though she had been sitting in the class for days. She sighed, raising her head to see everyone focused on the front of the room. What's the point? She thought to herself. Half of this information is useless, and the other half is just busy work.

She pulled out a composition notebook. After flipping through a few pages, she landed on a sketch of a woman, looking at her own reflection in a nearby pond. The girl's hair draped over her shoulders, covering part of her breasts. Her nipples poked out between strains of her hair, exposed. Her ears were pointed at the top. She sat among a scene of shrubs and trees.

Consumed in her thoughts, the blonde student let herself scan every inch of the page. Despite being ink on paper, she couldn't help but envy her. Before she knew it, her thoughts were interrupted by a sudden ringing bell. Everyone began packing their things. As she closed her notebook, a brunette girl to the left rolled her eyes, scoffing under her breath, "Freak."

The blonde girl packed her things, pretending not to hear, like always. As everyone funneled out of the room, she trailed behind.

"Ms. Sherwood," the teacher's voice cut through the air. "A moment?"

She turned to face her teacher, her empty eyes matching the focused gaze of her teacher.

"Are you doing okay?" The man's eyes looked over his glasses. "Lately your lack of effort has been catching up with you. Your As and Bs are quickly becoming a string of Cs and Ds."

The girl's gaze fell to the floor. "I'll be fine," she murmured, finally raising her eyes to meet his.

"If you need any help, just tell me," the teacher stated. "I don't want to see you fail."

She nodded, turning away and leaving the room. As she left, the brunette girl from class, leaning against the wall, called out to her.

"Hey, freak!" The girl sneered, walking up to her.

"What do you want, Stacey?" The blonde girl glared back.

"Come with me." Stacey titled her head, gesturing to the adjacent hallway.

"Mind if I join you?" A voice rang through the air.

Another blonde, shorter than the other two girls, but with longer hair, stepped up to the two.

Stacey glared at the new girl, groaning, before walking away from the two.

"Thanks, Alicia." The girl smiled at her sister.

"No problem, Rose." Alicia smiled back. "We have to look out for each other. That hasn't changed — it never will."

The two made their way toward the cafeteria, chatting with one another.

They sat together, alone. Rose picked up a French fry, poking her tray with it. Alicia watched her sister, scooping into her pile of applesauce with a spoon.

"Have you been experiencing any pain since we got these things?" Alicia asked, placing the spoonful of applesauce in her mouth.

Rose dropped the fry onto her tray, shaking her head. "No, but I don't seem to have much appetite."

"Things really haven't changed much, then." Alicia nodded. "Still, you shouldn't neglect your health."

Alicia took a French fry from Rose's plate, dipping it into her own applesauce. She then brought the fry up to her sister's mouth, who obediently opened it, biting into the fray. From the distance, Stacey glared at the two sisters.

Rose chewed on the fry, reaching down to her tray and continuing to eat.

"I know," Rose said between bites. "I'm glad we have each other."

"Of course. We're all we have." Alicia smirked. "Want to skip next period?"

"I don't see why not." Rose smiled. "Not like I'm benefitting from being there."

The two finished eating before leaving the cafeteria and heading outside to the school's football field, in silence.

The two snuck under nearby bleachers, moving through the space under the seats. The ground was littered with bottles, cigarette butts, and used condoms. It was clearly a favorite hangout spot for delinquents.

"Have you given any thought to who we should kill?" Rose asked, breaking the silence.

Alicia shrugged. "Do you think the old man was telling the truth?"

"I don't know." Rose shook her head. "Maybe if we kill someone who deserves it, then it won't matter either way."

Alicia watched her sister cautiously. Even though she was the younger sister, lately it seemed as though she was playing the part of the older, looking out for Rose.

"I just think we should really think about it." Alicia stared at Rose. "If it's bullshit, we could ruin the rest of our lives. I don't want anything to break us apart."

"I know." Rose smiled weakly. "But I just feel worse and worse each day. Everything feels meaningless."

Alicia stepped towards her sister, brushing her hair with her free hand.

"I'm sure you're not completely numb." Alicia smirked, placing her hand on her sister's neck. She pulled her toward her own body, meeting her lips with her own.

As their kiss ensued, a sudden flash erupted from their side.

"Sick freaks!" Stacey's familiar voice filled the air.

The two pulled away to see Stacey holding up her cell phone.

"I knew you two were freaks," she shouted. "Talking about murder, and then this? Well, I finally have proof now. I'll let the whole school know about you!"

Alicia stepped away from her sister, walking toward Stacey.

"Don't do anything stupid!" Stacey exclaimed. "If you want out of this, do exactly as —"

She was cut off by Alicia's hand tightening around her throat. Despite her stature, she was relatively strong. Stacey dropped her phone, raising her arms to try and loosen Alicia's grip.

"Rose," Alicia said calmly, staring into Stacey's eyes. "I think we found the right person for the job."

Rose slowly came to her sister's side.

Alicia released her grip, allowing Stacey to stumble onto the ground. The girl coughed as she struggled to catch her breath.

"How?" Rose asked, the two sisters looming over the girl.

Alicia glanced around, looking for a weapon.

Stacey lifted her head; tears begin to stream down her face. "I'm sorry! I'll delete the picture!"

"Too late for that." Alicia picked up Stacey's phone, putting it into her pocket.

"Are you stupid!?" Stacey yelled. "What are you planning to do?! You'll go to prison!"

Alicia picked up an empty bottle from the ground, smashing it against a nearby support beam. As she lowered herself over Stacey, she held the jagged glass against her throat.

"You threatened to hurt the one person I care about." Alicia glared at her. "I'll do whatever it takes to keep that from happening."

Stacey's tears intensified as she felt the point of the glass begin to dig into her skin. Blood slowly dripped from the tip of the bottle, and a warm liquid puddled around the ground around Stacey's body.

"Please!" Stacey shouted.

Rose watched, mesmerized by her sister's actions.

"Gross bitch." Alicia scoffed, dragging the broken glass along the girl's neck, splitting the skin and allowing blood to flow freely from her neck.

The red goop coated Alicia's hands and clothes as she dropped Stacey's body, allowing it to writhe on the ground before becoming completely still.

Rose came up behind her sister, looking down at the mess.

Alicia placed her hand, palm down, into the growing pool of blood.

"Put your hand on mine," Alicia demanded, looking up at Rose.

Rose nodded, doing as her sister instructed. As she did, the blood began to shimmer. In sync, both Rose and Alicia's bodies resonated, glowing in turn. The two, engulfed by light, disappeared in a flash.

"And," Alicia said to Evan, "that's how we got here. After that, Rose changed drastically. I could tell right away she was actually happy. Of course, I was happy just being with her."

Evan nodded, thinking back on Emma's death. On the people he had killed, all based around a lie. He was no different than Alicia. He did whatever it took for the only person he cared about.

"Then," Alicia exhaled, "we met you."

Evan met her eyes with his own.

"From the beginning, you were different than everyone else we had met," Alicia explained. "Most people relished in indulgence, and lust. But you single-mindedly focused on something else. And your reservations simply reminded me of how Rose had used to be. I wanted to protect you like I did her. Simply put, you reminding me of my sister is why I was so interested in you."

"That's…" Evan paused. "Reassuring?"

"Heh," Alicia chuckled. "Don't worry. As we traveled with you, I found myself falling in love with you. Not just what reminded me of Rose."

Alicia pressed her forehead against his.

"I was so scared after the battle at Alexa's castle," she frowned as tears welled, gripping him tightly. "I thought for sure we would lose you. I'm so glad you're okay. I don't know what I would have done if I had lost both you and Rose."

"All of this just feels like a consolation prize," Evan sighed. "We lost so much and were used and lied to. Yes, we have each other, but we lost so much to get here."

"Maybe that was necessary." Alicia wiped away a tear.

Evan watched tepidly, unsure how this was supposed to be good, or where Alicia was going with this.

"My sister had already given up," Alicia sighed. "I suspect she was only going on for me. She had nothing of her own. She went along with our relationship, but only because she was so depressed. A real relationship is what she wanted for me — just how you so obsessively latched onto the dead. Living in delusions, in the past, is not any way to live. Only after losing any hope of that unhealthy relationship, can we begin to move in the right direction."

Evan closed his eyes. He knew she was right. Emma never would have approved of his obsessing over her. He had been lost, and that made him easy to manipulate. His errors not only cost him, but several lives around him. He would have to live with that.

"Maybe you're right," Evan exhaled, opening his eyes to meet Alicia's.

She smiled weakly, pressing her lips to his own. Their eyes closed as they continued kissing, wrapping themselves into one another's legs and arms.

Evan felt a sense of peace. He finally felt like everything might end up okay. He could make a life here. Nearly forgetting what had just happened.

Suddenly, a deep, foreboding voice rang through his head.

"Hello."

Evan's eyes shot wide open, only to see a look of equal shock on Alicia's face.

"That voice," Alicia murmured.

"I know…" Evan said.

The voice eerily rang, "I should be speaking to every player in the game right now."

Evan and Alicia shared a look of dread.

"Allow me to introduce myself, as the creator of this game," the voice continued. "I'm sure you have all met me at some point or another. Although my form likely varied from player to player. Anyway, in one week's time the game will be receiving an upgrade. An expansion, so to speak."

"I don't like where this is going," Alicia groaned.

"Unfortunately…" The voice paused. "This will not be optional. So, I am giving everyone a week to prepare. Make any necessary arrangements, because this planet will be abandoned. Anything left behind will be forever out of reach."

Evan gripped the sheets tightly.

"So, enjoy your last week here," the voice elated. "We will be moving on to bigger and better things. Farewell, for now."

"Shit." Alicia scowled.

"Now that he's reached out to everyone," Evan started, "it's likely that he'll become a more active participant."

"Who knows what it has in store…" Alicia sighed. "Well, no sense in letting it ruin the mood."

She pulled him towards her, kissing more ferociously than ever. Evan felt more overpowered than ever.

"Shouldn't we…" he tried to interject.

"No," she dismissed him. "I'm too stressed. Fuck me now; we'll think of a plan later."

She continued kissing him, pinning him to the bed. He gave in, returning her affections as they further entwined their bodies. He allowed himself to be overtaken by her. Despite the situation, she was right. Having a clear head was most important.

XII
Prelude

Even after Evan had left on his journey from the town of Amaryllis, Leah, the supportive blacksmith, had remained all this time. She stayed, becoming a figurehead in the town, while helping to develop new players. Whereas others sought adventure and battle, she had never once wanted for such things. She merely sought to escape from her old life on Earth.

From her recently renovated stall in the bustling bazaar of Amaryllis, she and numerous beginners listened in shock at the sudden global announcement.

"...In one week's time the game will be receiving an upgrade," the voice eerily rang through Leah's head. "An expansion, so to speak."
It was a voice she had recognized; someone she had met on Earth before arriving here in Amaryllis.

"Unfortunately," the voice paused. "This will not be optional. So, I am giving everyone a week to prepare. Make any necessary arrangements, because this planet will be abandoned, anything left behind will be forever out of reach..."
As the voice continued, she gritted her teeth, slamming her hand in anger onto the wooden bench of her stall.

"Obviously," Leah sighed. "This is more than I signed up for..."

"You're telling me," a passing man with trimmed, dark hair replied. "I wasn't expecting to constantly be in danger, having to remain on the move. I thought this world we're in now was the change we were working for?"

"Yeah..." Leah looked down at her stand. "I didn't build this shop just so I could up and leave it on a whim."

"The problem is," the dark-haired man began, "a lot of people enjoy the indulgence and lust for power. Being out in the field is almost not even worth it lately. More and more people are ignoring quest lines and simply seeking to kill other players."

"I know," Leah sighed. "I've seen a lot of friends come and go. I thought we were trying to escape from bad circumstances, not create more."

The man gave no response, merely nodding his head somberly before continuing on his way. Her time in this place was filled with both good and bad memories, which was more than she could say about her life before coming here. She closed her eyes, reminiscing about her time on Earth, before she had escaped into this world.

She sat on her knees in a dirty gas station bathroom, dimly lit as a muscular figure loomed over her. He began instructing her on what to do. "Open your mouth, bitch." A gruff voice penetrated her ears as a sweaty mouthful of flesh forced its way into her mouth.

She endured his rough treatment. If this is what he wanted, then she had a duty as his girlfriend to make him happy. As the intensity of the thrusts increased, she began to cough, choking. Tears began to flow down her face; she didn't deserve to be just something that could be used and discarded. Her sole purpose in life was not to just please this man — a man who didn't even appreciate her and abused her.

As the man had his way with her mouth, she could feel herself gag and, unintentionally, clamp down; the man wailed in agony as her teeth broke the skin. A tremendous amount of blood flowed into her mouth and ran down her chin. Consumed in pain, the man stumbled back, falling onto the floor.
A deep, foreboding voice rang through her head. "Now is your chance. Finish him off. Kill him."

She got to her feet, barely registering what had happened as she staggered to the nearby sink. She spit out a mouthful of blood and looked up, seeing her reflection in the mirror. Dark circles ran under her puffy eyes, and a thick, red goop trickled down her lips and chin. She looked like shit.

Suddenly, she found herself sprawled on the ground, a sharp pain stinging her forehead. Looming over her was the man and all around her was shattered glass. A fresh stream of blood ran down the side of her face.

"What..." The man paused, breathing heavily. "have... you... done?!"

Instinctively, she placed a hand over a nearby piece of glass, her body trembling as she looked up at the closest thing she had to a family.

"I'm sor— "Leah began, before the man's boot struck her jaw.

"I'm so tired of hearing your excuses," the man growled.

He knelt down, grabbing her short hair and pulling her to face him. He clenched his fist, drawing his arm back. "I should've done this a long time ago."

"It's now or never." The deep voice rang through her head once more.

Before the man could land his first punch, she lunged a shard of glass into his throat. The hot, red liquid spurted from the gash, landing in various patches along her body and the floor. She watched as he gasped for air, writhing before finally falling to the ground, going still and silent. She smiled, breathing softly as the blood around her began to flow into a green, eight-pointed star tattooed on her stomach. Her body began to glow in turn, until all at once she shattered in several shards of blue light, disappearing from the bathroom.

After arriving in Amaryllis, she soon met Evan, and went on to continue to build a life as a simple blacksmith. She was lucky to escape such a bad situation; she couldn't ask for more than that. And, despite the blood on her hands, she had done enough killing. She certainly didn't want to continue adding to the bloodshed and suffering.

"I'm different," Leah murmured. "I just want to live a peaceful life."
Far away, Evan was asleep, laying on a messy, unmade bed within a quaint hotel room.

"Evan," a soft voice echoed through his head.

He found himself in a vast, empty, white space endlessly expanding in each direction. After a few moments, he heard the voice ring through his head once more. Finally, in the distance, he noticed the blurry figure of a woman. He began to struggle forward, barely able to lift his legs to take a step. It was as though his legs were strapped with heavy weights. In desperation, he stretched out his arm, grasping toward the hazy figure.

Suddenly, he found himself siting up on an unfamiliar, messy bed, his arm still outreached.

"Need something?" Alicia looked at him, confused.
She was sitting at a nearby table, naked, with a petite teacup held halfway up to her face.

Evan blinked, embarrassed, looking at his own arm before lowering it. "Nothing, just a dream."

"What kind?" Alicia inquired, sipping from the cup yet keeping her gaze focused on him.

"There was…" Evan paused, placing his hand on his head. "A girl."

"Emma?" Alicia immediately retorted, glaring at him.

"Erm," Evan hesitated, taken back by her sudden glare.

"You're so easy," Alicia smirked, taking another sip from the cup. "Don't worry — I'm not mad. I can't expect you to already be over her."

Evan exhaled, looking down at the sheets wrapped around him. "I honestly can't be sure; it was very hazy."

Alicia placed her cup down on the nearby table.

"Well, anyway…" She changed topics. "We have about seven days now. We need to come up with a plan."

Evan fell back, sprawling out onto the bed. If he was honest with himself, he was content with the current situation. Both he and Alicia had just lost so much; he didn't want to risk anymore. He certainly didn't want to end up losing Alicia too.

"Is there any real reason that we can't just live in solitude?" Evan exhaled, closing his eyes. "I just— "

He was cut off as a plump mass filled his mouth. Just from the taste, he could tell just what exactly it was. He opened his eyes to see Alicia planted firmly on him, her groin sitting cleanly against his mouth.

"Is this all your mouth is good for?" Alicia smirked, grinding against his face.

She moaned lightly as his lips vibrated against hers. She rolled off him, taking her place next to him.

"That was rude," Evan sneered.

"Well," Alicia smiled. "You were being stupid."

Evan chuckled. She treated him far differently than Emma ever had.

"Listen." Alicia lifted herself up onto him, straddling his stomach, and looking down into his eyes. "I love you. I would love nothing more than to just be alone with you forever. But it's not that simple."

Evan sighed, wrapping his arms around her body.

"I just don't want to end up alone…" he murmured into her skin.

Alicia smiled weakly, placing her hand on his back.

"I can't just let go of Rose," Alicia's voice trembled. "I love her. She was unfairly taken from me. I can never feel okay until I get revenge. But more than that, I don't get the impression that this demon will just leave us alone."

Evan gripped her tighter.

She smiled, leaning down and gently kissing his forehead. "It said it could use us, and that's why it spared us. I think no matter how hard we try to run, it would ultimately chase us. You were its vessel for a while after all."

"I know. I'm just scared." Evan's voice barely escaped his throat. "I've already lost so much. I don't want to just go on continuing to lose more and more."

"I'm scared, too," Alicia said, placing her hand against his face before leaning down to meet his lips with her own.

Their lips melded together as their hands ran along each other's bodies. Her touch seemed to alleviate his anxieties, calming him.

"It might seem sudden, but I want a child," Alicia admitted as the two parted. "But we can't have that sort of life… we can't live in peace unless we create a world where peace is possible. As long as that demon exists, we can't live freely."

Evan closed his eyes. *A world where I can live in peace. As a father, a husband, someone who isn't consumed by fantasy. Is that what I want? Do I even deserve that?*

"Is that what you want as well?" Alicia asked.

He couldn't keep running forever. If he truly didn't want to lose Alicia, she was right: the demon was a significant obstacle. He had lost far too much now. He wouldn't lose his future with Alicia. Evan placed his hand on the back of her neck, drawing her closer to him until their lips met.

"I want that too," Evan said as they pulled apart ever so slightly.

Alicia smiled, pressing her forefinger against her lips.

"Good," she affirmed. "So, any thoughts on a plan?"

"Do you think there are others like us?" Evan speculated. "Do you think everyone wants to kill or be killed? I have met plenty of people who haven't."

"I see," Alicia nodded. "You think we can instill some dissent in the masses."

"I know someone —" Evan started to speak.

"Is it a girl?" Alicia interrupted.

"Is that important?" Evan groaned. "Did you need to interru—"

"I mean…" Alicia glared, taking control of the conversation once again. "You only ever focused on Emma, and then Rose and me. You don't appear to have any guy friends."

"Jealous?" Evan asked, surprised.

Alicia bit her lip.

Evan smiled, leaning closer to her. "What can I do to reassure you?"

Alicia smirked, placing her hand onto his chest and pushing him back onto the bed, before straddling him once more.

In Amaryllis, Leah had been continuing to devote herself to her smith work. In the day since the announcement, she had become quite busy with clientele. Everyone seemed to want new and improved armor and weapons. Unlike her, more and more people were excited about going into this unknown terrain.

"Excuse me," a voice interrupted her thoughts. "I heard you're a fairly renowned blacksmith. I was hoping to get a few upgrades to my equipment."

"Of course," Leah said, wiping her brow before putting down her hammer and turning to face the tall, light-haired man. "What all do you need?"

"Are you able to enhance gear?" the man asked, brushing his bangs out of his face. "Increase the base stat parameters of my gear?"

"Yes." Leah nodded. "Simple enough. Unfortunately, with the recent announcement, I have a quite the backlog. So, the soonest I can get to this order would be tomorrow."

"No problem." The man smiled. "Should I just leave my stuff with you?"
"Yeah," Leah exhaled. "I guess that's fine."

A window popped up in front of her and, following the prompt, she accepted the trade.

"If you come back tomorrow evening, it'll be all done," Leah assured him.

"Great." The man nodded, walking away as quickly as he had arrived.

Leah sighed. "Guess I can expect another night without much sleep..."

"Maybe you should start denying some orders," a familiar voice cut through the air.

Her head shot up to see a boy with shaggy brown hair, his eyes much softer than last she saw. Wrapped around his arm was a girl with flowing pink hair.

"I thought I told you never to talk to me again," Leah stated calmly, yet scornfully.

"Well..." Evan smiled. "I thought the situation may have warranted an exception."

Leah stared at him blankly. "I'm not sure I understand what you mean."

"The announcement," Evan insisted, confused by her lack of concern.

"So what?" Leah's voice became increasingly agitated. "It's just an expansion; that's not abnormal."

"But —"

"No!" Leah's voice echoed through the bazaar.

Everyone in the area stopped in their tracks, stopping to see the commotion.

"I tried to help you!" Leah shouted, tears welling in her eyes. "But you refused, and then let yourself become a murderer! Now, you show up with some random girl, acting like we're close friends? Just leave me alone!"

Evan's gaze fell to the ground as Alicia clenched her fist. She took a step forward, only to be blocked by Evan's arm, halting her advance. He turned to her, smiling weakly.

"You're right." Evan turned back to Leah. "A lot has happened. All I'm asking to do is to give you an explanation. We'll be in this town tonight."

Evan placed a key on the wooden counter of her stall.

"This will get you into our hotel room," Evan told her softly. "If you want to hear me out, come by anytime tonight."

With that, Evan and Alicia walked away.

Leah looked down at the key, slowly wrapping her hand around it.

"Jerk," she whispered to herself.

In the hotel room, Evan and Alicia laid side by side, wrapped in a thin sheet but otherwise completely naked.

"Do you think she'll come?" Alicia asked, resting her head on his chest.

"I don't know," Evan sighed, brushing her hair with his hand. "She's the only one I could reach out to. She interacts with everyone on a regular basis. Even during our quests, I met many people who spoke of her blacksmithing. She's made quite a name for herself."

Alicia grumbled, biting Evan's nipple.

He clenched his teeth, pulling away.

"It's not polite to talk about other girls while you're naked in bed with your lover," Alicia scowled, sticking her tongue out.

Evan smiled, continuing to gently pet her head.

"You'll have to make it up to me," Alicia commanded, lifting herself up and planting her breasts into his face.

"Is this why you gave me a key?" Leah growled disdainfully. "I thought you were actually trying to reach out and mend this bridge."

"Jealous?" Alicia turned her body slightly to face Leah, smiling in contempt.

Leah gritted her teeth. "I'll just go…"

"Wait!" Evan called out, raising his arm up.

Leah glared at the two.

"We honestly weren't expecting you so quickly," Evan sighed, running his hand through his messy hair. "I'm sorry you walked in on us. Just give us a minute to get dressed."

Leah exhaled, shrugging, then made her way over to a nearby chair and taking a seat.

As Alicia and Evan got out of the bed, Leah turned her head, looking away from them. Alicia immediately took notice, making her way to the table, intentionally putting off getting dressed. Evan, who was focused on hastily wrapping himself in a plain white robe, hadn't noticed that Alicia was still naked until he had gotten to the table.

Leah shifted uncomfortably, continuing to avert her gaze as Alicia had taken a seat right next to her, her legs sprawled open, and her chest pushed out. Evan rubbed his forehead as he came up to the table.

"Alicia…" he exhaled, exasperated.

"What?" Alicia sneered. "I'm not embarrassed."

Leah looked up, staring intently at Evan, and continuing to force herself to avoid looking at Alicia.

"Come on…" he turned to Alicia, looking at her sympathetically.

"We're laying it all bare here," she insisted, standing up and going back over to the bed. "I'm just going with the flow."

With that, Alicia wrapped herself in a white robe similar to Evan's.

"So," Leah finally broke the silence, glancing from Alicia to Evan and back.

"Let's start from the beginning," Evan stated. "I came to this world with the hopes of reviving someone very special to me. I was told I could learn a spell that would do just that by coming here. Eventually, I learned that by killing other players as opposed to monsters, a person's skills could develop much more rapidly."

"So, you were willing to sacrifice others for your own selfish desires?" Leah glared.

"That day…" Evan sighed. "When you showed up during that fight, I was trying not to kill them. But they insisted on fighting until the end. That one girl wouldn't even let me spare her. She called me sexist for holding back against a girl, and told me that as long as she lived, she would hunt me until one day she died, or she killed me. I had no choice; I couldn't risk losing my life before I could learn that resurrection spell."

He went on to explain his meeting with Alexa, his confrontation with the mercenaries, fleeing through the forest to Alchemilla, meeting Rose and Alicia, learning about how people's real bodies exist in this world, and ultimately about the confrontation with the demon.

"I'm not sure what to say…" Leah rubbed her head.

"It's true," Alicia added. "That announcement was the demon — the progenitor of this world. If he's changing the setting of this game, he must have some ulterior motive."

"This may just be all a game to him," Evan explained. "But a lot of people have lost their lives as a result of this game. As such, Alicia and I are planning to confront it."

"No surprise there," Leah sighed. "But at least you're not alone now…"

"Jealous?" Alicia grinned, placing a hand on Evan's shoulder.

Leah glared at her.

"Anyway," Evan continued. "I wanted to see if you had a general feel for people's reactions."

"Well..." Leah nodded, regaining her composure. "As you saw earlier, I'm bogged down with requests. People seem pretty excited about this change."

"That's what we were afraid of," Alicia groaned.

"Why?" Leah inquired. "What difference does that make?"

"They are going to remain willing participants," Alicia grumbled. "Pawns."

"We could use a resistance force of our own," Evan stated. "I can't — we can't — do this all alone."

Leah stared at Evan, in awe. "You really have changed…"

Evan smiled, turning to Alicia. "Thanks to her."

Alicia smiled, reaching her hand out to grasp Evan's.

"I guess I am a little jealous." Leah smiled weakly.

Alicia smirked, feeling accomplished.

"Okay," Leah exhaled. "Myself included, I do know of some people who aren't all gung-ho about this whole situation."

"Oh?" Evan asked.

"What do you need form me?" Leah asked.

"Just gather people you can trust," Alicia told her. "Spread the truth. Let people know this isn't just a game. And, if possible, level up significantly. There are lots of higher-level players who will be on the front lines."

"We are going to go where the strongest monsters spawn, and grind until we are forced to move from this planet to the next," Evan explained.

"Got it," Leah nodded. "If that's all, I'll take my leave then."

"Unlucky for you," Alicia teased. "If this were just a few days earlier, I may have just invited you to stay the night with us."

Leah glared at her once more.

"Alicia," Evan scolded. "Don't be mean."

"Whatever." Leah chuckled. "I'll go and message some of my closer friends and keep an eye out for customers who aren't as excited about all of this. I'll be in touch."

With that, she left.

"Was that necessary?" Evan groaned.

"Just marking my territory." Alicia smirked.

Evan shook his head.

"Well," Alicia changed gears, turning towards Evan. "Let's go to the town near the Origin Forest. We can rent a room there and start first thing in the morning."

"Sounds good," Evan replied.

They began gathering their things, and after re-equipping their proper gear, withdrew a scroll. As it unrolled, a bright light flooded out, consuming the two. In an instant, they disappeared from the room.

The next morning, the two stood at the edge of the expansive forest. Alicia tightened her fist as flames enveloped it, while Evan held a spire of ice in his hand.

"Let's do this," Evan stated.

Alicia nodded, and the two walked toward the trees, disappearing into the brush.

XIII
Invasion

On Earth, a vast metropolis stood tall, bustling with life. Despite the daily news reports, life moved on. Political struggles waged, and people continued to fear an ever-approaching war between the most prominent nations. Even with the numerous, continued reports of missing youth, life moved on. As most people do, they continued to care only about their own situation.

In onc particular coffee shop, two well-dressed men were enjoying a brief reprieve before their daily grind began.

"Missing persons, murders, and the world on the brink of war," said a man with a clean-shaved face and slicked back dark hair.

"Yeah, everything is going to shit," the other man with silvery trimmed hair replied.

The younger man shook his head. "There are fewer and fewer interns at the office. There is hardly anyone to pick up the slack anymore. No one wants to work an honest job."

"At this rate, I'll never get to retire," the older man scoffed. "Selfish brats, always kicking and screaming about how unfair things are. They should just learn to accept their lot in life. What ever happened to good old-fashioned work ethic?"

The first man nodded. "Kids these days. It's a damn shame."

Suddenly, a loud bang echoed throughout the shop. The various glass windows and doors at the front of the building shattered. A figure wrapped in a black cloak with a gold chain hanging around its neck stood at the front of the shop.

The two men, now taking cover under the table they had been sitting at, looked at the individual in awe. While they remained composed, most of the people in the building had begun to panic, screaming and running in the opposite direction.

The figure raised its arm, gripping a curved knife.

"Die," it murmured.

It swung the knife through the air. The tip of the blade sparked as a wave of flame erupted, spreading through the space in front of it. Those who were closest to the flames were incinerated immediately. Then, two more figures suddenly appeared from behind the first, both wrapped in the same black cloaks. The three moved systematically, cutting down the people in the shop one by one with relative ease.

"Too easy," one of the figures said, removing its hood and revealing a young man with dark red hair.

The other two figures followed suit.

An older girl with medium-length blue hair and matching blue eyes scowled. "This isn't much of an expansion."

"I don't know," replied a black-haired man with scar along his chin. "I've always wanted to assault a public place like this. It's exhilarating."

"This is a pretty realistic expansion," the red-haired man stated, looking around at the damaged shop. "Didn't expect to get a reference to Earth."

"Reference, huh?" the blue haired girl murmured to herself.

"Something wrong?" the black-haired man asked.

She shook her head. "No. Let's go ahead and absorb the blood and move on."

The various pools and stains of blood around the shop began to glow before swirling and lacing through the air, flowing into the trio's respective tattoos.

All around the world, scenes like this played out. The players who had been spirited away were now transported to Earth, attacking businesses, schools, banks, and even military bases. To them, it was just a new expansion of the game.

Standing atop a hill looming over an adjacent city was a girl with curly, green hair — Leah. Beside her were two others: the first, a busty woman with flowing blond hair and encased in steel adornments. The second, a thin, dark-skinned man draped in a cloak with short, dark hair. The trio watched as smoke rose from within the city.

"This is undoubtedly Earth," Leah sighed. "Evan was right…"

The other two remained silent. Suddenly, one of the buildings began to collapse, as an explosion seemingly engulfed a small section of the city. Gunshots echoed through the air, followed by several more explosions.

Leah clenched a fist. "This is what Evan and Alicia warned me about." She gritted her teeth, closing her eyes. She felt bad that she had barely believed them. As well, she was almost certain that Evan had only wanted to flaunt his new relationship. Clearly, she owed him an apology.

The blonde woman placed a hand on Leah's shoulder. "Come on," she whispered. "We've prepared for this. We can minimize the casualties if we step in."

Leah nodded, staring at the crumbling city before her.

Across the planet, cities continued to fall. Players killed everyone: men, women, and children alike. Countries took immediate notice, and an emergency meeting was preparing to be held by representatives from each prominent nation. Three individuals spearheaded the conference, presenting information infant of a sea of somber faces.

"This threat is unprecedented!" A man with dark hair, a trimmed mustache, and a grey suit shouted to the convention. "We can't utilize conventional tactics! What can we possibly hope to do, Mr. Yamamoto?"

"Obviously, you're right, Mr. Williams," an older man with silver hair responded. "The world has been consumed by the supernatural. In every corner of the world, people — mostly young adults — have appeared wielding unique powers. Many nations, including my own, are stumped."

"And what's worse," a professional looking woman with shoulder-length blonde hair added, "most cases are involved in some form of crime."

"It is as Ms. Miller says," Mr. Williams continued, "and, interestingly enough, some of the identified people have been confirmed as those who have gone missing within the past couple of years."

"There must been some connection," Ms. Miller insisted.

"How very astute of you," a voice filled the air, echoing through the convention hall.

Everyone turned to see a woman clad in steel-plated body armor, with a crescent shaped scar etched around her right eye.

"Who are you?!" Mr. Williams yelled. "How did you get in here?!"

All eyes were focused on the woman as she confidently made her way down to the front of the room. Once centered before all of the congress, she smirked, addressing the group. "My name is Alexa," said the demon in her body. "You can consider me the leader of the people causing all these incidents."

Many of the representatives stood up, shouting and cursing at the woman, the entire congregation in an uproar as the hall was filled with chaos.

"Consider this a declaration of war," Alexa sneered. "I will be taking the lives of everyone on this planet."

A gun was immediately placed, point blank, against the side of her head. Before she had realized it, she had been surrounded by several men in black suits and shades.

Mr. Williams shook his head. "Absolutely foolish. You shouldn't have come so naively to us."

Alexa smirked as the air around her began to swirl and shift. Steadily the air currents sped up, billowing more violently. The gun aimed at her head split in half, and the limbs and heads of the several men around her severed and scattered amongst the floor. Before long, the entire room became a concentrated space of sharp wind. Blood, clothes, and limbs spiraled through the air as everyone was consumed by the attack.

Just as soon as the wind had picked up, it began to die down. Alexa stood, covered in blood, alone in the room.

"I'm not a fan of these wind powers," she remarked. "So messy." She glanced around the hall. "But they will have to do for the time being…"

She inhaled, and the blood that stained the room began to flow toward her like a mist, directly into her mouth. Her body flared with a black aura as the entirety of the spilled blood was consumed, leaving a room of shriveled corpses.

She scowled. "Just a snack at best. No matter, though — my meal will be prepared before long. The more these fools battle and grow, the more satisfying they will be to consume."

In a distant city, a brown-haired boy dressed in a shirt made of chains, stood before an illuminated building. The flashing, neon sign read, "Girls, Girls, Girls".

He smirked as he entered through the front door.

Inside, a center stage mounted with poles housed several naked girls. All around the stage were various men, seemingly ignorant to the chaos outside, hooting and howling as the women spun to the overhead music. The boy made his way left, towards the empty bar.

"Shot of whiskey please," he said to the topless, female bartender.

"I.D?" the woman asked, skeptically looking over the clearly underage youth.

"I don't think that's necessary," he barked.

"Look, kid," the woman snapped. "I don't think you've come to the right place."

Responding to the sudden commotion, a large man in a blazer made his way to the bar.

"Problem?" The gruff voice asked.

"This gentleman was just leaving," the bartender explained.

The large man nodded, placing his hand on the boy's shoulder. "Come on, then."

The bouncer shouted, immediately pulling his hand away, part of his palm already charred. "What the…?"

"Don't touch me, filth!" The boy turned, glaring at the bouncer.

"Damn kid," the man swung his fist at the boy.

As his fist approached, the boy's body erupted in flames, and the bouncer was blown back, his clothes ignited from the impact. Consumed in flames, he fell to the ground. Slowly, his body smoldered into a pile of bone and ash.

The bartender screamed and everyone in the club turned toward the bar. The boy grabbed the bartender's arm, her screams echoing through the building as her skin burned.

"Shot." The boy spoke slowly, glaring at the woman. "Of. Whiskey." The bartender screamed even louder as a group of men finally came out from the back.

"Hey, asshole!" A man dressed in a black suit shouted.

The boy turned to see five men wielding guns pointing at him.

"Have my whiskey ready," the boy murmured to the bartender. He stood up, moving toward the line of men. The sound of gunfire filled the air as

he walked, bullets racing toward him before melting under the intense heat he emitted. The men stared in awe for a moment before unloading the rest of their clips, each bullet as ineffective as the last.

"I'm not some pushover," the boy grumbled. He stretched out his arm, and all at once, the opposing men erupted into individual balls of flame. Screams of anguish filled the room as each man melted, becoming a black stain of ash on the ground.

The boy turned to the stage, looking at the men and women who stared in awe, frozen in fear.

"These girls are mine," the boy declared. "For slobbering all over what is mine, every man here will die."

One by one, each man sitting around the stage erupted in flames. Each of their screams cut off as one by one they turned to a pile of ash. All that remained were several nude women, many of which fell to their knees, shaking in terror at the sight of the psychopath.

"Anyone who doesn't want to die," the boy began, "needs to do exactly as I say."

He turned, walking towards the bar. A shot glass filled to the brim with an amber liquor awaited him, the bartender nowhere to be seen. He took it, drinking it all down in one gulp before making his way back to the stage.

"Lay down!" He pointed to a red head woman as he made his way onto the stage, undoing his pants.

Across town, a group of three people draped in dark purple cloaks stood in the lobby of a bank. The numerous patrons stared as they pushed their way up to the counter.

"Gather all the money you have," a deep voice demanded. "Then hand it over to us."

The well-dressed man behind the counter simply stared at the trio. Without hesitation, he pressed a small button under the counter, setting off the silent alarm.

"I'm afraid I don't have the authority to —"

The man's head flew off his shoulders, lobbed off by the stroke of an axe. The body fell to the ground, and the cloaked figure turned to the next nearby employee.

"Gather all the money you have," the voice repeated. "Then hand it over to us."

The woman nodded frantically, turning and making her way to the safe.

"Freeze!" A voice rang through the air. "Hands where we can see them!"

The three figures turned to see a line of police officers, guns drawn, slowly closing the distance between them.

One of the cloaked figures stepped forward, slowly walking toward the line of officers.

"Halt!" One of the officers shouted, accidentally firing a bullet.

The bullet flew forward, the force blowing the hood of the cloak off the figure's head to reveal a woman with a brown ponytail. Along her cheek was a shallow wound from the bullet, blood oozing down the side of her face. She stood still, raising her arms in the air to show she was unarmed.

"Hold your fire!" Another officer shouted, turning to his own men, before returning his attention to the woman. "Get on the ground!"

The woman positioned herself on the ground, placing her palms flat against the floor as the building began to shake uncontrollably.

The ground around the officer's cracked, and spires of earth and stone grew, piercing through their legs, chests, and heads. They remained held in place by the spires, lifeless, as blood pooled beneath them. The woman stood up, smiling at the sight and unfazed by the corpses, before turning and walking back towards her companions.

The civilians in the bank stood, frozen in fear. They were powerless, and none of them even considered trying to be a hero. This was beyond any robbery they had seen before.

"Now," the figure with the deep voice began again. "Let's not do anything rash. Just get us the god damn money."

Outside, several cop cars, as well as backup for the officers, congregated outside of the bank. A woman encased in plated armor with long, blue hair looked at the group of officers from a distance.

"What's going on over there?" She whispered to herself.

"Freak!" A man scoffed under his breath as he passed by her.

The girl smirked, watching as the man walked away. As he passed a fire hydrant, it exploded, a geyser of water erupting from the ground. The man stopped, stepping away from the sudden gush of water. At each nearby corner, the various hydrants began to explode. Water burst out from the ground, rapidly flooding the surrounding streets. Numerous people had fled the scene, but several remained frozen, unsure as to what was happening. The girl in armor made her way to the center square of the area, a large video screen looming over the street. She raised her arms, moving them fluidly through the air as though conducting a symphony. The pillars of water bent and shifted, spraying passersby. One by one, people were knocked over by the intense bursts of water.

A few police officers had made their way up the street toward the commotion, immediately noticing the woman adorned in armor. At this point, authorities around the world were well aware of the impending threat, and who to look for.

"Fools!" The girl laughed, watching as the streets continued to flood with water. "All shall bend to the whim of Ruto!"

Suddenly, the girl took a severe blow into her side. She groaned at the pop of her ribs cracking, falling to the ground.

Leah stood over the girl, mace in hand, and her companions at her side.

"Why?" Ruto asked, struggling to get to her feet.

"You're hurting people," Leah stated, looking down at Ruto. "Real people."

"We don't know that!" Ruto shouted, her body shaking as she brought herself to her feet.

"It's obvious that this is Earth!" Leah's dark-haired companion shouted, taking a step toward her.

"This is all just a game!" Ruto affirmed, her chest heaving. "It always has been!"

A sudden dialogue cut off the two. From a large screen looming overhead appeared a professionally dressed woman.

"Good afternoon," the professionally dressed woman greeted the viewership. "This is a breaking news announcement. In the wake of the recent World Conference Massacre, a woman claiming to be responsible has demanded a press conference, inviting all sources of media. We go live…"

The feed cut to Alexa, standing among numerous corpses, surrounded by tepid soldiers and officers.

"As you can see," Alexa sneered, motioning to the bodies around her, "the police and military are helpless to stop this. I slaughtered the major political figures at the world conference. This is a declaration of war. I have brought soldiers from another world. Those who were ostracized by your society are now in a position of power. Everything will bend to our wills, and those who had been oppressed shall have their just deserts. Send any force you like; we won't be stopped."

Alexa reached her arm out, and a burst of light engulfed the screen as screaming filled the airwaves. The video went blank before transitioning back to the original anchorwoman, who was left speechless. After a few moments, the breaking newsfeed ended.

"You'd have to be stupid to not acknowledge that!" Leah screamed at Ruto.

She sneered. "Even better — as Alexa said, we are in control. When I was here before, I got teased, abused, and rejected. Now I can get revenge on those who hurt me. I don't need to be the victim anymore!"

The flow of water intensified as the geysers erupted more violently than before. A deepening layer of water filled the streets as Leah now stood ankle deep in water. She gripped her mace tightly.

"This city is mine to do with as I please!" Ruto yelled. "I'll devour you! You're just another step for me to climb!"

If I cracked her ribs, I can do more, Leah thought to herself. *This isn't like a game; being more powerful doesn't negate damage.* She shot forward, swinging her mace horizontally through the air toward Ruto.

"Pathetic," Ruto scowled, leaping up and easily avoiding the blow.

While in midair, a beam of light pierced through Ruto's leg, throwing her off balance. Simultaneously, the dark-haired boy fell from the sky above, cleaving his axe deep into Ruto's shoulder. She grunted, hitting the ground face-up on her back, looking up to see the trio standing over the girl.

"How can we incapacitate her?" Leah asked.

"Isn't that a bit naive?" The blonde girl noted.

Leah shook her head. "There is absolutely no reason to kill her —"

She was cut off as a sudden shot rang through the air. Leah grunted as pain shot through her side. She fell to her knees, her free hand covering the fresh wound. Bleeding profusely, she looked up to see an officer pointing a smoking barrel at her.

"Why…?" Leah groaned, her vision blurring.

"Look!" The officer cheered. "They can be wounded! If they can bleed, they can die!"

The officers on site raised their weapons, aiming at the group.

"Who's the stupid one now?" Ruto coughed, blood running down her lip.

"You think you're safe? You think you're doing the world a favor? You're no different from us, and regardless of how you act, society will blame you just as much as it blames those who are taking advantage of their power."

Leah gritted her teeth, turning to face the officers.

"Stop!" She protested. "We aren't like her! We want to stop her as much as you guys do!"

"Don't listen to them!" One of the officers shouted. "Take advantage of this opportunity! Open fire!"

With several loud bangs, bullets sprayed towards the group. Leah's blonde companion pushed her aside, taking the brunt of the attacks, and dying almost instantly. She fell to the ground, her blood mixing in with the excess water.

Ruto closed her eyes. As her energy flowed out from her body, the water around her began to ripple. Concentrations of spiraling water began drilling upward, piercing through the various officers. They screamed in agony as their bodies fell limp.

Leah groaned, struggling to get to her feet. "Are you okay, Jordan?" The dark-haired man nodded, glancing down at their blonde friend. "Jessica didn't make it…"

Leah nodded. "I know…"

Ruto coughed up blood as her eyes struggled to open.

"She's helpless now," Jordan said, looking down at her. "She won't last much longer."

"She saved us, though," Leah sighed.

"We should be…" Ruto struggled, vomiting more blood. "Sticking together…we shouldn't rely on this society — just ourselves…"

Ruto's eyes fluttered shut, her body becoming completely still.

Meanwhile, Alexa stood atop a large hill, overlooking the city below. Skyscrapers reached endlessly into the sky, with buildings expanding for miles into the horizon.

"Humans are so pathetic," Alexa whispered softly to herself. "Building so much and clinging to growth. As if all this is supposed to make up for their mortality. I will make them realize their place in this universe. I will return everything on this planet back to the dust from which it came."

Alexa extended her arm, her palm opened, facing the expansive city. A small orb of red energy pulsated in front of her hand. Suddenly, it shot forward, flying down towards the city.

Citizens walking through the street looked up, noticing an ever-growing orb of scarlet. As the light came closer, it expanded until it struck the ground. All at once, the entire city was engulfed, and just as soon as the light of the explosion appeared, it faded away. Only a massive crater was left where the city once stood.

Alexa sneered, looking down at the crater in delight.

"Wiping out a few more cities should be a good way to kill time until everyone's powers have fully matur —"

She was cut off as a long, ornate blade penetrated her chest. As suddenly as it had pierced her, it was withdrawn, blood flooding from the gaping wound. She turned to see that the owner of the icy blade was a boy with brown hair.

"Time to end this," Evan declared.

"Once and for all," Alicia smirked, standing next to him.

XIV
Calamity

As Evan's frozen, ornate blade withdrew from the demon's body, ice spread outward from the wound.

"It... can't... be," the demon gasped.

Without hesitation, Evan stepped forward, slashing his sword through the air and cleaving the demon in half. He looked down at Alexa's body, feeling no remorse for the once human girl. She had already been claimed by the demon and had been nothing more than a vessel. She herself had once shared that sentiment; death was surely a better fate than being controlled.

"This isn't a game," Evan affirmed.

The demon lay in shock as the top half of Alexa's body lay severed, several feet away from the bottom half. Between the two sections was an ever-growing crimson pool. Despite this, flesh and organs began to creep from each section of the body in an attempt to reconnect.

"Don't think it'll be that easy!" The demon shouted in desperation, followed by an earth-shattering wail which seemed to hasten his regeneration process. Before long, Alexa's body was once again whole, standing to face the two interlopers.

"This is it," Alicia stated.

Evan nodded. "I know."

Alicia smirked. "Scared?"

"Nah." He smiled, turning to look at her. "I know you'll keep me safe."

Alicia smiled. "Good."

At once, the two shot forward, closing the distance between themselves and the demon. Alicia's hands and feet became wrapped in fire as she moved through the air. Once within arm's reach, she quickly plunged her flaming fist into the demon's chest.

The demon reeled backward, groaning as her fist burst out of its back. It grabbed her arm, and a black stain slowly spread across Alicia's skin. Her eager smirk transitioned to a frown of hastened desperation. All at once, she gritted her teeth and withdrew her arm from the demon. She sighed in relief as the patch of black quickly faded, her pale skin returning to its usual pristine shine.

The demon slowly exhaled, the hole in its chest beginning to slowly close in turn.

"Surprise, surprise," Evan murmured to himself as he approached the demon. Evan swung his blade through the air, severing the demon into two pieces once again.

Without hesitation, Evan held his free hand out, ice and air gathering in his open palm. As he slammed his hand onto the ground, a layer of ice spread toward the demon's body. It enveloped the creature, coating it in frost before ultimately encasing it in a sheet of ice.

Suddenly, a roaring ball of flames crashed through the air, engulfing the frozen figure. As the flames raged, the ice melted, and the boiling water and blood rose into a red mist. The fires began to smolder until all that remained was a charred, naked husk, hacked off at the waist.

Alicia watched tepidly. "Easier than expected."

Evan looked down, meeting the demon's fiery gaze.

"It's... not... over," the demon's voice trembled.

Evan stepped back as a bony, black arm shot up, tearing itself out of Alexa's chest. From the gaping wound, another hand reached out and, gripping the edge of the open wound, a large skeletal figured arose from Alexa's corpse.

"Its true form?" Evan asked.

Alicia nodded, staring at the gruesome fiend.

Towering over the two stood a long-limbed skeletal creature. Where its eyes should have been were two deep, crimson pools, and a large pair of wings draped over its shoulders.

"Is that why you use other people's bodies?" Evan asked. "Because you're so frail yourself?"

"Fool," the demon sneered. "You are nothing to me. I am the only reason you are alive. In the end, what was borrowed will return to me."

"Now that it's in its true form, we're going to need to be extra careful," Alicia murmured.

Evan nodded, his eyes fixated on the demon, poised to strike. He couldn't afford to miss any openings.

Alicia clapped her hands together, and as she slowly pulled them apart, a tiny spark floated between her palms. The spark began to grow and swirl, forming into a condensed ball of fire. She raised her right arm, the fireball hovering over her open palm. In an instant, the small orb expanded into a massive ball of swirling flames. Then, with a single step forward, she swung her arm, tossing the ball toward the demon.

As it approached, the demon reached out its bony arm, a point of light gathering at the center of its hand. The light extended into separate directions, forming a sparkling rod of pure light. The demon wrapped its fingers around the rod, gripping it tightly before swinging it through the flames. The ball cleaved into two before dissipating in the air.

From behind, Evan thrust his sword forward, only to have his attack parried by the demon's rod of light. Simultaneously, it reached out its arm, wrapping its rough hand tightly around Evan's neck. He gasped for air, frantically squirming until suddenly the demon's grip was loosened by Alicia's fist clocking it square in the jaw.

The bits of flame from Alicia's fist began to burn away at the demon's face as Evan quickly continued his own assault. He slashed the creature from hip to shoulder, as Alicia slammed her open palm into its chest.

As it stumbled back, its chest ignited, erupting and engulfing the demon in flames.

Alicia scowled. "Hard to say how effective that was when it has no real flesh..."

Evan smirked. "If ever we needed a health bar..."

"True." Alicia chuckled. "Although, at least we seem to be on equal footing."

Raising its arm into the sky, the demon suddenly let out a horrendous wail.

"DON'T THINK THIS ENDS SO EASILY!"

Dark clouds blanketed the sky as flashes of light occasionally erupted throughout the vast grey. Loud crashes roared through the air while bolts of lightning began to fall from the sky, striking seemingly at random points on the ground.

"Probably a good idea to start moving," Evan suggested.

The two rushed forward, intersecting one another's paths as they approached the demon, Evan raised his arm in the air, pointing his sword into the sky. As the lightning was guided to the tip of the blade, it dispersed against the surface of the frozen blade. Alicia, being much faster than Evan, had already closed in on the demon. As she moved to attack, sparks danced through the air all around the monster, spreading across her body as well. She collapsed to the ground, her body twitching and unresponsive.

The demon loomed over her, raising its arms up into the air. As it went to swing its arm downwards, it was toppled over as Evan's sword crashed into it. He knelt beside Alicia, a blue aura surrounding his hand as he placed it on her body. The twitching subsided as the aura flowed into her, the feeling returning to her body as she took to her feet.

Evan and Alicia watched their enemy from a distance, winded, but clearly at the advantage.

The demon trembled as it knelt on the ground, its body battered, covered in bruises and cuts. As it rose to its feet, appearing to be on its last leg, it glared at the two before it.

"Don't think this is over!" It cried out.

"That's all it ever says," Alicia sighed. "Still, it's probably best to not let it get too settled."

Evan nodded, tightening his grip around his sword.

With that, the two dashed forward, Alicia's fist engulfed in flames. As they closed in on the demon, a piercing screech filled the air. Evan and Alicia froze in place as a sudden burst of air pressure rolled over their bodies. Evan's sword shattered and the flames around Alicia's fists extinguished as they were sent flying backward into the ground.

They barely managed to lift their heads, pinned by the constant pressure and vibrations from the ongoing screech.

The ground around the demon began to crack and crumble, the excess dust and dirt levitating as it eroded away. The entire mountain, starting from underneath the creature's feet, began to shift apart. From the distance, several translucent blobs began to rush toward the demon. One after another, the creature swallowed each one, the pressure around Evan and Alicia intensifying with every gulp. Before long, the once vast mountain had become but a crater in the earth.

Suddenly, the vibrations ended, and Alicia found herself able to move. Promptly she clenched her fist, flexing her back as flames erupted from her shoulder blades. They stretched out like wings, allowing her to glide around the crumbling mountain debris. As she maneuvered around the falling rock, she accelerated downward, scanning the area for Evan.

Evan looked up at the sky as he fell. He felt as though he was falling in slow motion. He looked around as the debris spun slowly through the air. Before he realized what had happened, a large rock spiraled down, smashing into his body. As the weight intensified, he could feel his bones creaking and cracking as he wailed in agony.

This is it, he thought. He closed his eyes as he began to feel heavier and heavier.

Suddenly, the weight was lifted, and he felt his body slow down. He opened his eyes to see Alicia cradling him.

"Ah," Evan groaned softly. "Thanks..."

"Can't let my princess be in distress for too long." Alicia smirked as she gently touched the ground.

Evan glared up at her as she helped him to his feet.

"Heal yourself," Alicia instructed. "I'll cover us from the debris."

Evan nodded, closing his eyes and exhaling. It was all he could do to stay on his feet. His whole body ached as he raised his arms and clapped his hands together. A soft blue aura expanded from his hands, slowly enveloping his body. He let out a sigh of relief as the sharp pains he felt began to subside.

Meanwhile, as debris continued to fall, Alicia targeted specific rocks, incinerating them before they got too close while simultaneously keeping an eye out for the demon.

Evan stood up, now free of pain, with his body feeling much lighter than ever before. Still illuminating a blue aura, he made his way up to Alicia. He placed his open palm onto the center of her back.

"Oh!" Alicia cried out in surprise.

"Calm down — there will be time for that later," Evan teased. "Now, stay focused. I'll heal your wounds too."

Alicia pouted, thrusting her arm forward and firing off another ball of fire toward an incoming rock.

Before long, the falling debris subsided, leaving a vast, empty space before them. They continued to glance around, neither having seen the demon since the collapse.

"Where do you think its hiding?" Alicia murmured.

Evan shrugged. "It's not like we can sense it. I'm sure it'll show itself before long."

Alicia nodded. "You're right. Best to enjoy this breather while we can."

The two began to relax, taking a moment to stretch out the muscles in their arms, legs, and backs.

I've come a long way, Evan thought to himself. *It may not be what I had set out to do, but a lot has happened.* Alicia had found him and stayed with him in his time of need. *She held me down and kept me from going too far. I owe her my life. Now at the end, whatever the outcome may be, whatever happens, happens.* As he finished arching his back, his eyes lingered over Alicia, watching her light, pink hair wavering through the air. Taking a step toward her, he pulled her close and pressed his lips to her own.

"I love you," he whispered.

Alicia smiled, returning his kiss. "I love you, too."

Suddenly, a loud crashing noise shattered the moment.

In the distance, a cloud of dust rose up around the silhouette of a dark figure. As the smoke settled, it was apparent that the demon had become significantly taller. Where there was once just a bony figure were now plump, firm muscles. Red stripes ran vertically along the length of its legs, arms, and torso. Its eyes gleamed golden and protruding from its forehead were spiraled horns. In addition, a thicket of silvery hair now grew out from the scalp and down its neck. Its thin, black tail whipped through the air as a pair of dark, leathery wings folded against its back.

"What the hell happened?" Alicia shouted. "It's like it's a completely different being entirely."

The demon sneered, slowly making its way towards the two. Its feet stamped into the ground as it moved forward, leaving deep impressions in its wake.

"Simply put," the demon began, "my investment paid off."

"What does that mean?" Evan murmured.

The demon chuckled. "Too difficult to understand?"

"Don't get full of yourself!" Alicia shouted. "Being vague doesn't make you enlightened!"

"As if it matters," the demon scoffed, before continuing. "I am the source of everyone's power. The reason you all can fight the way you do is because I granted you that strength."

"Duh," Alicia retorted. "Are you hoping to win an award for being vague *and* obvious?"

"Shut up!" The demon's voice boomed, stretching its arms forward and pointing at the two.

The air around Evan and Alicia shifted, becoming denser. Suddenly, it was as though their bodies were strapped with numerous weights, and they dropped to the ground, pinned in place. The demon advanced toward the two, keeping its fingers extended toward its prey.

"Good job…" Evan groaned.

"Heh," Alicia smirked. "Can't help it."

"Now, listen!" The demon exclaimed. "When I first arrived on Earth, I broke off pieces of my own soul, fusing them with those who created a physical contract with me — the proof being those tattoos you all bear."

Despite their best efforts, Evan and Alicia were unable to move even an inch. As the demon moved closer to them, their heads were forced upward so that they were looking straight at it.

"However, that gift is not permanent," the demon explained. "Think of it as an investment on my part. I put a little up front so that you humans would cultivate it for me. You took that power to greater heights, and now that it's at a suitable level, I am simply taking it back. My power has increased due to the efforts of you foolish humans."

"Shit," Alicia groaned.

"So, this current metamorphosis is a result of taking back most of my power from everyone," the demon sneered. "Obviously, there are some people still holding onto their share."

"Like us," Evan murmured.

"Eventually, it will all return to me," the demon continued. "Then I will destroy this planet and move onto the next one."

The demon grinned, now looming over the two.

"Now it's your turn to give up your share," the demon declared. "I'll take great joy in absorbing your powers. You two have proven to be quite special."

"This sucks," Evan groaned to Alicia, still struggling in vein.

Suddenly, a burst of heat filled the air. Evan looked to see a surge of flames erupting around Alicia's body. She trembled as she slowly took to her feet. Her voice echoed through the area as the flames around her raged. The demon raised its arms, covering its face as the flames flared. The flesh on its arms began to peel as Alicia's flames burned away at its skin.

The demon leapt backward, distancing itself from the two, inadvertently retracting its fingers and breaking its spell. At once, Evan took to his feet.

"So." Alicia smirked. "Simply put, our powers aren't constrained by yours. Even though we got our power from you, we haven't been limited by how much we can grow. And, we've actually taken that power much further than you could imagine. It's safe to assume we are stronger than you."

The demon glared at them.

"No sense in holding back!" Alicia exclaimed.

Alicia clenched her fists, and the air around her body began to heat up drastically. A red aura began to envelop her and slowly flare up. Then, with a sudden burst of energy, the aura erupted, and flames poured outward from her body. The aura extended from her fingers, up her arms, and even extending out from her lower back, swishing back and forth like a tail.

She stomped the ground, cracking the earth beneath her. Then, with a sudden flash, she dashed forward at the demon.

Evan reached out his arm, opening his palm, and the temperature around him dropped. Flakes of snow and ice swirled in the air, and a shiny blue shard formed within his palm. As he clenched his fist, an array of light flowered out from it. Ice spread up his forearm slowly, encasing it as a blade of pure, white ice extended from his hand. He stepped forward and the ground around his feet began to freeze over, leaving a trail of ice as he advanced toward the demon.

Alicia swung her arm through the air, flames pouring off of her skin as the demon leapt back to avoid the attack. Immediately afterward, Alicia thrust her free arm forward. The demon smirked, grabbing Alicia's fist. She gritted her teeth as a flow of electricity poured into her body. With a sudden shout, her aura flared up, dispersing the voltage. Simultaneously, she swung her leg forward. The demon smirked, halting her sudden kick with its open palm. The flames radiating from her leg began to once again burn away at the demon's flesh. Furrowing its brow to endure the pain, it raised its free arm. A sudden bright light surrounded its hand, illuminating the immediate area. As it went to swing its arm downward, the aura from Alicia's lower back whipped around and pierced the demon's throat.

Rather than blood, a red steam rose from the wound as the heat around Alicia's body rapidly intensified. As her tail withdrew from violently the demon's neck, an icy blade erupted out from the demon's chest, and ice began to spread outward from the puncture wound, across its skin. The aura in the demon's hand faded away.

"Just a little more," Evan murmured.

With a sudden flash, beams of light erupted from the demon, causing the ice on its body to shatter and melt. The ground beneath it cratered, knocking Evan backwards. In midair, he stabbed his blade into the ground, halting his movement and bracing himself against the oncoming rush of air.

Meanwhile, Alicia had already closed the distance between her and the demon. She swung her leg upward in a kick. The demon quickly grabbed her leg, gripping it tightly, smoke rising as the flames seared the demon's palm. As Alicia struggled to pull free, the demon thrust its fist forward, striking her chest. With a burst of light, she was blown backwards, gritting her teeth as another surge of electricity ran through her body.

The demon quickly clapped its hands together, forming a dense aura of light and sparks. As it pulled its hands apart, a line of light stretched out, connecting both palms together, gaining shape as a surging spear. The demon grasped it in its hand, swinging it through the air and pointing at Alicia.

Evan watched as the demon dashed forward, flying through the air and clashing with Alicia. He looked down at his sword. The ice encasing his arm had begun to spread further up to his elbow and, across his body, smaller patches of ice had begun to form.

"This form is dangerous…" Evan exhaled. "I need to get moving."

He gazed out at the battlefield. Everywhere he had stepped had left patches of ice along the ground. Even now, beneath him, the ground was being covered by ice. He closed his eyes, inhaling and exhaling slowly as his whole body slowly sunk into ice.

Meanwhile, Alicia was matching the demon, blow for blow.

"What's wrong?!" The demon shrieked, stabbing its light spear forward and grazing Alicia's side. "You've been slowing down!"

Alicia thrust her arm forward, hitting nothing but air as the demon gracefully avoided the blow and retaliated, stabbing its spear toward Alicia. The impact against her gut forced her into the ground.

She laid on her back, looking up at the hovering demon. It was right: every traded blow left her increasingly numb. She had been shocked numerous times, and yet, the burns she had been inflicted seemed to heal almost instantaneously. Conversely, along her own body were various burns and bruises, her technique a double-edge sword. She exhaled, watching as the demon descended upon her.

"I see," the demon murmured. "You two are special indeed. However, you're left alone now. The boy has probably already abandoned you."

"Just do it already then!" Alicia cried out, spitting blood at the demon.

She closed her eyes, and thought, *this is fine. This demon was beyond us from the start. I'm okay with dying, as long as Evan can live. I guess I'll be coming to see you sooner than we thought, sis.*

A sudden wailing echoed through the air. Alicia opened her eyes to see a familiar blade protruding from the demon's chest. As the blade was withdrawn, the demon spun around, stabbing its spear forward. Evan immediately parried, his blade of ice shattering as the spear collided with it, sending shards of ice through the air and spreading along the ground.

The demon sneered as his spear continued forward. It pierced through the air as Evan sank into the ice beneath his feet. The demon stared in awe.

It glanced around, noticing various patches of ice along the ground.

It suddenly groaned in agony as it was pushed forward, flames spreading along its back. Meanwhile, Alicia had risen to her feet, facing the demon as it turned to look at her.

"Just die already!" The demon shouted, moving to stab her with its spear.

Suddenly it found itself falling face-first onto the ground. As it struggled to stand, it realized its legs had been hacked off at the knees. Its head reared to see Evan standing behind it, atop a patch of ice. It pushed itself off the ground, flapping its wings and taking to the sky.

"I see," it breathed heavily. "He uses the ice as a pathway."
Its legs had already begun to regenerate.

Evan turned to Alicia. "We need to end this with the next attack," he stressed.

Alicia nodded. "I agree."

The aura around Alicia had significantly waned, and the burns had spread more rapidly along her skin. Evan wasn't much better off. The ice had continued to spread along his body, further reaching up his right arm toward his shoulder.

"Fools!" The demon screamed. "You took your power to that extreme, thinking you could beat me?! Really, you've ended up beating yourselves!"

"Plan?" Alicia asked, glancing at Evan.

"I'll freeze him, then you hit it with everything you have left," Evan explained.

Alicia nodded as she closed her eyes.

What little of her aura was left shifted and began to flow into her hands.

Evan closed his eyes, exhaling as the ice began to spread faster. It climbed up his shoulder, spreading along his upper back and erupting out as a pair of frozen wings.

Alicia glanced at Evan tepidly, the ice spreading even faster at this point.

"I won't be able to contain it for long." Evan grimaced. "Be ready."

He shot himself upward toward the demon, flapping his wings to build up speed. The demon hovered in place, waiting, and a spear of light in each hand.

Evan thrust his sword forward as he came within reach. The demon sneered, matching his attack with its own. The spearhead clashed with the tip of the sword, halting the two attacks in place.

The demon hesitated as Evan rotated his body, pushing off with his wings to take to the creature's back. His left arm quickly solidified with a fresh coat of ice, a second sword forming in his free hand. Immediately, he swung the blade into the demon's spine, hurtling it into the ground and crashing against the hard surface.

Meanwhile, Evan had already made his descent, moving toward the fallen demon.

Its body wavered as it took to its feet. As Evan closed the distance, a spear of light flew past him, grazing his cheek. *Off the mark*, he thought.

He swung his sword down, the demon parrying with his remaining spear. The two weapons now held one another in place.

"I've won!" The demon exclaimed. "Look at yourself!

Both of Evan's arms, his upper body, parts of his neck and lower body had become encased in ice.

"All I have to do is hold out," the demon sneered. "Then you will freeze to death."

Evan smirked, stomping his foot onto the ground. A path of ice spread forward, enveloping the demon's feet. It quickly broke itself free.

"Foo —"

In that instant, Evan had bypassed the spear of light, stabbing the creature in the chest with both of his blades.

The demon gasped, held in place as ice began to spread across its entire body. It gritted its teeth, thrusting its own spear into Evan's exposed stomach. The ice had left him numb, so numb that he felt no pain. As a result, only specks of blood managed to escape from his open mouth. *My insides must already have started to freeze over*, he thought, but it was too late to turn back. He braced his body as the ice encasing him shifted, receding from his skin and transferring into the demon.

As the ice left his body, he clapped his hands together. All at once, the ice erupted, and branches of ice spread out in all directions, extending in the sky and rooting into the ground. As a result, the demon was frozen in place at the center of the ice.

Breathing heavily, Evan stumbled backwards. Slowly, he made his way toward Alicia.

She smirked, placing her pointer fingers and thumbs together to form a diamond between her hands. The entirety of her flame aura contracted into a condensed orb in its center.

It suddenly shot forward, crashing into the prison of ice. Several explosions chained together as a giant dome of flame encompassed the area around the demon. Evan and Alicia lay along the ground, holding one another to brace against the force from the explosions that passed over them in waves. As it faded, all that remained was excess steam rising from the demon's corpse at the bottom of a crater.

Evan, skin tinted blue and bruised, lay next to the burned and battered Alicia. They both watched in awe, breathing heavily as they began to help one another to their feet.

"Is it… is it over?" Alicia panted.

Evan stared at the wasteland before them. *It's finally over*, he thought. His vision became increasingly blurry as he collapsed to the ground, the hole in his gut still open. Alicia immediately knelt next to him, placing her hands over the open wound on his body. A light red aura surrounded her hands and slowly spread out around him.

"I'm not as good a healer as you," Alicia groaned. "But there must be something I can do. You aren't allowed to leave me alone here!"

Tears flowed from her eyes as the light around her hands became brighter and brighter. She was pouring everything she had into him. She hadn't realized it yet, but the red star tattooed on her breast began to tatter. From where the edges met, it split down the middle and began to be scratched away, leaving only half of a star tattooed on her skin.

The wound in his stomach began to close at a rapid pace and his skin returned to its natural color. His body continued to recover, but unbeknownst to either of them, a change had occurred within Evan's body. His usual blue flower tattoo had transformed, becoming a deep purple with now six heart-shaped petals.

Alicia exhaled, her body shaking as she struggled to stand on her own. Suddenly, she felt a familiar pain, as sparks spread through her whole body. A large gash opened up from her hip to her shoulder. Before she realized it, she was falling backwards, looking up at the demon above her.

In its right hand was a newly formed spear of light. Its left arm, meanwhile, had slowly began to regenerate.

"You've pushed me far further than I've ever had to go." The demon glared at the girl. "I will savor taking your soul."

It reached down with its newly formed arm, only to grasp at nothing. It watched in awe as its severed arm spiraled through the air before erupting in purple flames, incinerating. Evan stood next to Alicia, glaring at the demon.

"How —" the demon began.

The demon was suddenly forced backwards, crashing and sliding along the ground. Evan lowered his arm, kneeling next to Alicia. He placed his hand over Alicia's open wound, and from his palm, a small, purple ember dropped down. Sinking into her gash, his aura expanded, flowing through her. Before long, all of her wounds had been completely healed.

Alicia opened her eyes to see Evan above her.

"Stay here," he told her.

As he took a step forward, his body disappeared.

The demon took to its feet, its arm healing slower than ever, as Evan appeared before it.

"This is the true ending," Evan declared.

The demon glared at him, condensing his spear of light into an aura that wrapped around its hand. It raised its arm, and with a swift motion, swung it back down. With that, a pillar of light fell down toward Evan.

However, he simply raised his arm, catching the energy into his open palm. The energy circulated and sparked, and as Evan focused, he condensed the energy into a perfect sphere. He held it out, presenting it to the demon like a gift.

The demon stared in awe as the orb of white light was surrounded by purple flames. As the orb condensed further, it became stained by a pitch blackness.

Evan raised his arm, pointing his open palm at the demon. In a sudden flash, a black wave spread out, consuming the demon. As it passed over the creature, the energy carved deep into the demon's flesh.

Evan stood, watching the demon keel over. Its wounds weren't even healing at this point.

"No!" It shouted. "It can't end this way!"

"You've terrorized people for too long," Evan explained. "It's time for you to pay up."

The demon, barely holding itself up, cackled. "It's not over!"

Evan watched carefully, waiting to see how the creature would react.

"It'll never end," the demon howled. "Even if you disintegrate this body. I will live on!"

Evan smirked. "I highly doubt that."

With a flick of his wrist, purple flames began to form all over the demon's body. They slowly picked up speed, swirling and trapping the demon in a condensed whirlpool of flames. The demon struggled, burning and being pulled in all directions within the flow of flames.

Alicia stepped up next to Evan. "Is it stuck in there forever?"

"No…" Evan shook his head. "Unfortunately, whatever you did to me is about to wear off. I can already feel this power slipping away."

"Then what?" Alicia asked, clenching her fist.

"Don't worry." Evan smiled. "I can't feel its body resisting anymore." The flames dispersed, and a tiny black object emerged, floating in the air, before falling into the ground. Evan and Alicia made their way over to where the demon had been.

Evan knelt down, looking at the object. It was rounded on the top, with a sharp spear-like head pointing out from the bottom.

"What is it?" Alicia asked.

Evan poked it with a finger, before grasping it and pulling it out of the ground. Holding the jewel in his hand, a familiar voice filed his head.

"It's not over," the voice echoed. "This core will allow me to live on. After a little time, I will be born again."

Evan glared at the gem.

"What?" Alicia placed her hand on Evan's shoulder.

"We have to try and destroy this," Evan insisted.

"Futile," the voice rang.

Evan opened his palm, and blue crystals slowly began to gather into a single point within his hand. As an orb formed, it quickly shattered, and Evan exhaled feverishly.

"Shit!" He sighed. "Do you have any energy?"

Alicia shook her head.

"No matter," the voice snarled. "In this form I am invulnerable. And soon, I will hatch, and then you will be dead."

Evan stared at the gem.

"What is it?" Alicia asked.

"It's speaking to me," Evan explained. "It said this is its core, and it'll soon hatch."

"We have no way to stop it." Alicia gritted her teeth. "This sucks."

"If we have a vessel…" Evan murmured.

Alicia glanced at him.

"Something to contain the growth," Evan went on. "Something to control it."

He shifted his hand, glancing at the structure of the gem.

"Wait!" Alicia shouted.

Evan turned to face her.

"What will happen to you?" Alicia asked, stepping closer to Evan.

"I'm not sure," Evan whispered.

Alicia closed her eyes, tears beginning to well.

"Then don't!" She shouted. "We can face it together! We can…"

Evan placed his hand on her cheek, smiling wider than he ever had.

"I love you," he said before kissing Alicia.

Their lips entwined, both trying to overcome the other. They seemed to kiss forever.

However, before Alicia realized it, Evan had stepped away from her. She watched, tears flowing from her eyes as he plunged the gem into his chest.

Everything went black for Evan. He slipped off of his feet, falling. He reached upward, as his body continued to fall into nothingness. He felt as though he was being pulled further and further down. As he fell, a voice rang through his head.

"Heh, heh, heh…" it cackled. "Are you sad? Are you lonely? Surrounded by nothing, with nothing to grasp onto. It was beyond foolish to try and control me in this manner. In the end, I will take hold of your body, of your mind. Know that I will possess them."

With that, Evan was lost in a sea of black.

Epilogue
Celina

Humanity has slowly begun to rebuild itself. Most of those who had their powers during the initial assault on Earth have either been killed or committed suicide. Society, or what is left of it, has finally banded together. Cities have slowly been rebuilt over time by the combined effort of the remnants of humanity. In order to survive, people have begun to look past just themselves.

Meanwhile, most of the remaining players who survived have gone into hiding to avoid the consequences of their actions. The world as a whole is tepidly moving towards a more peaceful horizon. However, that isn't to say that everyone is enjoying this serenity. A familiar scene unfolds in one developing city.

A boy with dark hair and fitted with leather armor faced a patrol of soldiers. They raised their rifles, firing upon him. The bullets sliced through the air before drilling into a sudden wall of solid stone. Within an instant, the wall cracked, and then shattered. The shards floated in midair briefly before darting forward, piercing through the soldier's bodies and killing them.

The boy advanced forward, slowly moving through the barren streets. He looked around, glaring at each building, becoming increasingly impatient. At this point, he had grown bored of tranquil villages.

He thrust his arm forward, pointing his open palm at a nearby building. The ground around the foundation shook as the building sank and crumbled into the earth. Meanwhile, screams echoed through the air. The residents, without a chance to react, were pulled into the earth with their home. He felt a twinge at his heart and sneered; he almost felt bad for them. After the fall of the first building, people had begun to take to the streets before attempting to flee from their once home. He moved effortlessly, destroying building after building. The echoing screams only fueled his delight as he left nothing but ruin in his wake.

"No sense in wasting any more time here," he stated, swinging his arm through the air, pointing his palm at the last building. "After this one, I'll go ahead and chase down the reside —"

He was cut off, in shock as he recognized his own forearm spiraling through the air before falling helplessly onto the dusty ground. Before he knew it, blood had begun to gush from the open wound. In a desperate attempt to stop the bleeding, he grabbed it with his free hand, his eyes frantically scanning the area.

"What the...?!" He screamed out in pain, falling to his knees.

"Just like a boy to flail about haphazardly," a cool voice rang through the air. "Only to end up limp and helpless."

Before him stood a slender girl fitted with a steel breastplate, and with neck-length, wavy, purple hair. She knelt down, grabbing the severed arm before taking to her feet once more, glaring at the child before her.

"Who are you?!" the boy screamed as blood spurted out of the stub from between his fingers.

She merely looked on in silence.

Slowly, the boy regained his composure, struggling to ease his heavy breathing. His eyes stung, holding back tears, as he glared intently at the girl.

"Do you…" She paused. "Need a hand?"

She smirked, holding up his severed forearm.

The boy lost it, his wails of fury and agony echoing through the area as he slammed his palm onto the ground. The earth before him began to give way as suddenly, jagged spires of condensed gravel and sand erupted from the ground, traveling in a line toward the girl.

She welcomed the attack, rushing forward to face it. As the next spire rose up to pierce her, it caught nothing but the empty space where she had once been.

"Behind you," she shouted.

The boy turned around just in time to see his severed arm come flying toward him. Frozen in shock by the gruesomeness of her assault, he could only watch in horror as his own arm struck him dead in the face.

Before he had realized it, the girl had sprung forward, closing the distance between the two. Her arm reached out, with her hand wrapped in a dense, sparking aura. Her attack stopped just short of the boy's chest. From this distance, he noticed her pointed ears protruding between various strands of hair. Eyes wide open, he watched as she slowly placed her palm onto the boy's chest. His body shook violently, and he felt his teeth clench together tightly as the electricity surged through his body. After what felt like an eternity, the boy went still, and collapsed onto the ground.

"Stay still," she whispered. "It's almost over."

She placed her open palm over the octagonal tattoo on the boy's neck. Slowly, a silvery, wispy aura surrounded the boy, before gathering and condensing into the girl's hand. The aura flowed up her arm, gathering at a single point on her forearm. Where there was once a blank patch of pale skin was now the familiar octagonal shape, leaving a permanent mark among various other shapes that littered her arm. As she moved her hand away, the space where the tattoo had been on the boy was now just empty, pale skin.

With that, she turned, walking away from the scene.

"W… wait!" the boy called out.

She halted in place, reluctantly replying, "What?"

"What did you do?!" the boy shouted, glaring at her.

She turned, looking down at him.

"I freed you," she explained. "Now you'll no longer be tempted by your power."

She raised her arm out in front of her, pulling her long sleeve up to reveal numerous tattoos along her forearm.

"You're not the first," she said. "And you probably won't be the last. The world is unstable at the moment, and we don't need people like you disrupting the peace."

The boy stared in awe, placing his hand on his neck.

"I never want to see you again," the girl stated coldly.

The boy's body sunk, his gaze falling to the ground. She once more turned from him, walking away.

"W…wait!" he shouted out desperately.

Exasperated, the girl stopped in her tracks. "What?"

"Just…just kill me," he murmured. "I've got nothing left to live for. I can't face what I've done. I'm liable to be killed if I show my face anywhere. I've stolen, raped, and killed so many. What am I even supposed to do now?"

The girl turned to face him.

"You chose this," she said. "Learn to deal with the consequences of your actions."

He lowered his head, the ground beneath him stained with tear after tear.

Pathetic, she thought. And, with that, she left.

From a young age, she had been groomed for combat. Some of her earliest memories included sparring with her mother and father. However, unlike those who had made pacts in order to gain their power, she had been born with it. She was a very young child when she had first realized she had the power to take what wasn't hers.

The girl skipped gleefully, a spring in her step as she moved alongside her mother. It was a rare occasion in which she got to spend time away from fighting. Today, the two were visiting a nearby town to get some shopping done. The town, fairly simplistic, was attached to the ruins of a once much larger city. Various buildings stood on either side of a stretch of dirt road. As they moved down the path, the two came across a group of people. A towering, leather-clad man stood before three wooden pillars. Pinned to each was a woman, naked, with numerous metal stakes gouged through various parts of their bodies. Blood ran down from the puncture wounds, staining their bodies, and dripping onto the ground over which they hung.

The girl's mother placed a hand on her daughter's shoulder, stepping out in front of her as the man's voice echoed throughout the area.

"Listen up!" he roared. "These bitches refused to do as I say! So, they are facing crimes of treason!"

The crowd watched, visibly uncomfortable, many averting their eyes to the cruelty before them.

"Who is it that protects everyone in this town?!" the man shouted before pausing for a moment. "That's right! ME! To defy me, is to endanger everyone living here!"

He stretched out his arm, facing his open palm toward the ground. "The punishment is death," he stated coolly.

The earth in front of him sank into a crater as sand and dirt flowed together, condensing into a long, black rod. Wrapping his hand around it, he withdrew the rod from the earth and turned toward the hostages, sneering in delight. Many in the audience shuffled uncomfortably, exasperated but fearful, while some of the braver few had already begun to leave. It was clear that no one intended to stand up to this villain.

The girl's mother glared at the man, and yet, she was in the same position. She could no longer afford to think only of herself. She let out a sigh of frustration and turned back to her daughter, only to realize that her daughter had disappeared.

As the man turned back to check the reaction of the audience, he watched in awe as a small child darted through the air, closing in on him at breakneck speed. Despite this, he was quick to react.

"Fool!" he shouted, hurling the metallic rod toward the incoming child.

The girl, surrounded by a light blue aura and wrapped in sparks, spun through the air, easily avoiding the projectile. As she closed in on the man, she thrust her arm forward, punching a hole in his chest.

His eyes had begun to roll into the back of his head as blood erupted from his mouth. The girl's arm reached deep into his chest cavity, her fist protruding from his back. Her aura began to fluctuate, and after suddenly flickering to a pale white color, it instinctively wrapped around the man. It seemed to pull and tug at his now limp body as what remained of his energy flowed out of him and into the girl.

As the aura faded, a black cross appeared, tattooed onto the girl's forearm. The man slid off the girl's arm as he fell to the ground, dead. She stood over him; her entire right arm covered in a deep crimson liquid. She suddenly came back to reality, taking a step back and looking down at the fresh corpse before her, confused and growing increasingly frightened.

Before she had realized it, her mother was standing by her side. The pink-haired woman spun her daughter around to face her, and without hesitation, slapped the frightened girl.

"Don't ever do anything so reckless ever again!" she yelled, squeezing her daughter tightly.

That was the beginning. Ever since that day, she had ventured out, making use of her training and taking powers away from those who abused them. While her mother was reluctant to let her go at first, it was her father who had convinced her otherwise. "It would be necessary," she remembered him saying. At this point, the tattoos had even begun to spread up to her shoulder, creeping toward her chest. Her collection was a testament to her dedication, and she felt as though each time she cleansed the world of another deviant, she was another step closer to making her parents proud.

Before long, she stood on a small grassy hill, looking down at a familiar cabin beside a lake. Her home.

As she made her way inside the cabin, a heavy waft of various spices filled her nose: the familiar smell of her mother's cooking. She turned the corner at the end of the hall to find a slender, pale-skinned women with flowing pink hair running down her back. The ends of her hair reached just over a thin black string, tied around her waist. The woman turned to reveal her pale green eyes, a faint smile, pointed ears, and a black apron atop plain-looking clothes.

Alicia smiled warmly. "Welcome home."

The girl nodded flatly.

Alicia smirked at her daughter's disinterest, turning her attention back to the stove. She took care to stir the pot of simmering liquid a bit before breaking the silence.

"It'll be done soon," Alicia declared.

The girl shrugged. "Where's Dad?"

Alicia groaned, turning to face her daughter.

"It's always about your father," she pouted. "Aren't you happy to see your darling mother?"

"O-oh…of course." The girl smiled weakly.

Alicia glared at her, eyeing over her daughter for a minute before pointing to a nearby door.

"He's outside," she sighed.

The girl nodded, making her way to the door. As she placed her hand on the knob, she heard her mother whisper,

"Be careful…"

Outside was a man with broad shoulders and thick, dark hair that stopped just below his ears. As he held out his arm, a small blue light levitated over his broad hand. It slowly fell, sinking into his palm. A small patch of ice formed, steadily spreading out across his hand and up along his arm. He closed his eyes, inhaling as his entire body slowly became encased in a sheet of ice. As it spread up his neck, it stopped at the edge of his chin, cheeks, and forehead. He exhaled, slowly opening his golden, gleaming eyes.

He seemed to be doing calisthenics, flexing his arms and legs. The ice seemed to stretch as he moved, his mobility remaining without being compromised by the ice. As he stepped forward, the ground beneath him began to freeze over, spreading outward from where he stood. Simultaneously, the air around him seemed to have cooled down significantly, as his body was enveloped in a thin cloud of frost and frigid air.

"Father!" a familiar voice called out.

He turned to see his daughter standing behind him, and smiled gently. "Stay there, honey."

He once more closed his eyes, and as he exhaled again, the ice slowly began to recede from his body, flowing back toward a pale blue flower tattoo on the back of his palm. Once the ice around his body completely vanished, he made his way toward his daughter.

"Wait!" Her voice rang out.

He watched her tepidly.

"Today is the day that I defeat you, old man!" she shouted, pointing at him.

"Alright, then." He smiled weakly.

She smirked, clenching her fists. The air around her began to shift and spark. A blue aura flowed around her body, sparks jumping from one point on her body to another. She opened her fist, a concentrated surge of energy wrapped around her hand, stretching out past her fingers and converging, forming the shape of a spearhead. The sparks around her sped up, and the ground beneath her cracked as she crouched down, disappearing instantaneously.

Evan smirked back, flexing his hand. A single shard of ice formed in his palm. All at once, it expanded upward into a large crystal sword. The blade — nearly as long as his own body — extended out from a hilt that consisted of an intricate weave of ice and gems.

In an instant, his daughter appeared inches from his body. As she did, he gripped the handle of his blade and swung it through the air, cutting into her stomach. She gasped as blood poured from her open wound. The force of the blow pushed her backwards, her heels planting firmly into the ground as she slid back. Once she came to a stop, she knelt down, placing her hand over the cut along her midriff.

Her breathing had become labored, and the energy around her body had all but faded. A light blue aura surrounded her hand, and then expanded over the wound on her stomach. Slowly the gash began to close. She looked up to see the man was slowly advancing towards her.

"Foolish child," a deep voice echoed in the man's head. "Your arrogance shall be the end of your daughter."

The man raised his arm, pointing the blade up into the air. A faint black mist flowed around his body, and the usually blue tattoo on the back of his hand had now been stained black.

"Die —"

Suddenly, his body was engulfed in flames. The sword he once held quickly shattered and melted away, his skin beginning to char. Smoke rose off his body as he fell his knees. He breathed heavily, looking up to see a pair of hate-filled eyes. Before those was an arm stretched out, with an open palm inches from his face.

"Is today the day…?" The voice wavered. "Is today the day…I have to kill you, Evan?"

Her eyes began to water, as a small point of flame formed in-between his face and her open palm.

"…wait…" Evan managed to groan out.

The golden hue in his eyes faded away, returning to their normal shade of brown.

"Who are you?" Alicia's voice boomed, the point of light expanding into a condensed orb.

"Evan…" he coughed. "Evan Sherwood… your husband."

The orb slowly shrank before dissipating. Alicia knelt down, wrapping her arms around him as tears flowed freely from her eyes.

This scene had become a normal occurrence.

The younger, purple-haired girl slowly stood up, her wounds fully healed. Despite her power, and despite her training, she had never once beaten her father. She often challenged him, having been told she would eventually need to surpass him. The worst thing about it was usually her mother's reaction after the fact.

"Are you okay, Dad?" the girl asked, standing over her parents.

"I'm fine," Evan exhaled.

"I told you to be careful!" Alicia shouted.

"Calm down," Evan exhaled. "We're all well aware that she may have to face that seriously one day."

Alicia gritted her teeth, tightening her grip on Evan.

He began to stand, Alicia supporting him under her own weight.

The girl lowered her eyes, averting her gaze away from her parents.

After a moment, Alicia sighed, letting go of Evan and reaching out to her daughter to embrace her.

Evan smiled weakly, his wounds having already begun to heal.

"You've improved," he stated.

Alicia and her daughter parted, turning to look at him.

"You say that," the girl sighed. "However, I've yet to land even a single blow on you."

"There is no need to rush," Evan explained. "We should enjoy what time we have together as a family, after all. There is more to life than constant fighting."

The girl nodded, barely registering the note of advice.

"How about we just go enjoy dinner," he insisted. "Then you can tell us about how your morning went."

Alicia smiled, turning around and making her way back to the house. Evan walked alongside his daughter, both following behind Alicia.

"I can sense your fragility," a familiar voice rang through Evan's head. "This is all just about over. Soon, your body will be mine, and you will watch as your family lies dead at your feet. You have done nothing but stall the inevitable. All this time, for nothing! Hehehe…"

Evan placed a hand on his aching forehead, his daughter's gaze immediately focusing on him. The thing seemed to talk to him more and more lately, and it was certainly true that he felt he was barely hanging onto his own consciousness. He had hoped that in training his daughter, she would be able to stop him if he ever got out of control. However, it was still too soon for her.

"I'm okay." He smiled weakly as they made their way inside the house.

The trio sat around a set, wooden table. Spread across were a few large vessels containing mixed greens, a pale broth, fluffy bread, and charred strips of browned meat. The group took turns plating their own food before beginning to eat together.

"I managed to collect another tattoo today," the girl said between her initial bites. "I have no idea how many more people are left, but I have quite the collection at this point. It's almost inconvenient."

"Well," Evan began, swallowing a bite of meat. "No one said you had to steal so many…"

"If people weren't so terrible…" The girl stared solemnly at her dad. "Then I wouldn't need to. This guy was walking through a town, causing rampant destruction."

Alicia chuckled. "Who knows where you get your sense of justice from."

The girl looked from her mother, back to her father. "You guys, obviously."

"I find that hard to believe," Evan remarked, thinking back on his own adventures.

"Me too," Alicia snorted, caught off guard.

The family continued eating, talking about their respective days. It was a quiet reprieve from their chaotic lives.

"I'm going to get a little more exercise," the girl said, finishing her plate.

"Sounds good." Evan nodded, still working on some of his food.

She excused herself, making her way back outside. Evan and Alicia remained at the table, still eating.

"How are you feeling?" Alicia asked, wasting no time in probing her husband.

"Heh," Evan chuckled. "Nothing gets by you. It seems like it's closer than ever. I'm not sure how much longer it'll be, but I think it'll be soon."

Alicia sighed, looking down at her plate. Before she had realized it, Evan was beside her. His hands rested gently on her shoulders, leaning down and pressing his forehead against her own.

"I knew it was coming." Alicia's voice wavered.

"That doesn't make it any easier," Evan exhaled.

They remained silent for a few moments until Alicia finally asked, "What are we going to do?"

Meanwhile, their daughter remained outside, standing in the very spot where she had found her father earlier.

She closed her eyes, slowly breathing in, filling her lungs to the brim with air before just as slowly exhaling to free it from her body. *Dad's power seems like an insurmountable wall*, she thought. She had spent most of her life training and fighting; her arm was proof enough of that. From her wrist to her shoulder — and beginning to spread out across her collar and chest — were countless tattoos.

As she opened her eyes, she took a step forward, raising her forearm as though to parry an incoming blow. She followed this movement by another step forward, thrusting her fist straight through the air. She continued to move as though she was sparring an invisible foe, all the while thinking. *If only I could figure out how to activate all my tattoos simultaneously. Tapping into that much power would surely make me invincible.* So far, in desperate situations, she had managed to blend the power of a couple tattoos at once. Yet, pulling it off at will still eluded her.

A familiar voice cut off her train of thought.

"Seems like you're definitely getting more limber," her mother's voice rang through the air.

She turned to see her mother encased in a black leather garment. A large piece was fixed over her chest and torso, while her arms and legs appeared to be wrapped by numerous bands and belts.

"How about sparring with me a little bit?" Alicia asked, walking towards her daughter.

"Can't it wait until some other time?" she insisted, trying to spare her mother's feelings. "I'm trying to figure something out here."

"A new technique?" Alicia inquired, studying her daughter's face.

"Something like that," she murmured.

Alicia smirked. "Even more of a reason to have an actual sparring partner. There are certain things that can't be learned unless you're actually fighting someone. Not everything can be self-taught."

Her daughter sighed, nodding her head and reluctantly agreeing.

"Besides," Alicia whispered to herself, "you should spend some time with me too, while you still can."

The purple-haired girl didn't seem to realize what her mother had said as she took a stance in front of her. Alicia smiled weakly, doing the same and watching her daughter carefully.

The girl's body sparked, closing the distance practically instantaneously. Her fist thrust forward, moving through an empty space.

"Where'd she—" the girl looked around frantically, before getting the wind knocked out of her.

Alicia had appeared, crouched near the ground, her fist planted firmly into her daughter's stomach. She smirked, taking a step back and watching her daughter fall to her knees, breathing heavily. "Nice try. Boosting your base stats with an aura — great idea, if I do say so myself."

As the girl regained her composure, slowly rising to her feet, she felt an intense heat permeating through the air. Her eyes faced forward to see her mother wrapped entirely in an aura of flames, with two protruding, fiery wings. Her body froze in fear as she stood in awe.

"Still think you can just write me off?" Alicia asked, taking a step towards her daughter.

Her daughter exhaled, the sparks flowing around her body intensifying. She clapped her hands together as simultaneously, the sky above her began to swirl with dark clouds. A loud boom crashed through the air. With a sudden flash, a bolt of lightning dropped from the sky. She unclasped her hands, raising a free hand to catch the lightning. Alicia watched as her daughter held a sparking, ball of light in her bare hand.

"I doubt you'll be able to dodge this, Mom!" the girl shouted.

Alicia watched as her daughter thrusted her arm forward, the ball of light burst, and electricity sprang forward, taking the shape of a dragon. It danced through the air, weaving from one point to another as it moved towards her. As it closed in, she reached her arm out open her palm to meet its nose. The creature of light halted in place, unable to pierce through her flaming aura. She clamped her fingers down, grabbing its snout. Then, as she released her grip the beast shattered into small balls of light, dispersing in thin air.

The girl watched her attack shatter as her mother stood unfazed.

"I've got at least twice the experience as you when it comes to fighting," Alicia stated, her gaze focused on her daughter. "So, how about you let me in on what it is you're trying to figure out."

Meanwhile, Evan stood outside the front of their quaint home.

"It's time…" A dark, brooding voice echoed through his head.

"Maybe," Evan sighed. "But I won't let it happen easily."

His head throbbed, and he felt a sudden stinging pain shooting through his whole body. He fell to his knees, clenching his teeth to endure the pain. He had never felt something so intense in his whole life. His mind thought back to the first day, when he received his tattoo, watching Emma die in his arms, and barreling through so many bodies to reach his goal.

"Face it," the voice sneered. "This is the path you chose, the moment you allowed yourself to chase after that hollowed dream."

Perhaps it was right, Evan thought. He had spread his fair share of destruction and chaos. He had taken lives of those who hadn't deserved it. He followed the darkness as far as he could in the hopes of achieving his dream. Perhaps, it was simply his time to pay up.

"Yes…" the voice hissed. "Just give in; it'll be, much, much easier…"

"…no…" Evan's voice wavered. "I can't give up on what I have now. I don't want to."

Alicia had saved him, and together they managed to build something from nothing. They even had a precious daughter to think about now. He wasn't quite ready to go yet. The image of his daughter's face appeared in his mind, before slowly fading to black.

A long silence hung between Alicia and her daughter, who were now standing closer together, no longer amassed in any aura.

"I see," Alicia finally said. "Activating multiple abilities does make sense. As long as you have an understanding of how to do them individually, I'm not sure what would be holding you back from activating more than one."

"Well," the girl started. "It's more like…I can't access them. Other than my own abilities, trying to reach for others is like fishing in the darkness. I can take them quite easily, but once they are contained in me, they still feel rather far away."

"Ah!" Alicia exclaimed. "You're taking them for the sake of taking them, and not with the understanding of them."

"Uh, what?" the girl asked, clearly confused.

"How do I explain —" Alicia began, before she was interrupted by a loud *crack*.

The two turned in time to see a bolt of black energy fall from the sky, crashing into the cabin. The shockwave from the explosion pushed the girls backward off their feet, and where the cabin once stood was a mass of flames. Alicia stood up, watching as a figure emerged from the flames, slowly walking towards them.

As Evan reached the two, Alicia could see thick, dark circles around his shimmering golden eyes. It was time.

"RUN!" Alicia shouted to her daughter, before quickly wrapping herself in her usual flaming aura.

"Heh," the demon sneered. "You think that trick will work on me twice?"

"We've been preparing for you." Alicia grinned back. "I don't have to beat you myself. I'll just burn a hole in my dumbass husband and pull you out of him. Right now, you're even weaker than you were then, I won't give you the time to incubate and revive. Together, we can easily seal you again."

"You seem to be more clueless than I realized," the demon retorted. "I've completely corrupted his mind. It's not that I'm living inside of him, like with other vessels. I *am* him. Evan is already dead, even before I shed his skin and return to my true form."

Alicia hesitated for a moment. Was Evan withholding information from her this whole time? That wouldn't be unlike him. For a moment, her resolve wavered.

"Besides..." the demon continued, a familiar rod of black energy forming in his free hand. He pointed it toward her daughter. "I have no intention of fighting you directly."

Alicia panicked, turning to see that her daughter still hadn't fled.

"I TOLD YOU TO RU —" Alicia was cut off as the spearhead from the energy rod pierced through her chest.

She coughed, as blood began to run down her lips and chin. She let out a cry of agony as the spear was pulled from her body, and she collapsed to the ground. Her aura had all but faded, and she noticed a chill in her chest. Looking down and placing a hand to her wound, she saw fragments of frost and ice. It seemed as though he was integrating Evan's abilities. *Perhaps what he was saying wasn't a complete lie*, she thought. *He probably had to mix ice into the attack to pierce my aura, but luckily that's helped slow the bleeding.* Her hand was already soaked in a light aura, hoping to fix the wound quickly.

"As if I'll let you!" The demon shouted, moving to impale the woman once more.

However, before it could land a killing blow, it was suddenly blown back, crashing into the ground and skidding back several feet.

Alicia watched in awe as her daughter stood over her.

"Hurry up and finish healing," she called out. "Then we can save Dad together."

"Of course." Alicia smiled weakly before refocusing her efforts on healing her wounds.

By the time the demon took to its feet, the girl had already closed the gap. Her palm, wrapped in sparking energy, sliced through the air, cutting into her father's stomach. The demon, barely reacting in time, leapt back to avoid a fatal blow. The scene had shifted; it placed its hand over the shallow wound, watching the girl carefully.

"You realize," the demon began, "you're only hurting your father's body."

"Shut up," the girl replied. "As if my father would be hurt by something so weak. If he was in control, he would've never gotten hit by that. I can easily defeat you and get him back at this rate. Don't bother trying to squirm about."

This girl, the demon thought, scowling.

Before it could raise another argument, she had already gone on the offensive. She moved so quickly, as though she was simply appearing at the most convenient position for an attack. She slipped in and out of the space around the demon, swinging her arm about with precision, each slash cutting away at parts of her father's body. Eventually the demon found itself all but crippled, looking up as the girl loomed over him, Alicia now standing tall next to her daughter.

"W-wait…" Evan's voice rang out.

"Evan?" Alicia was taken back.

"Y-yeah," Evan coughed. "I-it's still m-me."

The girl looked her father over, before allowing the aura held in her hand to dissipate.

Alicia took a sigh of relief.

"FOOLS!" the demon's voice resumed. "IT IS TOO LATE!"

From Evan's widened mouth reached a long, bony arm. Its claws grabbed at the two girls. They quickly leapt back, building up their respective auras. The demon pulled itself up and stepped out of Evan as though slinking out of a sleeping bag. Evan's body, tattered and torn, lay on the ground beneath it. He suddenly coughed, struggling to open his eyes.

"Dad's still alive!" the girl shouted.

"JUST DIE ALREADY!" the demon shouted, turning and raising its arm to finish off the man.

Alicia, wrapped in flames, shot forward, grabbing the creature and darting off into the distance.

The girl quickly came to her father's side and, wrapping both her hands in a healing aura, began to move along the various wounds on her father's body.

"S-stop…" Evan managed to breath out.

"WHY?!" she shouted. "I can still save you!"

"N-no…" Evan coughed. "It's too late for m-me. S-so, quickly… t-take my t-tattoo for y-yourself."

Tears began to well in her eyes as she watched her father struggle to lift his arm. She reached out, grabbing his hand with her own.

"No!" She cried. "It's not fair."

Evan smiled weakly. "I kn-know. B-but, you have to be s-strong, and s-save your m-mother."

Evan had never felt so weak before in his entire life. It was as though he was a puddle on the ground, only able to look up but unable to reach out. Here at the end, he wasn't even able to comfort his own daughter. It was all he could muster to breathe out his last words.

"N-never forget…I love you."

With that, she wrapped her arms around him and yelled as loud as she could in frustration and despair. Seemingly unconscious to her, the wispy aura had already wrapped itself around her and her father, sapping the remaining energy from him and transferring it to her.

Her heart sank, as tears continued to stream down her face. It wasn't supposed to end like this. She wanted to defeat him, not lose him. What was everything she was doing up until this point even for? *What's the sense in having all this power if I can't even use it when I need it?* she thought.

After a few minutes, having calmed down slightly, she took to her feet. Her eyes, red and puffy, looked down at her lifeless father. Then, noticing an unfamiliar stinging on the back of her right hand, turned to see his light blue flower tattoo etched into her skin. She clenched her fist and looked up at the sky. After exhaling, she closed her eyes, she could feel something pulling at her. She turned her gaze toward its direction and made haste.

Alicia stood, exhausted, across from the ever-growing demon. Her black leather gear had become torn, and along her body were numerous shallow cuts and bruises. As her breathing labored, she could tell she was already at her limit. "It seems you're the one who has grown significantly weaker." The demon scowled, now looming over her.

It's not exactly wrong, she thought to herself.

"That man is dead," the demon taunted.

Alicia closed her eyes, sighing. "It's alright — I'll be joining him soon."

The demon smiled. "Glad to see you've accepted it."

"Don't get too excited." Alicia smirked. "You'll be joining both of us."

It clearly wasn't amused, leaping forward and closing the distance between the two.

"Die!" it shouted, slashing its arm through the air and cutting through her abdomen.

Blood spewed from her mouth and gut, as she fell backwards. *So fast*, she thought, looking up at the creature from on her back. She closed her eyes, readying herself to be finished off. Instead, a familiar voice called out.

"Wake up, Mom."

Alicia opened her eyes to see her daughter kneeling over her, starting to heal her wounds. She looked over to see the demon was several feet away yet watching cautiously.

"Don't worry about me..." Alicia said weakly. "Just…focus on that thing."

"Not going to happen," the girl mustered, tears flowing freely from her eyes. "I already lost Dad. I'm not going to lose you too."

"Sorry we put all this on you." Alicia lowered her eyes. "I know it's not fair to expect so much."

"Stop talking," the girl insisted. "Focus on getting better."

"Ce —" Alicia began.

A loud crack echoed through the air, as a pillar of black light fell from the sky towards the two girls. Before it could land, the girl immediately stood up, raising her arm and catching the energy in her bare hand. She clenched her fist, condensing the darkness allowing it to envelope her hand. As she turned to face the demon, Alicia caught a glimpse of her daughter's hand, seeing Evan's tattoo. Alicia smiled weakly, closing her eyes.

The girl glared at the demon, who was staring in awe, its arm still raised in the air from calling down the attack.

"T-that's…" the demon began.

"Stay out of this," the girl shouted, swinging her arm forward and throwing the condensed energy at it.

As the energy left her hand, it changed shape, jumping from point to point like a bolt of lightning. It reached the demon before it had time to react, piercing a hole straight through its bony chest, and knocking it backwards onto the ground.

The girl immediately turned away, refocusing her attention on her mother. She had already lost one parent; she had no intention of losing the other.

"Listen," Alicia insisted. "It's too late. I know you don't want to give up, but your father and I knew this would happen someday. We were prepared for it."

"That's bullshit," she shouted. "*I* wasn't prepared! If you guys were just going to roll over and die, then why did you even have me?"

Alicia's voice wavered as she placed her hand on her daughter's cheek. "I'm sorry, honey."

The girl's tears began to fall onto her mother's body as she leaned down to hug her.

"It's not fair," she wailed. "I didn't ask for this!"

Alicia felt a pull in her chest; she hadn't felt such pain in a long time. Not since she lost Rose. Her daughter was right: they had simply thrust this burden onto her and expected her to understand. They had done their best with what they had, but it was hardly a conventional upbringing. *I guess we were only fooling ourselves into thinking we were a real family*, she thought.

"If we had done nothing," Alicia's voice cracked, "you wouldn't have ever had a chance to be born."

The girl's heart sank as she watched the tears flow from her mother's eyes. Just earlier she had been pushing her mother away, and now she was watching her slip through her hands.

"What am I supposed to do without both of you?" she cried.

"You'll be free." Alicia smiled weakly. "You won't be shackled by this terrible burden. Please, forgive your foolish parents for what they've done. The fear of losing you was greater than we could've imagined. We knew we had to do something to keep you safe. We just wanted to make sure you would be able to survive."

The girl put her hand on her mother's chest, and, as with her father, instinctively the wispy aura appeared and wrapped around the two. Alicia could feel a pull, as though the very life was being drained from her and flowed into her daughter. As she felt her consciousness begin to fade away, she smiled one final time.

"I love you, honey."

The girl's eyes burned more than they ever had in her whole life. At this point, she didn't think she had any tears left to cry. The pain was so great, she didn't even notice the additional stinging on her right hand. Her father's tattoo had changed, blooming into six purple, heart shaped petals.

She stood up, knowing exactly what she was going to do next. As she turned around to face the demon, she noticed it was nowhere to be seen. She made her way over to where it had been blown back to and noticed a trail of blood. She promptly followed it.

It wasn't long before she found it limping away.

"Don't think you're getting away," she called out.

It froze in place, turning to face the girl, the hole in its chest having barely recovered at all.

"W-what are you?" it stammered.

She glared at the creature, visibly disgusted at it. *How could something this pathetic have just ruined my whole life in a matter of minutes?* she wondered. Exhausted of tears, she was left with a great weight in her chest, a vast emptiness like nothing she had ever felt before. She was alone and killing this demon wouldn't necessarily resolve that. Even still, her parents' tattoo on the back of her hand began to glow, and a brilliant white light enveloped her hand.

"I'm going to kill you now," she stated plainly.

The demon, desperate, took a step back, thinking frantically of some solution. It had always been able to take advantage of people's hearts; this time should be no different.

"W-wait!" it stammered, raising a hand in defense. "I-I can help you, I can show you how to reviv —"

In an instant she had flashed forward, swinging a beam of light through the air and severing the demon's head from its neck.

"Don't insult me with your lies," she spat at him. "My parents told me all about their adventures, and all about you."

Her eyes, now gleaming golden, were like daggers in the demon's.

"Y-your… eyes?" it stammered. "…I understand now… your power isn't borrowed. You were born with part of my power already inside of you, because I was inside that man when they conceived you. You didn't need to make a pact, because you're practically my daugh —"

The beam of light shot forward, piercing through the severed head's brain. The light faded, and she held out her hand, the purple flower tattoo beginning to glow. As the demon began to break apart and lose consciousness, it became a dark mist, flowing through the air, and gathering into her parents' tattoo. He heard one final thing from the girl.

"Burn this into your mind," she began. "I don't need to contain you into a core; I can absorb you entirely. You will lose yourself in my power, and you will cease to exist. I am not one of your puppets. I am Celina Sherwood, child of Alicia and Evan Sherwood. I have taken your power and being for my own, just as you have taken from me, and so many before me. Know that I possess them and that you will never reign free again."

With that, the long battle was finally over. Celina exhaled, closing her eyes to take in her victory. She would not have to worry about this demon in the back of her mind attempting to take over, as had happened with her father. After absorbing the creature, she began to understand more and more about the nature of it. Unfortunately, she was beginning to understand less and less about the nature of who she was. In a day, everything she knew and everything she held dear was taken from her. She would never be the same again.

Sometime later, she stood at the ruins of her house, two fresh mounds of dirt resting in what used to be her front lawn. Protruding from each mound was a single cross. This was the least she could do.

"Mom, Dad…" She spoke aloud, to no one but herself. "For now, I suppose I ought to seek out whoever remains with these powers. I want to continue to ensure that there will be no more victims of this demon's power. So, I need to leave this place for a while, but don't worry. One day I will return and rebuild the home we had together."

With that, she smirked, turning away from the graves and walking into the horizon, her eyes gleaming gold.

Made in the USA
Columbia, SC
23 December 2023

28159950R00108